Hood Misfits Volume 4:

Carl Weber Presents

Hood Misfits Volume 4:

Carl Weber Presents

Brick & Storm

www.urbanbooks.net

Urban Books, LLC
97 N18th Street
Wyandanch, NY 11798

Hood Misfits Volume 4: Carl Weber Presents
Copyright © 2016 Brick & Storm

ISBN 13: 978-1-62286-960-2
ISBN 10: 1-62286-960-5

First Trade Paperback Printing February 2016
Printed in the United States of America

10 9 8 7 6 5 4 3 2 1

Distributed by Kensington Publishing Corp.
Submit orders to:
Customer Service
400 Hahn Road
Westminster, MD 21157-4627
Phone: 1-800-733-3000
Fax: 1-800-659-2436

Hood Misfits Volume 4:

Carl Weber Presents

Brick & Storm

Chapter 1

Micah

After Candace sucked my dick and swallowed any chances of her having my children, I got up and went to shower. I'd never had a nut as painful as the one I'd just had. That nigga, Enzo, had stuck a wire hanger up my pee hole when it was scalding hot and that shit had fucked me up. For days he'd tortured me in an old, abandoned house after he had other members of the Nightwings turn against me to help him with his plan. He'd caught me slipping one time, but he wouldn't again.

As soon as the warm water hit my body, I let out a yell and punched the wall. Enzo had done a number on me and I intended to make that motherfucker pay. With everything I had left in me, he would pay.

It was just by fate that Enzo's little brother Drew didn't tie me back up the way Enzo had after the last day they had tortured me. A twist of fate, luck, and a crackhead had saved me from death at the hands of an Orlando. My history of beef with the Orlandos went back a long way. I'd never forget the way they singlehandedly destroyed my family in one day. I'd never been a man to cry and whine over my circumstances, but when a man took away lives like they meant nothing, something had to be done.

A knock came on the bathroom door as water rushed over my body like a waterfall. The crib I was in wasn't the normal place I laid my head, but because I wasn't into trusting Candace as far as I could throw her—actually I could throw that bitch farther than I could trust her—I wasn't about to have her take me there. The bathroom was small. The granite countertop was only big enough to hold my toothpaste, toothbrush, and shaving kit. The mirror was a regular small square with a medicine cabinet built into the wall behind it. There was a small window that had no curtain, only off-white blinds, and the toilet was rickety when you sat on it. The place in its entirety was small, almost claustrophobic, but it was a good place to be incognito. When I wasn't Micah Tems, the Nightwings' top sponsor and team manager, I was Micah Tems, the special agent in charge of ridding Atlanta of their major criminal enterprises.

"Yeah," I yelled out.

"You okay?" she asked me.

"I'm good. Give me a minute."

"Okay, but I just talked to Gina."

That got my attention. Shawn "Enzo" Banks had been a thorn in my asshole. Once Damien Orlando had been killed—supposedly by a group of Hood Misfits—all my hard work at infiltrating his crime faction, DOA, seemed to have been for naught. The operation I'd been heading up for years seemed to be on the verge of collapse until I'd convinced my director that there were others out there who still needed to be taken down. It had all been a ploy to stay connected to DOA any way I knew how. Since Dame, Dante, and their father, Lu Orlando, had all been taken down, I knew I was one step closer to getting the streets of Atlanta safe again.

While I knew there were other criminal enterprises that I needed to get rid of, like the African Queens, the Latin Kings, Russian cartels, and other big names like the Kulu Kings, I knew of one other Orlando who could be a tyrant if let loose on the streets of ATL. He was Enzo.

Phenom was another one on my list who I had a sneaking suspicion about; and he was just what his name alluded to. He was so skilled and talented at what he did that no law enforcement had ever been able to catch him with his hands dirty. He didn't exist. While his name was always floating through the streets, one had yet to see exactly what he looked like. Anyone we'd thought was him turned out to be just another dead end.

Finding out Enzo was an Orlando wasn't that hard for me to do. I knew the kid was an Orlando as soon as I'd laid eyes on him. Strange enough, when Dame was alive, he'd kept a close eye on the boy like he'd known too. After a little DNA test, courtesy of the fact that people tend to spit gum out anywhere and never think anything of it, I found out that he was indeed an Orlando. The way Dame would pass off the torturous acts to Enzo led me to believe he'd known something, even if it was just a hunch.

There was no way Damien hadn't looked at that boy and seen something, I thought as I started replaying things that had happened under Dame's rules. People had always joked that the boy was Dame Jr. with the way he would carry out acts in Dame's basement, which some had started to call the Underworld. Enzo, Trigga, and Big Jake: the three hood niggateers who no one wanted to see coming for them. While Trigga had been silent like a predator, Enzo had taken a public liking to offing others. He took way too much pride in the work he used to put in when it came to putting down an enemy.

I quickly stepped out of the shower, water dripping all over the faux, linoleum flooring, and snatched the door open. Candace jumped back like I'd scared her with my abruptness. I'd asked Candace to get her daughter to talk to her and bring her boyfriend, Big Jake, along. Jake and Enzo were close and I'd use any means necessary to draw Enzo back into the fire again.

"What did she say?" I asked her.

When Candace started to shake her head I knew I'd have to find another way to get what I wanted. I growled out in frustration and slammed the door in her face.

"You don't have to be a dick, Micah," she yelled at me from the hall. "I tried, but she wouldn't listen to me. She hung up in my face."

I drowned Candace out and finished my business in the bathroom. With any luck she would be gone when I stepped out. Luck was on my side. When I walked out of the bathroom Candace was gone. I didn't bother to dry off. I lay across the bed and let my mind wonder back to a time when I was an innocent ten-year-old little boy. Fucking Orlandos were going down once and for all. They would no longer snatch young girls and boys off the street to be pawns in their debauchery.

I reached over to the nightstand and opened the top drawer. I pulled a picture out that I kept close to me at all times. I looked down at the smiling faces of two kids. They'd grown up poorer than the poorest, but they were as close as siblings could get. The young girl smiling, holding her little brother in her lap—even though he was as tall as she was—would always be missed. Erica had been only sixteen when Lu Orlando took her like she had belonged to him.

I'd never forgive myself for her being taken as she was.

That day, Mama and Daddy had to work late and Erica was supposed to cook dinner. I was a bad ass kid at the time. She had cooked rice and bacon, the only things we had left. Our neighborhood was one of the poorest. There was no other way to put it. Vacant houses sat on our block, boarded up. Crackheads decorated the block like street signs.

Kids rode around on makeshift bikes with two differ-ent kinds of wheels. Had been to the dump and found pieces of bikes myself and put one together. That was how down in the dumps most of us were around there. I typically ate whatever Erica put in front of me since it was she who took care of me most nights when Mama and Daddy had to work. But I'd been eating rice and bacon for two weeks by then. We had cereal but no milk. So I whined and whined for cereal until Erica finally gave in.

"Okay, okay, Micah. Damn it, li'l boy," she snapped, pretending to be angry; but I knew she wasn't.

I was only ten, but my big sister had spoiled me. She got me anything I wanted. I used to ask where she was getting all the money from, but she just told me to mind my business. Erica made me promise not to tell Mama and Daddy that she had been sneaking out late at night and then coming back home before anyone could miss her. So I didn't. She dressed me, threw my coat on and a wool hat over my head, and then we headed out the door to walk to the corner store. A snow white BMW pulled up as we walked into the store.

"Ooohhh, bingo," I called out, making Erica laugh.

My sister had the prettiest laugh of any girl I knew. We always played the bingo game, where if we saw a car, whoever said "bingo" first owned the car in our minds.

"Wait, that's not fair, Micah. You didn't give me time," she cajoled.

"So? I saw it first and that ride is slickkkk, sis," I replied, trying to sound like the cool kid I wasn't.

She giggled. "Okay, okay, what if I told you I could get you a ride in that car?"

My eyes widened. "For real?" I asked, beaming with excitement.

"Yes. I know the man who owns it," she bragged.

I looked up into my sister's face. Most people mistook her for a white girl because of how light she was and the texture of her hair. She had golden triangle-shaped earrings in her ears. The Gloria Vanderbilt jeans she had on my parents couldn't afford. In fact, nothing she had on my folks could afford, but she was getting it from somewhere.

My eyes got even wider. "You do?"

She nodded. "Yeah. His name is Lu."

I frowned. "What kind of name is that?"

She giggled. "A nice one. His name is Lu Orlando."

"The bad, bad man? Daddy and Mama said for us to stay away from anybody with that last name."

Erica kneeled in front of me with a frown on her face. "Mama and Daddy just misunderstand them like everybody else. Lu's a good guy. Look at me," she quipped then held her arms out. "Ain't I fly? Who you think gives me money to get you all that stuff you got?"

I was confused. "The bad man gives it to you?" She nodded and I didn't really understand. "Why? Mama and Daddy say he ain't no good for the hood."

Erica tsked. "Don't listen to them, bighead. He's good people."

Just as she said that the BMW's back windows slowly rolled down.

I'd never forget the day I first laid eyes on the men who would forever change the dynamics of my home life.

"Erica, let me talk to you for a second," a man with coal black eyes called out to my sister.

Even at ten years old, I could feel the air get colder around us, but Erica smiled then stood.

"Stay right here, Micah, okay? Don't move," she told me before walking over to the car.

Before she made it to the door, the back door opened and out stepped the tallest men I'd ever seen before. Both men were built like statues. One was the older version of the one who had called my sister over. Women gawked, but started to walk faster. Men cringed and refused to make eye contact with them. Both men were dressed like they were going to church or something. That was the only time I'd seen men in their good suits like those men were.

"This is my father, Caltrone," the younger man said.

My sister's cheeks flushed red and she dropped her head a bit before glancing back up at the older gentleman. While the man's face was stoic, the way he was gawking at my sister's overly developed body made me feel some type of way. I knew they were too old and she was just a kid.

"Nice to meet you," Erica told him.

All he did was nod, but the younger version of the man carried a slick smirk. He grabbed Erica by one hand then spun her around as if showcasing her for the older man. I was confused because she was all too happy to do it. For the first time, I felt like I didn't know my sister.

"So, I need you and my father to get better acquainted. He's only in the States for a few days until he goes to Cuba. Think you can hook my old man up with your specialty?"

"I can do anything you want me to do," Erica answered.

Specialty? What's that? I thought.

The younger man nodded toward me. "Seems like you have a tagalong," he said.

She glanced over her shoulder at me. "Oh, that's my little brother, Micah. I was going to get him some milk for his cereal," she told him.

The younger man reached into his pocket and pulled out a wad of cash so big that I openly gawked and walked a little closer. I'd never seen that much money.

"*Get rid of him,*" *the younger man told Erica as he held the money out to her. She nodded and eagerly took the money.*

Erica turned and rushed back over to me. She kneeled down again. "Hey, I gotta do something for Lu. Think I can just buy you something quick out of here and then take you back home?"

I was still busy looking at all the money in her hand. "Why the bad man give you all this money?" I was loud and didn't even realize it.

"Shhh." She placed her hand over my mouth then glanced over her shoulder. "Just come on, Micah. I have to make money so we won't be hungry and poor. You can't tell Mama and Daddy though, okay? Don't ever tell them, no matter what, okay?"

I foolishly nodded and followed my sister. I was just an eager kid, happy to please his sister and happy to see all of that money. Erica rushed inside of the store and bought me anything I asked for: candy, chips, cookies, juice, some chicken they already had cooked, and a little action figure toy I wanted. I was a happy kid.

It never occurred to me that as my sister walked me back home, that would be the last time I would see her alive.

She quickly fixed me a plate of leftover rice to go along with the chicken. "Hey, I have to leave now, okay?" she told me.

I nodded. "Okay, where you going?"

"To take care of something."

"When you coming back?"

"Later tonight like always. Leave the window unlocked for me like last time, okay?"

I nodded once again as I bit into the chicken. "You going with the bad man?"

"He's not a bad man, Micah."

"He looks like one. Only bad men look the way he do, like Mama said."

Erica just rolled her eyes and shook her head as she stood. *"Lock the doors, okay? And hide this in our secret spot,"* she told me as she handed me half of the stash of cash she had.

I nodded eagerly because Erica had told me she was saving up enough money to take me to Universal Studios in Florida. She grabbed a bag she had put some extra stuff in. I ran to look out of the window to see the white BMW waiting by the curb. Just as Erica was walking out of the house, my daddy's small green Toyota truck was pulling up. The truck made a lot of noise and was barely running, but it was all we had, all we could afford.

"Go in the house, Mena," my father ordered my mother as he stepped out of the truck and slammed the rickety door.

My mother was petite and short. Most people didn't know she was deaf in one ear. It had come courtesy of physical abuse when she was a child. Her big 'fro swayed in the wind as she took one look at the car and rushed inside.

Pops was a prideful man. He was dark skinned, the color of chocolate, and had eyes that could scare the God out of Jesus. While he was nowhere near as big as the two bad men in height, his pride made it seem that way. Pops rushed up to stop Erica as my mama rushed into the house like a woman who'd just seen a ghost, completely ignoring the car. My mama locked every door behind her and ordered me to my room. I rushed up the stairs to my room, only to run back to my window to see my father trying to drag Erica back in the house.

"No, Daddy, stop," she yelled. *"Let me go,"* she screamed as she bucked and kicked.

"I will not let the streets have you, if I have to lock you in the house myself. Do you realize what you're doing?" he yelled at her, his baritone loud enough to cause neighbors to come out and see what was going on.

Erica fell to the ground, tears streaming down her face. *"Yes, I'm trying to do better. I'm sick of this place and I'm sick of you. I'm tired of all the damn rules and the curfews. I'm tired of only having one thing to eat for weeks at a time. Tired of having to see Micah tape the bottom of his damn shoes and Mama patch his jeans."*

Pops didn't care about the car sitting behind them or the men in it. When Erica stood and tried to rush past him again, he snatched her back. Although he was as tough as nails, I could tell he was hurting from my sister's words by the way his face frowned and his shoulders slumped a bit. The back door of the BMW opened again and out stepped one of the men: the younger one I'd seen earlier.

"Why don't you leave the girl alone?" the bad man asked my father. *"She's old enough to make her own decisions."*

My father let Erica go and turned around to face the man who was trying to lure his daughter away from home. *"And why don't you just get the fuck off my property? You may own every other motherfucker around here, but you don't own me and mine,"* my pops stated.

There was a look on his face that said he was seconds away from going head-on with the man. My pops' fists were balled by his sides as he stepped closer to the bad man.

"I'm going to need you to back up off my person. I feel threatened," Lu told my father. His upper lip twitched, but his hands never left his pockets as he stood there casually.

"That ain't all you gon' feel." My father stood his ground. Didn't back down at all. Lu's eyes turned to slits as he smiled coolly. "You don't scare me, Lu. Never have, nigga, and you never will. You think throwing money at a girl child is cute, nigga? It ain't, and you won't get my baby girl. You won't."

"Already had her, nigga," Lu taunted him, then shrugged. "Sweet, tight piece of pussy, too. So good gotta introduce my old man to it."

Before I could blink, my pops had taken a fist to the bad man's face, rocking him backward. My mama was yelling for my father not to do it. From my window I could see people staring on in shock at my father, who dared to go up against an Orlando.

"No, Michael, no," my mama screamed and tried to run outside.

"Stay in the house, Mena," he yelled back at her as she opened the front door. "Go in the house and stay."

She backed into the house again. "Michael, please come in the house, please," she pleaded as she closed the screen door.

"Daddy, no," Erica cried when she realized our father wasn't listening to our mother.

Lu found his balance and then reached behind him. When he brought his hand back around, in his hand was a silver gun, the biggest gun I'd ever seen. I knew what was about to happen before my pops had any idea. I knew I should have said something or even run downstairs, but I couldn't move. Fear had me glued to where I was. While my father's back was turned, the man in the white suit walked up to my father and pulled the trigger, hitting my pops in the back of the head. My mama's screams blended with Erica's as she fell backward. Erica's eyes were wide with fright as she screamed louder and louder.

"Daddy," she cried and then, in a hurried crawl, made her way over to his limp body.

I could tell she hadn't been expecting that to happen. I could see that by the wild look of panic in her eyes. I heard my mama running back down the stairs in a frenzy. As Erica tried to pull our father into her arms, the man walked over to his body and emptied more of his clip into my father's back. With each shot that rang out, Erica's body shook and trembled like it was she who was being ripped apart by bullets. My eyes widened. I couldn't move. Couldn't even breathe. My throat swelled as I watched my mama rush outside then fall to her knees as a shot to her chest from the same gun hit her. Her body slumped over and fell next to my father's.

As Erica tried to run back into the house, the man grabbed a handful of her hair and tossed her back down the front steps. He snatched Erica up from the ground then shoved her into the back of the car despite her struggling. I finally was able to move my feet and I rushed outside. I knew I was running fast, but it felt as if I was moving in slow motion. It took me forever to make it to my parents. By the time I made it outside, all I could see were the taillights of the car driving away. Tears streamed down my face as I watched my mama struggle to breathe. Nobody did anything. Nobody came to help.

Even though my mama survived, she was never the same. She ended up dying six years later of a drug over-dose. I'd been orphaned long before then anyway. Rumor had it they found my sister's body weeks later. My mama refused to go even identify the body and I was too young to do so.

I never forgave myself and I never forgot the Orlandos. Maybe if I had just eaten the rice and bacon my sister would have never walked to the store. Then maybe, just maybe, my family would still be alive. A few hours later, I sat in the locker room of the Nightwings, dressed to impress in a suit that would always tell my role of being the team manager for the Atlanta Nightwings. My PR rep had already been working in the media to explain my absence. There was nothing like a serious car crash to explain my injuries and sudden disappearance. I looked around at the players in the room. They all had a look of greed in their eyes.

"So what'chu saying is all we need to do is either fuck this nigga up in practice or let him get fucked up on the field and the dough is as good as ours?" a player asked.

Just that quick I was back to being Micah Tems, the Nightwings' manager. I took on the persona I'd been playing for years and smiled even though the pain in my face was almost unbearable. I casually pulled some Vicodin from the pill bottle and popped three, then slid the bottle back in my pocket.

"I'ma say it like this: whichever one of you motherfuckers take this nigga's legs from under him and make sure he never gets back up gets all the dough you see in this silver suitcase," I answered. "I want this nigga to never think he has enough fame and power to walk away from the Nightwings, you feel me?"

I could see money signs flipping in all those niggas' eyes as they greedily eyed the suitcase. I knew the ones who were on my team and I knew the ones who needed a little convincing. That brought my attention back to the one tied down to the gray folding chair in the middle of the room. Dragon was sitting there surrounded by the men on the team who were in my back pocket. He and Enzo were the closest on the team. You could tell by the way he protected the boy when he ran the ball. If Enzo got the ball in his hand, he was end zone–bound and part of that was thanks to the man blocking for him: Dragon.

"So, you rethink my proposition, my man?" I asked him as I tilted his bloody face up to look at me.

I wasn't surprised that he spit in my face.

"Fuck you, nigga," he barked out. "You still on your own."

I chuckled then shook my head. "Nah, see, anything I do or ask, I always have a backup plan for if niggas like you get to having a conscience and shit, feel me?"

I snapped my fingers and the back door opened. In walked a little girl with long plaits and eyes of the man who sat tied to the chair. She slowly walked over and tried to run to her father, but I snatched her up before she could make it to him. The little girl started to cry and toss and turn in my arms as she reached for her father. One look at his daughter, and it took about five men to hold Dragon down in his chair.

"She's beautiful, like her mother," I said with a wicked smile. "But check it, if you don't move to allow what I want done to happen, I'm going to sell both her and her mother to the highest bidder. I mean, after all, the man you protect on the field has ties in human trafficking, right? I'd get a pretty penny," I teased him, as I looked at the little girl who'd started crying after seeing her father, "for this one. And oh, yeah . . ." I said, snapping my fingers like I'd just remembered something.

The girl's mother's naked frame was shoved into the room. She, too, had been beaten up. Blood covered her beautiful dark skin. One of her eyes had swollen shut as blood dripped from her bottom lip.

"Oh shit, Lenika, I'm sorry, baby," Dragon growled out.

"That one is a fighter," I commented. "You know she took down two of my niggas by herself?" I asked like I was really impressed.

The dark-skinned beauty lying on the cold floor looked up to see me holding her daughter. She took one look at her daughter's crying face, hopped from the floor, then rushed at me. I backed away knowing my men would stop her.

"Give me my baby," she shrieked out, jumping at me as two guards held her back.

While they were busy eyeing her shaved pussy and bouncing tits, I kept my eyes on the man she lay with every night. Being naked did nothing to deter the fight in her. The wild bitch clawed at the eyes of one of the players and wildly swung at the other one before they let her go. She came at me again. I calmly pulled a Taser from my waist then lit into her. Dragon's baby mama fell backward, shivering and shaking as the high voltage of the gun assaulted her. The woman's hair spread out behind her on the floor like black silk. Their daughter's wails lit up the room as she cried for her mama.

"Now, Dragon, your answer?" I asked him again.

That nigga was foaming at the mouth, bursting at the seams to protect his girl and daughter. I smiled when the man dropped his head and gave in. As I smoothed the lapels down on my suit jacket, I walked with a renewed purpose. Even if I died trying, the Orlandos would pay for what they had done to my family. I wouldn't stop until I had erased the whole bloodline.

Chapter 2

Angel

"I need to talk to you," Tino said as he grabbed my arm when I walked out of the Bounce Girls' locker room.

All had been quiet on the home front for me. In the past three weeks, I'd seen Enzo in passing when I had practice or when I had been helping his aunt with her treatments, and even then I could tell that no love had been lost or gained between us. I was angry with him. Pissed the hell off that after all I'd tried to do to show him I wasn't who he was perceiving me to be, he still treated me as if I was. After all the plotting and scheming to get that nigga Micah off our asses, he still saw the worst in me. For that I would always be angry at him.

"About what?" I asked, noticing the urgency in Tino's voice.

He walked at a fast pace, pulling me with him as he did so. Tino was one of the three male dancers on the Bounce Girls dance team. He was as flamboyant as the night was long. He had some shiesty ways about him, but had proved to be an ally when Enzo decided he wanted to take Micah down. Tino had a way of getting information and making dudes talk. A lot of those niggas in the NFL were on the DL and Tino could get all the dirt in exchange for whatever he was offering at the moment.

"Girl, ya boy Enzo has been put on the chopping block," he told me once we had bent a corner and no one could hear or see us.

I wanted to pretend that I didn't care about Enzo. In my head I told Tino that I didn't give a fuck about what would happen to Enzo, but I couldn't. Whether I wanted to admit it or not, I . . . I was deep in my feelings when it came to Enzo.

Still, I nonchalantly shrugged and asked, "Put on the chopping block? What's that? They're cutting him from the team?"

"Nah, bitch. Micah done put a bounty on this nigga's career. So you know we play the Angels in two days and shit, right? Well, a few of the players are on my roster, if you know what I mean, and I heard the bounty has even been extended to them. Micah wants them to take this nigga legs clear from under him. You feel me?"

Nervousness made the muscles in my stomach clench and my heart rate speed up. I tensely brought a hand up to scratch just above my right brow and switched my weight from one foot to the other as I adjusted my Bounce Girls bag on my shoulder.

"When did you hear this?" I asked him as we both looked around to make sure nobody could hear us.

"Just left the players' locker room."

He was about to say something else until his cell rang. He quickly looked down at it and his face fell. He held a finger to his lips telling me to be quiet as he answered the phone. Just judging by the way Tino's whole body went rigid I knew who was calling him.

"This is Tino. If you paying, I'm playing," he answered casually.

For a few seconds he just stood there with the phone to his ear then he passed it over to me with a look that I couldn't read. I didn't even have to say hello.

"I'm going to kill you, bitch, but before I do, I'm going to make sure you feel every kind of pain imaginable," Micah said coolly into the phone. "All you had to do was make the right choice, Angel, but like the whore you were bred to be, you chose wrong." He chuckled low, hissed like he had burned himself, and then I heard him swallow. "I had big plans for you, Angel. Would have made you an honest woman. Okay, that part would have been impossible since you like to sell your pussy to the highest bidder, but still. You would have at least been more than another Orlando's whore."

I frowned because I knew Micah had cameras trained on us from somewhere. Even still, I was more confused about what he had meant by calling me an Orlando's whore. But there was something like defiance that arose in me in that moment. I was no longer going to let Micah turn me into a victim. I was sick and damn tired of being the victim. So if this nigga wanted me, he was going to have to fight to take me.

"Fuck you, nigga," I responded to him causing Tino's eyes to widen. "You walk around like you run this shit and we both know with one word from me I can end you," I threatened him.

I didn't even have to tell him what I was talking about. His silence on the other end of the phone told me he knew exactly what I meant.

"So you bucking the system now, Angel? Think you can rumble with the big dogs? It's one thing to join an alliance with a nigga such as Enzo to go against me. It's another one altogether to think your pussy fat enough to rise up against me alone. Don't you see?" He chuckled and I heard something crash, sounding like he'd thrown something. "I'm motherfucking unstoppable. That nigga tried to kill me and I'm still here. If Enzo couldn't take me down, what the fuck make you think a two-bit whore can?"

"I may be a two-bit whore, but I'm the two-bit whore who's going to ruin you. I'm the whore who you were so obsessed with that when she was just sixteen you bought her. You fucked her in your condos and hotel rooms. The pussy had you so gone that you slipped up and told her a few secrets. Let's see how all the underworld bosses in Atlanta will feel once they know a snitch for the Feds is in their midst."

I pressed the end button on the phone and shoved it back in Tino's hand. His almond-shaped brown eyes were so wide that they looked as if they were going to pop out of his head at any moment.

"Bitch, Micah a snitch?" he asked. I could tell he was fizzing from the mouth for the gossip.

I shrugged, feigning ignorance. "I don't know. But since he wants to keep fucking with me like I've personally done something to him then I'll do the same to him."

"This nigga was fucking you when you were sixteen?" Tino asked again.

I looked at my watch and then back at Tino. I knew players were on the field and whether I wanted to or not, I had to get to Enzo.

"I'm going to tell you something I never wanted anybody to know: I was snatched up by Damien Orlando at the tender age of fourteen. You know who that nigga was and you know what he specialized in. You do the math in your head."

That was all I said to him as I headed down the long corridor to the field. I could feel the hairs on the back of my neck stand up. I'd learned to always go with my gut. When Tino called out behind me frantically, I looked behind me to see Micah coming around the corner at the other end of the hall. The way his face was bandaged with a patch over his right eye made him look every bit of the madman he was. As soon as he saw Tino, he swung on him and with one punch put the flamboyant gay male on his ass. Tino was out cold. Sucker-ass nigga had to catch him when he wasn't looking. I knew he was coming for me. When I saw three other players with him chasing after me, I knew what time it was. I had to get to that door and onto the field where I was sure cameras, other sponsors, players, owners, coaches and, more importantly, Enzo were.

"Let me school you right quick, baby girl, because you seem to have shit all wrong. The women I take under my wing, I don't allow them to be victims. I don't allow them to play the 'woe is me' game. Understand? So, you tell me right here, right now, if you're ready to stop being a victim and start being a survivor."

I'd never forget those words Anika spoke to me as Shy looked on. Even as I ran full speed ahead, those words echoed in my mind. It was a day after Enzo had damn near beat me down in his condo because he thought I'd been trying to have sex with his thirteen-year-old brother. I'd called Anika that night scared and crying because I'd found myself, once again, on the receiving end of an ass-whooping from a man. The same man I was running to. He and I had yet to talk about what had happened between us: the sex, the bad, and the ugly. Ain't shit really ever been good between me and Enzo. From the moment we found ourselves thrown into the abyss of the psycho Micah and his need to rid the earth of Enzo, me and Enzo always found ourselves on the opposite ends of friends and foes.

That night, I was hurt, physically, emotionally, and mentally, and beyond distraught. Couldn't believe that after all had been said and done, Enzo still saw me as an enemy. I didn't even know why I had been trying so hard to make him see differently anyway. I would never willingly try to fuck Drew. He was only thirteen years old, for crying out loud.

"You can only play the role of a victim for so long before I start to call bullshit and allow you to start fending for yourself. I only help those who help themselves. I'm telling you the same thing I told my niece, Diamond, or Ray-Ray as you may know her. Dame's dead. While what he did to you was beyond low, I won't allow where you've been to dictate where you're going," Anika told me.

"She's right, Angel," Shy chimed in. *"I know you and Shawn kind of got some issues with one another, but he, too, has to get that monkey off his back. That nigga, his brother, and his soulless father are all rotting in hell as they should be. So don't you let another nigga like Micah come and try to turn your lives upside down because he has an agenda. Every nigga got an agenda and now it's time that you and Shawn come together and have one too. No bullshit, just business,"* she said.

"Grab that bitch," I heard Micah yell behind me.

I almost made the mistake of looking behind me, but something made me look to the left of me. If I hadn't, I would have surely been football tackled by the meaty player charging at me from another entrance in the hall. I did a quick step and slammed into the wall. The beefy player ended up going into the wall head first. I yelped out and by instinct alone, kicked him in his dick for good measure. The pain in my elbow made me inwardly curse, but I didn't stop moving. I was a few inches away from the door, and could hear the commotion on the field.

My breath was caught in my chest. I felt as if it was hard for me to breathe and even though everything in me said to keep running and keep fighting, there was still that modicum of fear riding me. I was so blinded by trying to get out the door that I didn't see a few of the Bounce Girls dancers running for me. By the time I realized it, two of them had grabbed me. If I had learned anything from

Enzo, I learned to always have a weapon on my person. I struggled with the two dancers, head-butting one and then sending an elbow to the face of the other. Another one of the dancers came from behind me, grabbing the bag I had on my shoulder. The force of the pull took me down to the ground as the strap from the bag choked me. I fought my way out of the entanglement, saw Micah closing in on me, and hopped to my feet.

I reached in the pocket of my jacket and brought out a pocket knife. At that point, I no longer gave a fuck. As soon as another dancer came for me, I jumped up and gave her a nice cut across her face for the affront. Bitch wanted to work for Micah then I would end her career as a dancer. She fell back against the wall with a loud scream. I stomped that bitch for good measure. A hard pull against my ponytail brought my attention back to someone behind me. I didn't know if it was another dancer or a player. Either way, my knife caught them in their gut with a slash. Blood covered my hand and I knew that if I ran out those doors, all hell would break loose. The fuck if I cared anymore. Micah was a few feet away from me. I stabbed and cut up any person I thought meant me harm. I grunted, yelled, and screamed like I was in a *Mortal Kombat* match. I backed all of them up off me by any means necessary, shoved the doors open, and rushed out. I saw a broom. Sweat dripped down my face and blood saturated my hands. I quickly grabbed the broom and slid it through the bars. I jumped back as a body slammed into the door trying to open it.

I looked up to see I was in the area that was still hidden just before you walked onto the field. I quickly pulled my jacket off and cleaned my hands and face as best I could with it. Leaving nothing to chance, I rushed through the tunnel and onto the field. It didn't take me long to find the man of the hour. Photographers surrounded the area he was in as he ran drills with the quarterback. Sweat drenched his body, and his abs clenched each time he angled his body to run around a cone. His cheeks inflated each time he blew out air. He was focused. The head coach tried to stop me, but I was too quick. Enzo saw me before I even made it over to him. I couldn't read his face and in that moment I didn't care.

"I need to talk to you," I told him.

He stood there with sweat drenching his face and the Under Armour apparel shirt he had on. He stood with his hands on his hips breathing calmly, but the rise and fall of his chest alluded to the fact that his cardio was in overdrive. Something was on his mind I could tell. The sight of him caused an array of different emotions in me. His light eyes took me in. He glanced down at my hands and the look that passed his eyes made me look down at them too. Blood was still there so I slid my hands into the pockets of the jeans I had on.

"Talk," he said to me.

Being that close to him made me remember the time when I shared my body with him. I'd never had pleasure from a man the way he'd given it to me. I felt as if he had turned his back on me without a thought in a sense. I couldn't help that I still thought about him at night. I couldn't help that I often cried when thinking about him and the time we'd shared, albeit volatile; we still had a connection. He'd been the only man who had killed for me. The only man who ever protected me beyond the scope of keeping Dame's pussy under lock and key when I used to dance at Magic City.

It kind of hurt my feelings to know that whatever it was that we had was done. Yeah, the nigga was crazy as all hell, but . . . he gave me something I'd never, ever had. He gave me protection. He protected me whether he wanted to or not. I didn't know how to explain it. A girl like me never had a father or any kind of man around to protect me. All my life I'd had to protect myself from men. So when Enzo came around and we found ourselves in a mess, it felt good to finally have a man who would kill for me even if we weren't together. Enzo had killed for me and something in me would always be attached to him because of that. Always. I wanted to protect him even if he didn't want me around him at times.

I spoke frantically. "Micah has a bounty on your head. Come Sunday your teammates and some of the Angels are going to be gunning hard for you. He caught me and Tino in the hall and ambushed me."

Enzo looked behind me toward the direction I'd power walked from and then back down at me. "You okay?" he asked.

I didn't expect him to ask me that, but I nodded anyway.

"Good. Tell me what else you know," he said.

I shrugged. "That's it for now. How did this nigga get away? I thought you had him handled."

I was scared, still amped from the adrenaline and the rush of the fight from the hallway. I knew he probably thought I was trying to jump stupid with him, but I wasn't. I was just tired. Tired of running and tired of playing that fucking game of cat and mouse with Micah.

"We ain't got time to hash that out right now. Shit happened that I didn't foresee happening. Get back to my aunt's place and wait there for me."

"I know Micah is probably going to try to follow me."

Enzo shook his head and nodded up to the sponsors' box. "You just get to your car. I'll handle the rest. Get to the sponsor box and a friend of a friend is there. You'll get to your car and where you need to go."

For a second I just stood there and looked at him. I wasn't expecting any of that. I was prepared to fight him, be annoyed with his attitude. I was prepared for anything but what he gave me. I didn't know what to feel or what to think.

"So you're not—"

"Angel, we ain't got time to be jawing, shawty. Get the fuck on like I told you," he snapped. "Go up the stairs toward the west exit through the stadium seats. Somebody will meet you there. I'll see you when I see you," he finished.

Just as he finished talking, I saw Micah and a few of the players who were chasing me come rushing through the tunnel then stop abruptly.

"Oh shit, my nigga, Micah," Enzo yelled and threw his arms up in the air like he was about to go and hug the man. "Yo, Micah is back and walking around. Good to see you back on your feet, nigga. Shit, I thought you were a goner for a second. It's funny how life hangs you upside down, huh?" Enzo said with a sinister smirk.

Reporters and photographers flocked to the dark-skinned male in the tailored Brooks Brothers suit. Micah gave a sneer at Enzo then smirked as reporters shoved microphones and cameras in his face. Enzo put on a smile for the camera and walked over to throw an arm around Micah's shoulders.

"I ain't ever been one to let one little accident slow me down," Micah countered. "I always come out on top. Always," he said coolly as he sneered at Enzo.

"Even still, you've got to be more careful, man. Everybody always got their own agenda and you never want to get caught in the crosshairs of another man's agenda. You'll find yourself locked down somewhere near death and the only thing that can save you is fate."

Enzo gave a laugh that reminded me of the rapper Jadakiss when he did that kooky laugh at the beginning of all his tracks; then he slapped Micah on the back. As the reporters looked on, a bit confused at the exchange between the two, I got the hell up out of there.

Chapter 3

Enzo

Ooh wee, we seemed to be back at the same ol' bullshit for another same ol' day.

As I was conversing with Angel, I definitely wasn't expecting to see that nigga Micah surrounded by the media. Flashing lights and chatter had me on edge. Them cats with their cameras and shit seemed to surround us both, pointing their cameras as if we stood in the middle of a execution gun line, but I was chill with it. Wasn't shit but a ploy for Micah who thought it would shake up my world and stop me from getting to my agenda.

Thumbing my nose, I crossed my arms over my chest with an amused look. But what he wasn't realizing yet was that I was trained by the best. So, I stood there playing the beloved athlete. I gave them some grins, winked, and spit some jokes all while speaking in code to a nigga who had me feeling like I was chewing on shards of glass.

Honestly, I was amazed at myself, because I was in the middle of blacking out again, yet I was functioning. Nothing but hatred poured from me; but to the lights and cameras, I came off as suave and enthusiastic about the game and my manager. Funny thing was they had no damn clue what was really going on, and I couldn't wait for them to find out. So the moment that the cameras started to spread out and turn their backs on us, I immediately dropped my arm and my eyes darkened like soot.

Micah shifted on his feet in a turn and glared at me through narrow slits.

His intimidation didn't faze me a bit. I stepped forward then jetted toward him so fast that I was able to bypass his fuck-boy security. My hand swallowed the side of that nigga's face to slam him directly into the wall of the tunnel we stood in while I spoke to the side of his face.

Searing hatred had my nostrils flaring but a creeping sinister humor bubbled from me and had me laughing at this nigga's pain. "It's unfortunate that our little meeting was cut short, but I promise you, we will . . . hang again. Feel me?"

Micah gave a grunt; then a menacing sneer peeked out from under my hand. "Maybe, but next time I'm thinking it'll be you. But, check it, whatever you are about to do, I wouldn't do that, if you feel me."

My gaze stayed on Micah but I wasn't stupid. I knew the cameras were still around. I also knew his security was getting up. Which was why when I felt the tap of a gun against the back of my neck, it had me slowly dropping my hand then backing away.

"Me and you have unfinished business, nigga. You a little too uppity for my taste and you've had your hands in my pockets for far too long, Shawn. You think you are invincible like your brother Dame, but guess what? That nigga is kicking up dirt and you're about to join him and his twin, asshole," Micah snarled.

The moment he spit out that he knew about my blood tie to the Orlandos, I realized that this nigga had been possibly setting me up from the gate. My jaw clenched tight as I stared this nigga down. I could feel the nerve in my jaw ticking when my facial expression went blank. His admission of truth pissed me off even more, but in a good game of cards, you never show your hand, so I did what I did well and that's play dumb.

"Oh, yeah? Don't even know what you talking about. But I have checked that you got a bad obsession with a nigga I didn't even like being forced to run with. But that's cool though, you do you and I do me." I snatched my arm out of Micah's security's grasp then pushed them niggas back to get out of their zone.

The sound of the news crews circling back around with a group of fans and football players to where we were let me know the show was back on. That was when I noticed Micah giving a nod and suddenly the tunnel was crowded with teams of FBI agents. Agents pointed their Glocks my way. Fans backed away in shock, hissing out questions as camera crews shot on.

"Shawn Banks! I am Special Agent Reyes. You are under arrest!" one agent barked out.

Anger had me looking that nigga's way in confusion as I pushed that fool off me and went off, "Man, fuck you! Tell me what the hell I did! Huh? Huh? I thought so. Kiss my ass, nigga."

I understood in that moment that Micah had played his high card. Bitch nigga was serving the law, as if he had a fucking right. With what I knew about him, all I could do was laugh and be dragged away. Several of my teammates who were against me laughed, and threw up middle fingers to show me whose side they were on. Others stepped forward and tried to pull me away from the cops.

A huge smile played on my face while I resisted. I slammed my shoulders into officers and shouted in protest, "I ain't do shit! Tell Coach to hit my emergency contact! Let them know what's up!"

The crowd who watched on seemed to become just as angry as I was and I felt pride in that moment. That was until I saw Micah on the sidelines of the tunnel speaking to the Feds. This cat had the nerve to be looking concerned. Suddenly all that knowledge about that fool flashed before me and all I saw was red. I would have spit on him but the Fed who held me back kept me from doing so. So, all I could do was vehemently watch Micah play some snitch shit, "I am law" bull crap.

"I'm trying to tell them that you aren't some drug dealer, Enzo. That those drugs ain't yours, but all I can do is try! Take care of my player. I don't know what is going on, fellas, but this is a prized player and if you hurt him, it makes us lose money, respect that," he said with fake concern in his eyes.

Drugs? So this nigga got some shit planted somewhere and is setting me up? Oh, okay. I saw some silence exchange pass between him and several other agents. Several agents came to his side and pushed him back, telling him to stay with other citizens.

A nerve in my jaw ticked, causing me to bristle. "I ain't do shit. But I bet that the one who did it is right in front of you, ain't that right, Micah . . . Mr. *Federali.*"

I shook forward as best I could and spit at his feet. That was when a beefy arm snaked around my neck. It quickly snatched me back and pulled me away. I swear I was on some blackout shit but this crap just kept getting worse.

"Don't worry, Shawn! I'm not sure what is going on, but we will send you the best legal representation Atlanta has," Micah yelled out, brushing his blazer off while looking down at his Italian leather shoes. Twisted laughter followed right after.

Then my fans immediately started throwing drinks at the officers and other objects that littered the field. Chants of, "Enzo, Enzo, Enzo," followed me through the tunnels.

Reporters tried to follow, spitting out questions, and all media was on me. I was loving the hype. Because whatever Micah was playing, I was about to twist that shit and turn it into my favor. It was his move and he called checkmate.

It was my turn and I had some fire just for him now that I knew the truth to the other half of me. "Loyalty, pain, and mayhem" was my personal motto. ENGA for life, for sure. All gloves were off and now I was going to turn into the beast while I kicked my feet up in hell and tried keep my sanity.

I was surrounded by nothing but bullshit. See, motherfuckers know when they are feeling extra that they ham that shit up to the fullest and, right now, the five-o in front me was on some major bullshit. One oversized motherfucker was sucking up life with the way he kept taking breaths, and his partner, a wandering-eye, Deebolooking nigga, stared me down as I sat in a cramped interrogation room. Now, I was wondering exactly what case I was catching that had these punk-ass niggas sweating me so hard. But at the same time, I was enjoying how they kept stretching out the time.

The Feds and five-o had been serious about my shit. I had thought my lockup would be only a few hours. But when it stretched out to more than one day, more like three, I knew they were sniffing around trying to trump up multiple bricks on a brotha. It was all good for me though because I knew my PR rep, with the guidance of my mother, Shy, was out twisting this to my favor, which had been privately negotiated after learning about Micah's vendetta against me.

Angel had hit me up to it while I was practicing before the big game. Our words were short but it was what it was. There were too many eyes and ears. Thinking about her, our whole interaction with each other, was on some sour shit. The majority of it was on my part and I felt bad about it, having seen that she'd been proving that she was here for the team. As a man, I knew I was wrong for putting my hands on her, in turn treating her like another bitch on the street.

I had low tolerance for bitches, but she was put in a situation that she had no control over or wanted to be a part of; yet she still made sure not to be a foul bitch in her mind. Micah had destroyed our lives, causing us to be monsters, and I helped to add more fear in her. Shit, Shy ain't raise me to be that way. The streets did. But I knew better so there was no excuse, so I was sorry about it. Still, if any harm came to Drew, I'd kill the pope if I had to and that was the truth. So I sat back, and relaxed with a knowing smile on my face with what Angel told me, thankful for it while inhaling the scent of stale cigarettes and weak coffee.

"I take it you two aren't Nightwings fans huh?" I laughed with a sly smirk when Uncle Phil's bushy brows and bloodshot eyes glanced my way a little too long for my taste and comfort.

"Cute mouth, kid." Uncle Phil licked his overly glossy pink lips and cooed my way while shifting in his chair causing it to creak with his stocky build.

In my mind, I was disgusted with how the nigga was trying to play me in the moment, but I kept it cool and collected, kicking back and not letting my disheveled experience give anything away. My hand reached up as far as it could, being that I was handcuffed yet again, and scratched the side of my bushy beard.

"But, no, you're wrong. My partner and I are number one fans of yours, so much so that we've been following your every movement since your start," he said in a too gleeful and gloating type of way.

Deebo gave a laugh then crossed his arms over his broad, budging chest. "Where's the body, Shawn?"

My brow quirked upward in question while I continued to study each cop in front of me. Something in the way they were in my face let me know that they were puppets for Micah, and I wondered how I could play it to my advantage.

"Body? I'm not clear about what you're talking about, my man. You all pulled a foul big time and dragged in one of ATL's golden kids on some bullshit about a body? Oh, damn, y'all must be bored today," I goaded them.

My hands were still cuffed due to the scuffle I had with several of the cops and it annoyed me that they were still bound as I spoke to Thing One and Thing Two.

Laughter came from both men and Deebo spoke up again: "Word on the street and evidence show us that you've taken out several people for your enjoyment. Scottie Kruger has been reported missing for several weeks now and surveillance shows that he was in the area of your complex. So again I ask: where's the body, Shawn? Don't you want to get back to your ailing aunt?"

Frowning, I gave a bored sigh and murmured out loud to myself, "I'm 'bout tired of you motherfuckers bringing her into shit. That's a fucking queen move if ever—"

"Excuse me?" Uncle Phil barked out, causing me to glance up at him in annoyance.

"I said I'm sure she'll be fine. My aunt is a survivor and she knows I'm a good man. Ask me whatever you want but it's all going to be the same answer. What body? Where, who, and why? Send my condolences to the family of that missing person."

Uncle Phil sucked his teeth then spit into a cup near him. He glanced at his partner then slammed a fist on the table. "We have evidence that you had a hand in the murder, Shawn!"

He held his hand out and Deebo slapped a folder down in front of him then pulled out a photo. In front of me was a chick I remembered running into some weeks back when Angel and me were hiding out at the Dixie Motel. She and her whore friends had tried to kill Angel and I'd had to turn into that nigga I didn't want to be again. The woman in the photo lay on her side bashed, battered, cut up with pieces of her in different containers. Her skin seemed to be graying from some liquid she was soaking in. I had to remember to thank ol' boy who worked at the hotel for getting rid of the bodies for me, if I ever laid eyes on him again. Shit was like something out of *Hostel* and it piqued my curiosity. I calmly looked around the room and gave a slight shrug.

"Is that your missing cat? She or he got worked up damn good. Wonder what shit she was into," I responded, leaning back into my chair.

A fist went flying into my face with a slam. It would have broken my nose but I turned my head to the side in time to just feel it against my jaw. Pain sliced through me, making my teeth chatter, and I coughed. Heated anger had me side-eying Uncle Phil's way in a flash of malice.

"Yesterday, this woman was found in a dump yard near your old stomping grounds, the Trap. This all has your MO on it, Shawn. You were known to be sponsored by one the biggest drug kingpins in ATL and several of the Feds report that they also found drugs and weapons in your locker. Just keeping your hands in everything huh?" he spat out, slamming his fist down in front of me, as if I'd be scared of his intimidation.

Uncle Phil leaned in and covered me with his sour coffee-scented breath while glaring at me harder as Deebo spoke up.

"Queeniesha Jackson was just a young girl forced to sell herself and you ordered her hit? Assaulted her at the Dixie Motel and because you thought your manhood was in question, you ordered a hit out on her for being transgendered? Sounds like some shit Dame Orlando used to order his street runners to do, ain't that right, Enzo?" Deebo spit out.

My nerves were being pulled thin. They had me locked up without knowing why they had me, for several days. Plus now I was sitting looking at a picture of a broad I wasn't very familiar with outside of that one meeting that ended in a fight. Micah was full of shit and it showed just how deep he was out to get me.

I wondered what the fuck was about to drop on me next because it was just too convenient how that shit was found. As they said, this shit was becoming sloppy and foul. Now I had racketeering and corrupt organization charges along with gun possession and drugs? Yo, in my twenty-one years of life, I had never seen so much bullshit. Nah, that was a lie. Dame had lived nothing but that.

Yawning, I widened my legs then rolled my shoulders, still stunned by that punch. "You run prints? You see anything on it connected with me, my nigga? No. I like how Micah got his fucking hands even in this. Tell him to move his chess piece better because this shit right here is pitiful and boring as fuck. Can we move on to something more fun? Because saying I beat that broad up for being transgendered is wack as fuck and ain't me. Next, my nigga."

Another punch came my way. It landed into my solar plexus, causing me to hunch forward in pain and gasp for breath.

"Hold that little nigga down and, remember, he said not to work him up too much. He still has money on this monkey," Deebo hissed out in front of me.

Several punches flew into me, causing me to rock back and forth in my chair. I tried to push with my elbows but the beating continued until they got tired. Wheezing, I glanced around the room and licked my cracked lips. I knew I had some aces up my sleeve, so I let them do them and waited for the right moment to move forward.

Uncle Phil had his back turned to me while wiping his bloody knuckles and laughing. "It's going to be fun fucking with you, kid. We have so much more to bless you with. But since you staying stupid and smart mouth, we just want you to know that the pain is going to continue coming your way. We get cases daily that no one can explain that seem to fit exactly who you used to be in the streets, kid. How you feel about that?"

Blood mixed with spittle pooled in my mouth and I spit on the concrete floor then shrugged. "Do what the fuck you want. I don't care. You ain't got the answers, niggas! All you niggas do is run your mouth like y'all got shit to say, but I got something none of you all are comprehending. You ain't got the answers!"

Pushing up in my chair, I slammed the chair over causing Uncle Phil's fat ass to fly into Deebo. Deebo fell backward, banging his head into the wall. Hooking the chair with my foot, I stared down Uncle Phil's bubbly ass and dropped the chair right on his beach ball–sized stomach, then on his neck. Sitting on it, I glared at him as he choked.

"My name is Shawn fucking Orlando! That's right, Lu Orlando, that nigga is my pops, and all the heat you think you gonna get from Micah ain't got shit to do with the heat you about to get from me. Say good-bye to your family and your life, because they are done. What was once my enemy's becomes mine. That death you tryin'a put on me is now spoken into existence, bitch! Pain is my pleasure, nigga!" I roared and squeezed hard enough to the point that I almost was able to hear the snap of his neck.

Luckily, life was on his side because cops burst into the room full force, pulling me off of fat bastard and his lover Deebo.

A jarring maniacal chuckle erupted from me as I struggled. "Check the cameras, niggas, they put their hands on me. I'm defending myself. Tell those niggas to wipe their blood up and I'll take care of the hospital bills. I'm an innocent bystander. Shawn Banks-Orlando is an innocent bystander regardless of what you bitches are sayin'!"

An instant hush of chilling silence erupted through the police station. Multiple cops looked my way and I saw in their eyes a tie and a loyalty that almost made my stomach churn. Even after death, my sperm donor had a hand in the law. A team of cops dragged me back to my private cell, throwing me on the ground. I could hear them talking, wondering if I was lying; but, as a few kept saying, I was a mirror image of the Orlandos, no doubt.

That was the truth. My name was Shawn "Enzo" Banks, the seed of Lucifer, and now what was his and his sons' world was now going to be mine. Micah had made a major mistake in opening up Pandora's box and a war was about to follow. Like I kept telling him, he should have left me the hell alone.

Chapter 4

Shy

Dreams are a guide to give you lessons on what is needed in your life, or what is harming you in your life. My dreams were what I wished would have happened had my life gone the way I had wanted. Before me were my sons as children, running around me as they played. Little Andrew was giving his all in keeping up with Shawn. Mindful of his baby brother, Shawn was slowing his movements just so Drew could keep in step with him while they ran.

That in and of itself was a message directed toward me in that moment. It was something that had my heart swelling in sadness, but also with love. Behind me was my big sister vibrant in life and happiness. Her belly was swollen with life and the man who should have been her love was by her side holding her close. I missed her deeply and it hurt to know that in this lucid dream my sister Sade had lost so much just to protect my children and me.

A warm breeze flowed over the surface of my skin, kissing me in its soothing touch as the sound of my grandfather's booming laughter ebbed around me. It was so close that it had me turning full circle. The ends of my white maxi dress swirled around me, with those of my long brown locs. All around me were my family: my mother and father, my grandmother, Anika, Fatima,

Ahmir, and Jamir with his grandfather. We all stood in front of a great house. Those were lessons. I knew that before I left this earthly plane I had business to take care of, business that laid down a secure foundation for my children.

No, I didn't want my sons to step into the world of criminal activity. I wanted nothing but the best for them, but I understood that as a mother, a queen, their protector, I had to lay down something that would take care of their needs. I did that. Money was set aside for them both from my time working as a nurse and money I gained from poetry gigs. My sons each had property in the DC-Maryland area with land that went on for days.

My sons were protected on the legit front. Now with their true lineage coming to light by a corrupt mother-fucker I had strong issues with, I had to step into a world I never thought I'd have to go into. Yes, I was a creator, a founder of a crime syndicate that was making moves not only in ATL but also internationally; but I had stepped away from that, once my attacker died in prison and once I knew I could be invisible again. However, as my sons were learning, life has a way of putting you in situations you do not want and now I was back in that situation.

A mother could be the fiercest lion in the jungle. As the old saying went, you messed with her cubs then you walked into death. Micah Tems had messed with my sons. He really must have believed that they were weak stock, that they had no protection; however, Micah was far from the truth in that. I knew men like him and sur-vived men like him, and the fact that he was FBI didn't scare me at all. In my opinion, he was just another carbon copy wannabe Orlando.

That nigga was nothing to me. I'd survived worse. My vacation home was hell and if I had to walk back into the valley of death again, I would. See, what that piece of scum didn't know, or maybe he did not realize, was that the moment Lucifer touched me, I became his Lilith. I did things that would make the strongest of men shit themselves and soon Micah would learn that. See, survival was of the fittest and that bitch would learn today.

I was a queen, a lion. I was an anaconda in the thicket. He had no idea who he'd just awakened. The devil wanted me so bad that a contract was created. That contract stated that not only did the father of the devil want his grandsons, but he also wanted the one who created prime stock: me.

Micah may have thought he had the upper hand, but he did not even begin to understand that Pandora's box had been opened and would bring down hell in the A. He had no idea that a mother had to resurrect her own family blood power, and officially take the steps to meet in hell by accepting something she never wanted as well: to be the true queen mother of DOA.

As my dreams spoke to me, the dripping of holistic medicines in my IV played a song of vengeance. Old poison was in my system and dying was the least of my concerns. Niggas wanted to play and wake up a dragon, then that would be what they were going to get: a motherfucking dragon. Tapping my stiletto-shaped nail against my brow, my eyes narrowed while I watched my son being taken down by the law. All the major news outlets kept replaying it over and over again. Yes, Micah was playing with the wrong one and on the chessboard called war he'd just made a grave mistake. He fucked with the wrong mother.

The specially designed red and tan thin smoking pipe that held the contents of sweet ganja between my lips kept me calm as I thought on what to do for my son. Micah had to go, and the quicker that happened the quicker my sons could get some semblance of normalcy, even with the Orlandos coming for them. Reaching for my cell phone, I got ready to text my son's PR rep, Dymetra, but I was stopped by the image of a tall, slightly thick and muscled cocoa smooth male dropping a stool in front of me. On his shoulder was a long white towel; in his hand was a bucket of hot, sudsy water that wafted a calming scent that reminded me of the healing candles Anika would light at night for me when she visited.

"What are you doing, Mirror?" I lightly asked him as I removed my pipe and set it next to me.

The man before me was dressed in casual dark jeans that hung just right on his warrior-built form. He sported a simple open white button-down and a black tank underneath. He was damn calm, very quiet, very lethal, and very sexy. It was bringing up old memories of the man he resembled. When he smiled in that same way but slightly different, I sat up in my chair, keeping my view on his handsome, chiseled face. Mirror pulled off the simple hat he wore, revealing his deep-set black waves that fell into clean-cut sideburns that lined his jaw. Like Phenom, he had the occasional gray but it wasn't enough to make him look any older than the area of age we were: late thirties and early forties.

Revealing a bag, Mirror gave me a wink and dropped his hands on what I could only imagine were concrete-hard thighs. "Today is taking care of di woman of di house and yuh that woman."

A slight smile played across my face. He reached down, picked up my bare foot, and held it between his two large hands, rubbing it. "Remember what you were told, if yuh want yuh sickness ta go, den yuh have to work on that stress."

Mirror had a deep and rich melodic, sensual British- and Jamaican-accented voice, one of the many differences between him and Phenom. It made my body warm with the way he watched me. From the way my smaller foot sat comfortably between his larger hands, I could only imagine that on his downtime this man was a sculptor or painter. It made my heart heavy but also made me smile in the way my mind was working.

"Yes, I remember that, Mirror, but I have a responsibility to this family and one major one was just flashed across the screen; did you not see it?" I asked, trying to ignore just how good it felt as he rubbed, then dipped his hand in the bowl of water before me to wash my feet.

The man before me gave a slight nod while sliding his now oiled and wet hand up my calf then down to my foot again, focusing on the arch.

"Of course I saw it. I swear down, woman, yuh don't listen." He glanced at my monitors as the medicine pumped into me but also noted my stress levels. "It's being handled. His bail will be met, but there are some things that have to go a specific way before the true game can be revealed. And right now, yuh need to sit back before yuh make yuh king be taken in this chess game, queen," Mirror calmly explained.

He said so much in so few words. It amazed me. Had me assessing the man more deeply, had me wondering just what his agenda was. "Tell me something, Mirror."

"Be my guest, love. What you have to say?" Mirror simply stated.

My lower lip trembled at the sensation of his wonderful hands. They had me wanting to arch up and just purr; it felt that great. "How is it that a man who is the exact carbon copy of Phenom, with only subtle differences, can be loyal to Kulu Kings . . . well, Phenom's house, but be in the house of a woman who's been stamped DOA? Does that not cause conflict for you?" I gently asked.

We sat in my private home, nestled in the southwest hills of Atlanta. Around me were pictures of my past in

NYC, pictures that capture the true history of a group of kids who came to the A just wanting forge their own lives, until the criminal pasts of their parents and grandparents got in the way. My awards from poetry shows sat in a display case that also was home to the awards Shawn received from playing sports, and the awards Andrew received from his intelligent mind and sports. Next to those accolades were my prized possessions: my college diploma for nursing and my ultrasound pictures of Shawn and Andrew.

A comforting warmth surrounded me in my French château-styled home with its cream-painted walls, accented with music legends from the past, next to African masks, paintings, and Harlem Renaissance legends. This was my true home in a sense, my spiritual oasis, and as I glanced at pictures of me holding Shawn and Andrew in the hospital when they both were born, my eyes watered and I put my focus back on the man before me. I almost gasped when I noticed how he watched me. I knew I was blushing but I brushed it off to keep cool. I was too old, sick, and dying to feel this way with him.

"Tell me what you think," was all he said.

In the moment, I had to laugh. I relaxed in my seat then smiled. "Do you know the tale of two brothers?"

Mirror gave a slick smile, and then settled my foot in the hot, but not scalding, water. He reached behind him to hand me a bowl of dragon fruit, kiwi, melons, and other cancer-fighting fruits. He then shifted, reached in his bag, and pulled out more oil. "Tell me your interpretation."

This man was a purposeful enigma and the longer we were together, the more I was enjoying it. "Okay. The tale is in various different forms, from Egyptian to Native American, but basically it's the story of two brothers' loyalty to each other and how it was tested once the love for one woman was involved. Love, fights, sex, murder, drama was all in it, and ultimately the brothers ended up having to lose each other to get back together again."

My toes wiggled in his hand, and I enjoyed the comforting way he chuckled deep in his chest before responding, "A very good story. I know it well. Tell me yuh point, or theory, because I can see you have a proper idea in your mind. Yuh pretty eyes sparkle with it."

"Okay. It's my mission to keep my sons from living that story. Shawn was privy to that with working for one of the twins of hell," I explained.

"Yes, an' what does that do with me, love?" Mirror calmly asked while rubbing my feet.

"It relates because it makes sense for Cozy—I mean, Ahmir—to keep his business secure by keeping it in the family. By also using a relative who resembles him so much that no one can pinpoint exactly who he is. This is brilliant, especially when that person, a cousin, is actually a brother, a twin," I continued explaining, trying to read any little twitch or change in his body language.

However, nothing changed. All I read was possibly that this man was checking for me, and it had my body humming in quiet need.

The feel of smooth, firm, and plush lips kissing the top of my foot had my eyes almost bucking as my yoni clenched and throbbed.

I gripped the side of my large, plush rocking chair and cleared my throat. "What . . . what was that?"

"That was me giving thanks for being in the presence of an intelligent sista. I swear down, many people have been around me in our close circle and none the wiser except those who truly know us. But, you are off on one thing. I'm over the twin shit." He chuckled.

Welcoming, nervous laughter came from me, and I smiled. "Me too."

"We aren't twins; we are brothers. You understand the code of secrecy in why we say what we say, yes? He and I have separate mothers, but we were born the same day. He in the States, me in Kingston, then moved to London. So, to answer yuh previous question, the conflict is not there for me because my loyalty is to my brother and only my brother. You are King Kulu's direct blood; Anika is too. Your sons carry his likeness as well, even though that DOA blood is there. We know the true history. I enjoy my role in the shadows, so no threat is there, because I work for Kulu via my brother. I work for you and I work for those two innocent young men," he continued.

I sat quietly in what he shared. My gaze stared at the large fading picture of three drop-dead gorgeous and rough men, in suits posing with large smiles. Truth of hidden secrets was all around me and here this man sat in the middle of it with me.

It had me reaching out to cup his face. "Mirror, you're a gatekeeper like me."

He nodded, and then turned his hand to kiss my palm, which had me blushing.

"I am and I enjoy it. It makes being a right hand very comforting and now I see what my brother was always talking about," he said.

He leaned forward then whispered something that had me melting in my seat: his true name. His hand slipped under my chin and then dropped away before going back to washing my feet.

"I'm too old and dying for this," I muttered while blinking several times.

"Too old for what?" Mirror quietly laughed.

"This, whatever this is. I loved your cousin . . . your brother. Was basically his other wife for a small moment until the devil destroyed my body," I rushed out in embarrassment.

"So? What does that have to do with me? In the past, Ahmir believed that he should have two lionesses. He did that, and still believes that, though now he's in the same mindset as me. I don't need two women or more to feel like a king or uphold me. One is enough, especially if she's as bad as you and Anika." Mirror shrugged.

"I know what I want and besides, yuh not dead yet and yuh health is definitely improving, love. Besides, mi old nan told me as a kid that after I finished sowing my oats, I would care for a fading lioness; and it was when I was bending before her, washing her feet, that I would know my wife. I'm not a young punk anymore picking up batty chicks," he matter-of-factly stated.

His words had me sitting in shock. "I mean, we're both grown, but that can't be why you've been single all this time, to wait on a dying woman."

"Godblind me. You American women are something else! I swear down yuh all don' listen or accept truth in your face. Your fading gives you the gift to read people, but yuh not reading me well. I didn't wait for nothing. It just happened that way and here yuh are. I'm not blocking blessings especially in this game. Now what yuh think on that?" Mirror laughed almost boastfully.

It had me smiling again, and I shrugged. "If you get down with sleeping with invalids, then I won't deny you. I'm dying; it would be nice to go out with a bang, but before that, I need to protect my sons. Is that why you really are here and not feeling conflicted? Because of your feelings for me?"

Mirror reached up, and pulled my chair to him, where he sat between my legs. He checked the monitor to make sure I was okay, smiling at how my pulse levels had jumped. He then gave me a flash of a smile while shaking his head. "No! Ya zeet? My true agenda is that I'm here because of your feelings for me, then my feelings for you. I'll be yuh king and we can be chill in how we do our dealings with our enemies."

What he said was enough for me. I touched his face and nodded. He was like me: a gatekeeper and a person content with playing the right hand. He could help me ease back into my role in comfort and not shame, while letting me do things by my own accord. I was down for that, so we stared into each other's eyes and we began our think tank.

"I'll take your secret to the grave, and no one knows?" I said stating my loyalty.

"No one knows, and I know you will. Our circle is tight except for one," he explained.

I gave a slight frown knowing who he was talking about. "You know, I still say that is no *bueno* for that child to be there. Traitors need not be in that circle and it worries me that she's there. Did my two misfit boys not learn from my lessons?"

Shifting in my chair I continued, "I never liked that girl from the moment I saw her; and when Bianca told me how that ho almost got her cut by your nephew, I was ready to off her then."

Mirror gave a bold laugh and winked. "Oh no, we don't want that, love. You have a good read on people and you taught that well to your three Misfits. Trust me they have this. Of course they listened; remember when you were young, how you learned your agenda, love?"

A flicker of a smirk flashed across my face and I sighed in relief. "Okay, so that's their agenda then. They did learn well. Keep your enemies close and traitors even closer."

"Most definitely, trust, she'll get a proper killing real soon and any secrets she thinks she knows are not factual." Mirror smirked.

My appreciation for this man bloomed. I relaxed and softly asked to move forward. "Do you know the story of Br'er Rabbit?" My body hummed in want for this man, and I felt vibrant in life for the first time in a long time.

"Old Br'er Rabbit? Cha, yuh I know that trickster's tale. He's also Anasai." Mirror stated with a sensual laugh.

"Well, my son is now Br'er Rabbit, or Anasai, and Micah is the enemy. We need to make sure that—" I was about to explain my plan but Mirror slid back in his seat, then picked my foot up and tilted his head.

"I think it's best you share it with the ears that listen," he calmly stated.

Looking over Mirror's shoulder, I saw both Angel and Drew pausing by my healing room. Something had happened because Angel looked scratched up and was breathing hard. Her hands were clenched beside her and I saw blood on her knuckles. Awareness hit me hard and I knew it was time to ante the hell up and be about business. Mirror's hand rested on my calf and I knew my stress levels had shot back up. I couldn't freak out like I wanted, and I needed to be calm though both children in front of me held worry in their eyes. So I turned into the caring mother and swallowed the fear that threatened to take me out.

I gave both my son and Angel a loving smile that reached my heart, and I motioned to them. "Come in. We all need to talk. I have a few things to say."

Drew and I were still having a tricky time since I revealed that I was his mother, but I could only hope and pray that through my words and actions he could see that I loved him and Shawn. I hoped that they could understand that, as a young girl, I did the only thing I could do at that time to protect them from the Orlandos.

"Hey, man, why you on my *tía* . . . mom like that?" Drew fussed.

The distance in his eyes melted away to reveal a flash of emotion. My baby boy moved forward by my side to hand me my pipe again and then kissed my temple. His sudden protectiveness had me laughing but it also gave me a sliver of hope that all would be okay.

"He's doing what he does: helping this family, Drew. Don't trip," I teased with a wink and a smile.

Drew gave a slight grumble then poured me some water and soursop juice. Angel was on my other side, fluffing my pillow and smiling at the burgundy dye job she did on my short 'fro. I could see she was wanting to tell me something and that she was hiding her hands in the process. It had me shaking my head as I played dumb.

"Thank you, Bianca. I love what you did to my hair." I smiled as I called Angel by her real name, studying her movements.

"You're welcome, Shy. I just picked up Drew; that's why we kinda heard you two. We all need to talk, though. Micah went after me and I just heard on the radio that Shawn's locked up," Angel frantically rushed out. She rested her hand on mine in respect and tried to read my facial expression.

I smiled up at her and my gaze went to Mirror as I chuckled. "You were right. I have a good reading on traitors and on who is to truly trust. I only hope my boys take those lessons and use them well. Drew, you get your homework in?" I quickly asked narrowing my eyes.

"Yes, dang. But did you hear Angel?" he asked with a flash of fear in his voice.

My head shook and I sighed. "Okay, just making sure. Did you still drop your friends for those little niggas on the street? And yes, I did; I want to take care of home first before we speak on a nigga I intend to have killed."

"*Tía!* Be cool. Damn, why you in my business like that? Wait what?" Drew barked out then gazed at me in shock.

I knew I had to rein it in, but Angel stepped in for me. "Why you tripping, Drew? Stop it. She's just checking on you. And yeah, what?"

I gave a weak smile and tried to focus on Mirror's hands. "Thank you, Bianca. And because I can, Drew. Shawn has been arrested. My son is sitting in jail with parasites all around him. I don't do well with niggas who play foul so, yes, I want Micah's head."

"That's why I'm here. I was coming to tell you," Angel rushed out.

She was still in her uniform, so I could tell that she rolled out in a straight shot from the stadium. Glancing around at one son who stared at me with a swollen chest in conflicted emotions, I tilted my head to watch a young girl who I knew if trained right would be a force to be reckoned with, especially in her love for Shawn. I then smiled at a man who still kneeled in support to whatever plans I had for my family and our forming emotions. I placed a hand to my heart, and then reached for my pipe.

"We all are going to sit here and make our own plans to help Shawn. That nigga Micah really believes that we are unintelligent monsters. But, that's copasetic, though. I am here to let him know that if you are going to go after someone like Shawn, you better make sure his whole foundation has crumbled totally. That was how I trained three young boys to think back in the day, and that is how a group of Misfits took down an empire then created their own. It's time we build our empire back up. So I need you all to listen to what I teach and take it in, because I may be sick, but I'm not dead yet, so there is no fear of that nigga Micah in me at all. Now listen."

Lighting up, I explained the story of Br'er Rabbit, and how we had to help Shawn be the trickster in order to survive Micah and eventually survive the Orlandos. Every nigga had an agenda in this plan and the first start in that was to draw out Micah through using our status as a united football family with money and pull. In the great words of Sun Tzu, "Secret operations are essential in war; upon them, the army relies to make its every move."

Besides, I had people who could give me whatever information I wanted on men like Micah, so-called law enforcers, Feds, CIA, and more. As I quietly told myself, he knew nothing about the daughter of King Kulu Okoye, the king of NYC's crime syndicate.

I was Iya "Shy" Okoye-Banks. Micah messed with the wrong family and the wrong mother.

Chapter 5

Micah

When the door to my office opened and Enzo walked in, the gun in my hand was already trained on him. That nigga hadn't even bothered to change out of his prison garb to come see me. The cocky disposition he carried made me want to fire the gun, but I knew I couldn't. If he had found a way out of jail then I knew he hadn't come alone. The fact that Enzo was supposed to be tucked away in a jail cell but had found a way to be in my office told me he had found out just how much power the Orlando name possessed.

He took a seat in front of my desk like he owned the place. "What it do, my nigga? Still trying to lock a nigga down I see."

He looked like the thug he was, a fucking menace. Eyes bloodshot like mine, but he still hadn't learned anything.

"How the fuck did you get here?"

"Doesn't matter. I'm here. You see me. See how close I can get to you even while locked away, my nigga? You shouldn't fuck with what you don't understand."

"And you shouldn't think you can't be touched," I retorted, cocking the gun.

Enzo shrugged and then leaned back in the chair as he watched me. "A gun don't scare me, nigga. Guns never fazed a nigga like me. Guns used to be a way of life for me." He leaned forward as he spoke. "All you had to do was leave me alone, big homie. That's it. We ain't even have to be here. I told you, *told you,* nigga, to leave me be."

"Fuck you, Enzo. Fuck you, nigga. You think the world is yours because your last name is Orlando."

"Nigga, I didn't even know I was one of them niggas until you came fucking with me," he yelled and slapped a hand down on my desk. He placed his head right into the aim of my gun, not even caring that I could pull the trigga and end him. "All I wanted to do was play football. That was all I ever wanted to do before niggas like you and Dame decided to play God." He laughed. That nigga laughed with a madness in his eyes that was unmatched by anything I'd seen. "Niggas like to play King Kong in this bitch, but remember it was a motherfucking plane that took that monkey down, and, nigga, I'm that plane."

I knew those words. Had used them to taunt him at one time. Rage burned in me. Staring that young nigga in the eyes, I could see the monster he was lurking behind them. All I had to do was pull the trigga. Cock back and let a bullet speak for me. The world didn't need Enzo. The world didn't need another nigga like Dame, Dante, Lu, and Caltrone. All I had to do was pull the trigga, so I did. I pulled it twice. *Put two bullets in that nigga's skull and watch the life drain from his eyes.*

Only when I pulled the trigga, nothing happened. I cocked the gun back and tried to fire two rounds and all I was rewarded with was Enzo's cocky chuckle.

"Dumb nigga. You still a dumb nigga, Micah. Fucking with me this whole time and you still underestimate me, homie," he taunted.

Before I could react, Enzo snatched the gun from my hand and brought it down over my head. That nigga had caught me off guard and rocked my senses, I couldn't lie. I lay back in the chair feeling my blood spill down my head as I looked at the boy who'd become everything I knew he would be. He turned to walk out of my office.

"I was right," I called out behind him. He stopped and turned to look at me. "I knew you were your father's son. No matter how you try to deny it, you still that nigga."

Enzo grinned at me. Grinned like he'd won the lottery. "You're right. I am my father's son. I'm every bit of that nigga, I've come to learn. Just like he took out your old man, I'm going to take out you. Tell your sister hello for me when you see her," he said with an arrogance that sent me over the edge.

Images of my sister being thrown into the back of that white BMW started to haunt me. My mother's screams and cries, father's lifeless body hitting the ground all had me rushing behind the boy only to be met by men in black suits, guns trained on me. They kept me at bay until Enzo had gotten back into the black-on-black Hummer and driven off.

After the day the Orlandos took my whole family away from me, all I heard were the whispers of how my father had been stupid to go up against them. People talked about my sister like she wasn't even human. Said shit about her getting what she deserved for fooling with men like them. She was a fucking kid! Just a fucking child! Someone, somebody, somewhere should have done something. Then to know she was found days later, beaten, raped, murdered, and then tossed like yesterday's trash, was when the little boy was no more.

I became something that I didn't even recognize anymore. Now, the man who'd all but sent his son after my sister was back because his arrogant grandson thought the world was his. Thought he could have anything he wanted simply because he had Orlando blood in him. *Fuck him. Fuck the bitch who bred him and fuck the nigga whose nuts he came from.*

"I tried, Pops. I really did," I mumbled to myself as I stumbled back into my office. "Tried to get the niggas who got you, Mama, Erica . . ."

Hot tears rolled down my face as I finally realized I'd failed my family once again. Couldn't save them then, couldn't avenge them now. I'd failed. The darkness in the room engulfed me like flames in a building drenched in gasoline.

"Took a lot of them down, Pops, I did. You would have been proud of me. If them niggas hadn't . . . If they hadn't been cowards, shot you in the back of the head when you weren't looking, Pops . . . Fucked up. Cowards, the whole family, buncha fucking cowards, Pops."

I was in such a fit of rage I didn't even realize that what I assumed were my thoughts had actually manifested in the room. By the time I realized that I was talking out loud, I'd gone through my office like a madman. Chairs had grown wings and flown across the room. The oak wood bookcase lay on the floor. Glasses of liquor had been tossed around like they had been juggled and dropped. I needed to get it together or my whole operation would be in shambles like my office. I felt like shit was coming undone. Needed to get it together so I could get that nigga and the rest of his family off the streets.

Chapter 6

Enzo

My feet slammed against the door of my new cozy cell as I sat pissed all the way off, making sure to make mental notes of everything that was going down. I used my connections to get me in and out and then back into the jail again. I could have just escaped, but that wasn't a part of the bigger picture. Niggas had me twisted, and it was crazy how quick people loved you as an athlete then turned their backs on you. Was I shocked by that shit? Nope, not in the least bit; but I still was annoyed.

Deebo and Uncle Phil had moved me into a general population cell where I walked straight into a setup.

"Ey yo, look at this pretty nigga right here," one black-gum and crooked-eye-looking nigga popped off.

I rolled my shoulders and walked in with a slow stroll, checking my surroundings and saying nothing. Bitch-ass niggas always thought by pointing out that a nigga was "pretty" it would piss him off, make him pissed at the gay undertones. But in reality, I was just counting the offenses.

A deep laugh sounded off and another cat stepped up to plate. It was just me, Jabba the Hutt, and Jar Jar Binks. Around me were two beds. I figured this must be where the prison population who was about to be transported chillaxed, because it was a little too cozy for my taste. Something in me realized that it was probably that way so they could get away with fucking me up. I was ready for it, excited and expecting it. Which was why I casually moved to rest against the wall and check out my enemies.

"Pretty? Shit! That nigga is pussy ready. Ey yo! You that Enzo cat huh? Heard 'bout cha. It's true you an Orlando man? Fuckkkk do you know that last time an Orlando went to prison, that nigga got got?" Jabba sputtered out, getting closer in my face to glare into my darkening eyes.

I kept quiet and gave a yawn. A nigga was bored, but I was going to let them do them, just to see how much they knew.

"Ah yeah, I heard about that shit on the block. Nigga was found with his dick in his mouth. Got dayum shit was bloody 'n' ya know what? We got the same shit for any nigga claiming to be him, don't we, Chunk?" Jar Jar taunted as he also came up to me with his ashy hands rubbing together.

"So is it true? Yeah, we know it's true. Micah got a little gift for you, nigga, since you like hanging an' shit," Jar Jar continued.

From the moment I walked into the cell until the moment I was escorted out, everything that went down was like a wonderful haze that I clearly remembered. A menacing smile spread across my face. My hands clutched at my sides, digging into my palms. All it took was one head butt to that nigga Chunk's nose and a quick arched punch on the top of Jar Jar's matted locs to set everything just right. The rough sound of grunts and hisses surrounded me. I pushed my way out of being surrounded by the two dudes. Don't get me wrong, this battle was hard since I was outnumbered, but it was all about perspective that helped me survive.

Chunk's beefy hands slammed me back against the wall, where Jar Jar snatched me to slam my head against the bed. Spit shot out from between my clenched teeth.

My abs constricted so I could center my core and push back with my foot and a clean uppercut. I watched Jar Jar stare in shock while I pushed up to rush him and slam him into the bars.

The sound of Jar Jar's yelp gave me fleeting satisfaction. Chunk came up behind me and snatched me up. Nigga squeezed my rib cage so tight that I thought I was going to black out, but that was cool because I lived in that zone. I dug at his arms then rolled my shoulders to unhinge them. This allowed me to slam my fist into his temple hitting hard enough to black that nigga out. I watched him stumble then growl like a drunk pit bull as he tried to snatch me.

Jar Jar stood confused and I just smiled and wiped the blood off my face. "What was that shit you said you knew about that Orlando cat? You said he was my pops? Shit, I don't even know that, but it seems you know a hell of a lot. Let me holla at'cha real quick." I smirked then headed after Jar Jar.

Chunk was still squirming from the pressure point hit I gave him and I paused to snatch him by the head and slam it into the concrete floor. I figured that would make Jar Jar think I was ignoring him and it pretty much worked out in my favor. As I kept smashing that dude's head in, Jar Jar rushed me and sent me sideways into the wall. Blow after blow came at me, but I used a football move to slip to that nigga's side in a smooth swipe, twist his arm behind him, and wrap my arm around that goon's neck.

I gazed up at the ceiling studying the lights as I squeezed. Something like a sensation of pleasure mixed with raw hatred washed over me. It had me so hyped that I started laughing. Nigga tried to struggle but it only made it worse for him. He grunted and wagged around, then spit blood spewing from him, until I heard a pop and I sighed in pleasure.

"Why the fuck do I enjoy this so much? It's like butta, my nigga. That choking sound you making? Shieet, priceless. Now let me tell you a secret that nigga that got got in prison. Yeah, that's my pops; but guess what? It was my mom who helped get the man in prison who offed him. Side with who you know; and, nigga, you know nothing about me. You played wrong, night-night, nigga." With that, I took the bed sheet off the bed, roped it around that cat, and let him swing from the top bar over Chunk's dead and battered body.

Blood was everywhere. I wiped theirs off of me, sat on the bed, and shouted, "Oh shit! Fat bastard just fucked up this gangly looking nigga then had a heart attack! Y'all niggas need to do something with that! I wasn't supposed to be in here. I'm a celeb, man. This the fuck y'all do to celebs?"

After that, I was dragged off and both Deebo and Uncle Phil glared at me, pissed off. Now after my fun with Jar Jar and Chunk, I sat in my private holding cell ticking off the time.

"Where's my fucking phone call? I got a lawyer I need to get, too!" I shouted, hoping to piss off more cops.

A deep voice softly penetrated my cell, making me glance up to see a tall nigga with short locs and cardboard-brown skin approaching me. He rolled his sleeves up to show me his forearm, which had the branding DOA on it. Disgusted, I pushed myself up to study the nigga's beard-covered face. He seemed to be in his mid-twenties. He was almost as tall as I was from what I could tell when he walked into the cell with me.

"Whatever you need, I got for you. I'll set you up with a lawyer and get you out of here and back on the field, fam; just know you got backing in the law," he explained, brown eyes locking on me to make sure I was paying attention.

"I ain't got no fam through you and I don't need a lawyer by you, either," I retorted. I thumbed my nose and definitely kept my chin up while watching him. There was nothing in him that I could trust. Which was why I kept my distance while wondering what this cat was going to say next. Blood stained the front of my tee and oversized jail-issued pants, as my fists clenched by my sides.

"It's a code I have to stand by and that's helping fam, cousin. You're an Orlando for sure. Chill and relax. I'll get you out of here," he said again, keeping his words low to where only I could hear.

"A'ght then, but check it. I wasn't playing. I want my call. On a secure line, in private," I countered.

"I got you. Just sit still, fam," I heard this nigga who said he was fam say. I watched him walk out while slamming the door and that was the last I saw of him until what felt like two hours later.

He walked in and tilted his head up. "Get up. It looks like you don't need your call, fam."

"What you mean?" I hesitantly stood and kept my distance.

"You have guests; follow me. I got you set up in a private spot, no ears or eyes," he explained with a smirk while walking out.

See, how my mind works, I already was thinking that I was being set up on some more shit, but I followed anyway. Shock hit me hard when I saw Shy with Angel by her side, sitting quietly and waiting. My aunt—well, mom—sported a black-and-gold scarf that wrapped around her head like a hoodie. She had on all black again, but this time it was a simple fitted black long-sleeve top and leggings with boots that reached her thick thighs. My mom sported a pair of glammed-out shades and she tapped her long nails on the table before her.

Angel sat beside her, pulling out a water bottle I was sure was mixed with the healing fruit juices my mom always sipped on. Bianca also had on all black. She sported a pair of jeggings, with open black utility boots. She had a hoodie short black jacket that covered her long white tank and her breasts were peeking out in a caramel hue. I shifted on my feet and noticed that her natural hair was styled in a way that hid her face under the hood she wore as well and I gazed at both women with a smile. I wondered what they had to say.

Heading inside, I glanced around and sat with my cuffed hands in front of me. "'Sup, *Tía?* 'Sup, B. What's shaking?" My words were coded. I didn't trust anything that was around me. Unfamiliar surroundings did that to people.

"We came as soon as we could, especially since there was no call," Shy explained while taking a sip from her bottle. She held up her hand then continued. "Which I know wasn't your fault."

I gave a nod and let her continue.

"Several things are going to happen. We have your lawyer on retainer. As you sit here, we have some things working on your behalf right now. One is your release okay?" she coolly said, keeping her emotions level even though she allowed me to see her true feelings in her eyes.

It was tripping me out because I hadn't seen that side of Shy in a long time. The woman in front of me was the woman I got a glimpse of when I was a kid and told her about my coach. She was the woman who went stone cold when I explained that my assistant coach had reached out to touch my shit, and she was the woman who disappeared for days, only showing up several weeks later after that same assistant coach went missing. A killer was in front of me and I understood that she was only there to see if I was safe and to take names and memorize faces.

It had me smiling and leaning back in my chair. "Yes, ma'am. I'm cool with that. Do the plan and I'll wait this shit out."

Shy slowly stood. She walked to me and kissed my temple, whispering in my ear, "Your shadow is with some Misfits for extra safety and to make sure you are able to concentrate on the big picture. You don't have to worry about a thing; we have you." She wrapped her arms around me and then headed to the door. "You two need to speak. I'll be getting some air. I have people here to speak with."

In the moment, I turned quickly to glimpse the woman I was becoming accustomed to having as my mother. "You good though?"

Shy turned and gave me a calm smile then blew a kiss my way. "Like a predator, yes, I am. I love you, Shawn."

I frowned and she walked out leaving me with Angel. I turned quickly to see Bianca eying me wearily.

"Is she good for real?" I asked low.

Angel gave me a nod and played with her fingers on the table before me. "I'm making sure she is. Yeah, she is. So, you just okay with being in here?"

I chuckled and shrugged. "No doubt. I'm keeping my cool. Besides, last time they had a problem with holding an innocent cat, the whole place got shot up. I doubt they want that trouble again."

A lighthearted laugh came from Angel. She knew very well who I was speaking about and she sighed. "Look, I'm making sure—"

"Hey, do something for me?" I calmly interrupted.

"Ah, yeah?" she muttered glancing at me.

Her eyes were a nutty tone to the point of turning dark and I sighed. "Just listen, a'ight? There's no time to say I'm sorry in a deep way, but I am. A nigga has very few people to trust, and since I appreciate how you handling my *tía,* all I can do now is deal with whatever comes with trusting you; and that is me saying I'm sorry. A'ight? Also, with that comes this: I need you to hold down my fam. Handle whatever you gotta do to get close to a nigga we both know. I'm depending on you to be smart, cunning, manipulative, and lethal, a'ight? Like how you made it into the NFL: use those skills to take this shit further. I'm counting on you to be my hands when I can't. Like now. Can you do that? If you can't, if you too chicken shit or if you really just plain dumb, just ride out now. Ask my *tía* to set up you up nice and go somewhere and disappear, a'ight?"

Angel gazed at me and, for a moment, I thought she had tears. It caused me to glance away to calm my own emotions and wait for her response. When she muttered, "Okay," I turned my head to study her.

"Thank you, shawty, but what does that mean exactly?" I asked for clarity.

"Means I'm here for your aunt above all things, and even . . . you know who." She glanced around then rubbed her shoulders. "I'm not feeling you in here, so you need to come on okay? Whatever you need I'll help and do it because I'm not some basic bitch like you thought I was, so I'll learn what I have to and make it work for your safety," she passionately stated.

I watched her stand and move to rest a hand on my cuffs, but what she did next shocked the shit out of me. Her hand moved like lightning striking a tree to slap my face. She gripped my jaw and leaned down close so that only I could hear, "Don't put your hands on me again because I'm not some sour foul bitch. You did me dirty, nigga, when I was on your team. I did everything, everything, you asked of me. Other niggas were gunning for you and I had your back. You held me down and protected me; that gave me something I ain't ever had and now I'm giving you that back. But don't you ever, ever put your hands on me again, Enzo. I'm telling you, or I promise on everything I know, I will try my best to kill you, nigga. Tell me okay."

My dick thumped in my pants and I gave her a smirk. My eyes slightly turned dark as I stared at a woman who I could now read like a book. "Kiss me and hold my dick for a moment and I'll see what I'll say."

Her eyes narrowed and I chuckled when she tried to fight a smile breaking through. I thought she was going to back up, but she gave me that kiss, and our tongues danced. She tasted like fruit, strangely, and I enjoyed it, especially the feel of her soft lips against mine and then her hand on my dick. I heard her sigh; then she frowned, stepping back.

"Where're your piercings?" she quipped.

My head shook again and I shifted in my chair. "They made me remove all that shit. It's cool, just how they do it. B. Remember what I asked. I know my *tía* got you handled in what we do in cases like that. Listen, follow, do your thing. I need a Bonnie, be that."

"I will. I should go," she whispered, eyeing me hungrily.

A smile spread across my face and I watched her walk out, her ass jiggling in a way that had my dick in pain. Turning in my seat, I moved on to the next plan on the list. Time was my friend. Deebo and Uncle Phil's friends came into the room I was in, snatched me back up, and threw me back in my cell. I swore these niggas were a little too enthusiastic about this shit but it was what it was.

Several hours later a man—who resembled the dude given to my aunt to watch over her whenever she needed to head out of the house—appeared in my cell. I was lying back on my cot with my arm over my face when I heard the lock to the bars open up. I felt like being a prick so I was spitting out T.I.'s "Trap Muzik."

With my foot tapping against the wall, banging out a beat, I beasted the lyrics: "'Man wherever I be, the Feds got me scoped out, motherfucker let my nuts hang.'"

"'Block out the duc canes, cook it to it bubbles, double fast as a mustang.'" I heard an accented deep voice finish the lyrics.

My head turned to the side and recognition had me standing up quickly as he walked into the room with his briefcase, a crisp gray suit, and slick, shiny shoes. He rubbed his light white speckled lined goatee and in his dark eyes he held amusement and something else: surprise. Calling him Mirror wasn't going to happen in this case. I understood he was playing another role, so I kept quiet until he spoke.

"It appears they have been holding you wrongfully, Mr. Banks," he explained, while taking two strides to my cot and sitting on it. "Looks like it won't be a thing to get you out of here. Wrongful accusations about a past they can't prove was part of a RICO lifestyle. Holding you longer than is protocol as well as unnecessary physical assault against you, quite a mess it is, mi friend," Mirror explained, his accent lilting out from time to time.

That familiar nerve in my jaw ticked the more I clenched my teeth. It took everything in me to keep my words back so I took several breaths while Mirror's voice dropped into a faint whisper. I also kept my eyes on the door just in case and gave him responses with a nod of my head.

"Has Micah been in here?" he questioned and I shook my head no. "Just so you know, he's on the premises. I saw him. Also your aunt"—he paused, letting me know that he knew the truth of my creation—"filled me in on everything. I noticed that cop with the branding is one of DOA's former cunts. Whatever yuh agenda is, use him to yuh fullest, mi friend."

Mirror stood, scribbled some notes while looking around the cell, and then gave a curt nod, returning to a British accent. "Your civil rights were violated. This is going to go in your favor, and don't worry about those two missing people. The real culprit has been identified and they are seeking him out. Foul scum in the streets but the most ruthless know how to die poetically. I'll work your bail; just keep your fist out of cops' mouths. This will only take a few, mate."

"What about the drugs and gun?" I asked.

"We'll see what we can do about that. If anything, people love the bad boy, but for now, let's focus on your bail, mi friend. Don't worry about a thing. Yuh family has you as yuh just saw," Mirror reassured me.

Another nod came from me, to let him know I understood. I sat where he had, rested my ankle on my knee, and laid my head back against the cold brick wall with an internal smile. I needed to shave, shower, and get back on the field. Micah and me had some things to discuss and since he was somewhere around here, I figured that conversation was going to be scheduled very soon.

An hour later, Mirror came back with the DOA cop behind him. I checked how that cat eyed me as I slowly walked out of my cell with Mirror behind me.

The cop stepped forward and I muttered low, "Wherever the rest of them are at, you let them know what's up. We'll have a family reunion on my terms when I want it, a'ight?"

"No doubt, cousin. I'll relay that intel; anything else you need?" the cop asked me and I gave a shrug before responding.

Keeping my hands behind my back, I did a rundown just for this dude's comfort. "It's a nigga gunning for me. Having me step in to make sure that he doesn't get his hands on power that ain't his to have. Nigga is a turncoat,

a pussy-ass bitch who has been manipulating what is my
birthright. He has eyes in here; get those eyes corrected
or dig them out, a'ight?" Not watching the cop anymore,
I stared straight ahead down the hall waiting, seeing how
this would work out.

Like clockwork, the cop cleared his throat and gave
a nod. "I got you. If you need me, you can find me as
Lieutenant Bryant. In the streets they call me Fuego
because I play with fire."

It was then that I noticed a slight accent to his voice.
"You really fam then huh?"

Fuego gave a nod then slipped me a card with his
contact info. "I'm ya cousin, and I'm the sane one. Let's
ride out, fam."

Heading through the hall, I eyed the nigga. He carried
some of my looks, though I looked better. He had light
eyes, and the short locs that fell around his face were
actually braided up. On his neck, I could see a Cuban
flag and a US flag merging into one. He said he was the
sane one but fuck that lie. I got a quart of the same blood
and I was fucked up. Shaking my head, I gave an inward
sigh not wanting to deal with the bullshit that came with
being an Orlando.

Incessant talking sounded around the three of us as we
strolled by. I tilted my head up with a smirk, watching
Uncle Phil and Deebo stare at me with all hate, but also
smelling and reflecting fear in their eyes. I purposely
turned my head to smile at them, reminding them of
my words. I meant every bit of them. The cold darkness
in me was going to hunt down every last member of
their families, and end their lives, while saving the main
culprits for last. I had no love for those who attempted
to destroy my livelihood. If you weren't family or an ally
then you weren't shit to me.

The feel of Mirror behind me disappeared and I noticed he had vanished. I knew cameras weren't his thing. Though he could change his appearance, he still was cautious and I had mad respect for him for that. So I stepped out into the cool air, noticing that he was pulling up in his blacked-out Bentley. Mirror stepped out of the ride behind the press and fans and waited.

My PR rep, Dymetra Clarke, stood with her hands out in a tight maxi skirt that had her calves looking like sex as she sported a pair of cream and black heels. She was thick, her ass poking out, and I gave a sigh. She was also linked to the African Queens and I had no clue about that until my mother let me in on that info. She had just finished saying something to the media in defense of me and all that had been going on.

Her hair was sideswiped into a fishtail braid of micro-braids. She had sumptuous tits, lush lips, and was sexy in an "around the way" kind of look. She also was the color of bourbon and smart as fuck. We boned a couple of times when we were both bored. But outside of that, she was married to another sports nigga who played ball, and I really wasn't invested in her outside of trusting her with my career and trusting in her hand at murder.

"Damn," I heard Fuego mutter by my side.

A smile played across my face as I stepped forward. "Pussy is like yack, shit is sweet and tight, but she that type who only give it when she want to, so she ain't worth it, fam. Besides, I had her first and the chick is married. One. We'll speak later."

Heading toward my PR rep, I felt the burning sensation of hatred on me and it had me turning to the left with a slick grin. Standing in the doorway of the police station was Micah. He was still fucked up, bruised up, and had a bandage on the side of his face. I gave him the thumbs-up, then turned back to head to my ride where

Mirror stood waiting. I could tell he saw what I did to Micah due to the way his shoulders shook with laughter.

Reporters rushed after me asking me various questions and I turned to address them.

"Shawn! Shawn! Are the allegations true? Were you being held for two murders and RICO charges in association with Dame Orlando?" one reporter passionately asked.

My gaze went to Micah who studied me with his own sneer. I knew he had leaked that part of the information. My PR rep stood beside me as I spoke, occasionally whispering in my ear, telling me what to say and what not to say.

"Baby, I am a lover, not a fighter, or a killer. The only deaths I cause are on the field, so yes, the allegations are true, but the facts behind it all are all lies," I responded.

I hammed it up for the cameras, flashing a smile and acting like the media-loving athlete. "I know nothing about Dame's hand in any of that except from what I've heard in the streets. I was born and raised here in Atlanta and was trained here. All I know about him is that he supported us kids as athletes and created a program to get us off the streets; that's the only business I did with him indirectly. Men like Micah Tems had direct involvement with him through picking us kids out of the camp. So please understand that my life is the game and not some debasing, slanderous lies meant to stop me from doing what I was born to do: be the King of the A!"

My tongue ran over my lips while I glanced up in that moment at Micah knowing he understood what I was saying in those words. My media training with what Shy taught me gave me all the ammo I needed. Which was why I hoped that my words would also act as bait for one question I was waiting to be asked.

"Speaking of, we heard the name Orlando being tied to your name; is this true?" another reporter asked.

There it was. I let my face drop in sadness, which really wasn't a hard stretch for me. I bowed my head, ran a hand over my face, and nodded. Dymetra rubbed my back as I spoke. "This is news that I only recently was given but . . ." I gave a sad sigh and that was when Mirror stepped forward, taking over.

"Mr. Banks' birth was that of an attack on his birth mother. She was but a young girl in college when she was stalked and assaulted against her will. The attack resulted in Mr. Banks and in his mother's death as well. Sadly, it is this dark past that Mr. Banks is not proud of; however, he wanted those children in the streets of Atlanta to understand and relate with it, that he too knows the struggle. That he too knows how it is to try to survive in a world that would try to hold you back and turn you into something you wish not to be. Mr. Banks has used his past as a strength to help him be the athlete you all love and cherish. He is not a murderer or killer or any other label you wish to give. But he is a young man eager to bring a new change to Atlanta and be a mentor for the youth," Mirror passionately explained.

Like I said, Mirror didn't like cameras. But when he had to, he made moves and he usually did it with his face being altered in some manner, like it was tonight. It was those words that had Micah punching his fist into the wall near him and storming off. I gave a flash of a smile and stepped forward with the rest of the icing. A raise was definitely coming for Mirror after this.

"Please respect my need for privacy in this moment. I just learned of this and I wanted to explain that I am a child of Atlanta and Orlando is my blood. I am here for the people. Please don't lose faith in me. I send my prayers to those who have gone missing who were also found murdered. I offer myself as a help to those people's families, and I know that justice will be had. God bless." With that, I turned my back on the flashing lights, climbed into the car, and waited to pull off, leaving Dymetra behind to answer the rest of the questions.

The nigga I learned was my cousin gave me a nod then walked back into the precinct as Mirror hopped in the ride, revved up the engine, and then pulled off.

"You know he's going to come hard at yuh again, mi friend?" Mirror asked me.

Watching the precinct disappear, I knew he was right. I scratched the side of my jaw in thought about my family and career. "Yeah, just make sure what is mine is protected; then whatever happens after that just happens. I'm game."

"Sounds like yuh becoming a kingpin already. A'ight, mi friend. Listen though: whatever yuh need, yuh have one house backing yuh as yuh build up yours." Mirror chuckled while driving.

Sighing, I joined him in the ironic laughter. "I didn't want this but yeah. Looks like I inherited it, so yeah. Let's build this shit and let me call my *tía* to tell her what went down."

I may have been young as fuck. I knew for damn sure I was too young to be able to hold my own like I just did, but I was schooled by the very best: Shy. My mother was a queen. The streets were my backbone, and the chess piece I just moved was called checkmate. Micah wanted a war and he now just got it. One day he was going to learn not to fuck with what you didn't understand. It was his move.

Chapter 7

Angel

Bullets. Live rounds. A barrage of those motherfuckers came at the car Shy and I left the jail in. While all the windows and the truck were bulletproof, Shy assured me, the tires weren't. And they shot those fuckers right out from under us. My first mind was to protect Shy. Enzo had just asked me as we left the station to look out for his aunt and brother until he could get out. It was as if he expected to be locked up for the long haul, which puzzled and bothered me.

We had been sitting in traffic, heading toward a venue Shy had said she needed to go to and scope out for the charity event she was going to be doing. I didn't think anybody would be following us because of how cautious Shy was and how thorough she was with her security detail; but, alas, there we were hunkered down in traffic in the middle of downtown Atlanta as someone tried unsuccessfully to riddle the black Escalade with bullets.

"Don't worry about me," Shy said as she crouched down in the truck then reached underneath her seat. "You arm yourself," she ordered as she opened the steel black suitcase she pulled out.

"What are we going to do?" I asked. I still ducked and cowered as if the bullets could somehow breach the steel contraption and get to us.

"We're going to fight back because that's the only way we're going to get out of here," she said as she looked up at me and loaded two Desert Eagles.

"Boss, I'll use myself as a distraction to buy you and the girl time. You two get the fuck up out of here as soon as I step out this door, you hear me?" the driver asked as he stared straight ahead.

"Jennings, you don't have to do that," Shy told the man.

"How long I been employed by this family, Iya?" the man asked Shy as he turned to look at her. The gunfire had abruptly stopped and we could see about five men closing in on the vehicle from the front.

"Since I was a child."

"How long have the Kulu Kings taken care of me and my family?"

"Since before I was born."

"So don't you go telling me what I don't have to do," the elderly but stout Italian man said sternly. He looked to be Sicilian because of his dark features, but just judging by the look of complete devotion on his face, I knew his loyalty belonged to the African Queens.

"If by chance the wrong thing happens, Bonita, the girls, and your grandchildren will always be taken of," Shy said as she laid a hand on the man's shoulder.

"I never doubted it," was all the man said before he grabbed two M-10s from the seat next to him and opened the car door.

As soon as his feet touched the black asphalt, bullets started to fly. One caught him in the shoulder and another in the leg, but the man stood anyway. When he let his bullets spray, the men took cover.

Shy kicked the back door of the Escalade open on the right side, fell backward, and let her bullets rain down on the streets of Atlanta. I had to admit, I was surprised at her agility since the woman was damn near on her deathbed. Still, I jumped out of the other side of the truck and covered her. My utility boots hit the pavement hard as I ran through a maze of abandoned cars. The two 9 mm Sig Sauer handles resting against my palm as the muscles in my hand struggled to control them sounded off like fireworks. The recoil from the fire of the bullets shook my hands as I ran behind Shy and covered her six.

For her to be a cancer patient, she wasn't acting like one. As she ran and slid over cars, shooting niggas, I saw a glimpse of the woman she used to be, of a woman she had to become because the devil wouldn't leave her alone. The woman who had just taken the butt of her gun and knocked a man twice her size on his ass looked like an assassin as she ran in all black with the scarf around her face making her look like she was from a foreign country.

I took her lead, followed her, watched her as I took aim and fired at an approaching man who tried to come from her blind side.

"We need to get to Peachtree Street on the northeast end. There is an abandoned building that used to be a restaurant called the Pleasant Peasant. You'll know it because it's a mix between pea green and shit brown in color with a light blue building attached to it. It's a safe location," she said as we ran side by side.

A Tahoe came skidding to a halt in front of us, as we ran down Linden Avenue. Shy stopped running and took aim like the skilled shooter she was. Even if the windows in that truck had been bulletproof, the Desert Eagles Shy was busting would have broken through the glass. Two bullets, one to the head and one in the heart, through the windshield took the driver out. When the passenger tried to escape, I was on him. As soon as he turned his back to run, I caught him in his spine. Once he fell, I ran over to him and pumped two into his skull.

I heard Shy yell out as her body hit the ground. I tried to run for her, but I was snatched up from behind by the hood I had on. I did a quick spin move and slid it over my head then kicked the man who had grabbed me in his dick so hard I swore I heard one of his balls pop.

"Arrrghh. You bitch," he roared out as his knees hit the pavement.

"All day," I responded before going on the attack again.

I gave a running kick to his face as I heard Shy struggling on the other side of the truck. The man in front of me went down hard. I rushed around the truck expecting to find Shy in a sticky situation. Instead, I found that she had brandished a knife from somewhere and was in the process of slicing a man from ear to ear. Those grunts I heard had been her fighting, judging by the way the man's face had been busted open. She kneeled over the man and as she cut him there was a look of pure elation on her face, one I had only seen on two other people: Enzo and Drew.

She then stood and brought the sharp, pointy heel of her boot down into the man's eye. "That'll learn you not to fuck with a woman in heels, bitch," she said then spit on the man's body.

People ran around us. Screams and yells could be heard in the melee as sirens closing in on us alerted us to the threat that loomed over us. I grabbed Shy by her hand and hit the corner of Linden and Peachtree. The building that Shy had referenced was one building down. She rushed up to the door, hit a hidden panel, and then punched in a code so quick that I wasn't even sure she knew what she had entered. We rushed inside and slammed the door behind us.

I finally realized that I needed to breathe. Chest was burning like it was on fire. The establishment was barren except for a telephone and a flat-screen wall monitor. The

walls were brick; the area where I was sure the bar had
been sat dusty and empty. The floors needed to be swept
and polished of the dust and cobwebs.

I watched on in silence as Shy picked up the phone,
punched in some numbers, and waited. She was ex-
hausted, barely standing as she waited. Her chest rapidly
heaved up and down and I could see what color she had
left slowly draining from her face.

Once someone answered the phone, Shy pressed the
speaker button and said, "Hello?"

"Good day, love." A British accent came through the
phone. I could tell it belonged to Phenom. Unlike Mirror,
Phenom's Caribbean accent didn't blend in with his faux
British one.

"I wish this were a social call, but it isn't. I've been
attacked."

"What?" Phenom belted out.

"I . . . I was . . ." Shy stopped and caught her breath
before continuing. "I was on my way to a venue after
leaving Shawn at the jail. Micah sent men to follow me
and they attacked me in the middle of fucking downtown
Atlanta," she fussed. Mixed with her fatigue was anger
at the audacity that Micah would have the unmitigated
gall to come after her. There was a fire burning in that
woman's eyes.

"What in bloody hell do you mean this wangster sent
people after you? Does he realize—"

Phenom's words were cut off when Anika's voice came
on the phone. "You're at a safe haven. I got you pin-
pointed on the tracker."

"Good. Please get here quick, I'm . . . I . . ."

I'd been busy scoping the streets peeking through the
blinds when I noticed Shy's words fading. Shy didn't
finish her sentence. She started coughing and couldn't
stop. She pulled a handkerchief to her mouth and came

back with a pool of blood. I quickly rushed to her side. She was weak, had been without rest for too many hours.

"We're on our way," Anika spoke loudly.

The phone fell as Shy doubled over in pain.

"Iya," Anika screamed again.

"Please hurry," I pleaded frantically when I noticed Shy was bleeding from her side.

My whole world shattered.

"Oh, God. Oh, God," I cried as I held the woman in my arms.

"I don't think God ever heard me when I cried out to Him so maybe you can put in a word for me," she said as she weakly smiled up at me. "Maybe my demons are too much for even God to take." Tears filled her eyes as she looked at me. "If by chance I don't make it through, you take care of my sons for me," she said.

I could see the physical and emotional pain she was in. I was in pain with and for her. Tears rolled down my cheeks the same as hers. I'd only known the woman a short time and she'd been more of a mother than I'd ever had.

"You're going to make it. I know you will," I tried to convince her and myself.

She gave a light smile, licked her blood-laden lips, and took a deep breath. "Just in case I don't though, you keep my boys on the brink of sanity. Don't let them go to the point of no return. Promise me that, no matter what, you will protect them by any means necessary, as I've done. I'm putting all the trust I have left in you to do that for me."

"Shy, please. Just hold on, okay?"

"Answer me."

"I will. I promise, I will."

"I never doubted it. The love you have for Shawn will see to it that you do."

I was crying like she was my mother or my aunt because, in the last few weeks, she had been like family. All of our little talks and training sessions had led to this. As I got my balance to help her up, she hugged me tightly. I could feel her tears wetting my shoulder.

She took a deep, shaky breath. "Don't let Micah hurt my baby, Angel. I'm not just talking about on the field, either. I probably won't get to see my son take the Nightwings to that win in the Super Bowl. If I don't, you make sure he remembers me not in my weakest moments, not as a victim of anything, but as a woman, a strong woman, who battled through the depths of hell to protect him and his brother," she whispered in my ear.

Her grip loosened around my neck and I panicked. Part of me died in that moment. I never got to see or know how my grandmother passed, but to know that she died alone without my love there to see her through it, to know she didn't get to hug me as Shy was doing right now, broke me down. I wanted to help her up so no one would see her like she was, but I couldn't; and I thought, by the way she held me, she knew it too.

"No, no, no," I yelled out, rapidly dropping to the floor beside the woman I'd come to love.

I'd cried to her and told her a few days prior that I had no idea where my grandmother had been buried or when she'd died. She and I had spoken candidly about how I was still a little girl lost. At eighteen, I still felt as if I was that fourteen-year-old girl Dame had snatched from Garden Walk Boulevard in Riverdale. As I rocked her in my arms I remembered those tears she shed with me and I knew I would never forget the way Shy had impacted my life in such a short time.

Minutes later when Phenom and Anika rushed in from the back of the building with medics in tow, they found me on the floor with Shy's arms languidly hanging around my neck and my arms holding her limp body. She wasn't gone just yet, but the pain and exhaustion had put her to sleep for the day. Still, I was afraid of the moment, petrified that, once again, I'd be alone. Scared that Shawn and Drew would lose the only peace and love they'd ever known.

A few hours later, machines beeped around us. Drew sat in a chair next to Shy's bed. My soul was heavy and, seriously, for the first time since this whole thing began, I was just plain old tired. My body was tired. Mind was tired. Soul was burdened. I had never liked death. When Dame had killed Coco, another girl who worked for him, he had done so in front of the whole house then left her dead body, lifeless, in the middle of the floor for two hours before he allowed anyone to move it. I had nightmares of her death and her lifeless body for months after the whole ordeal. Death scared me and when Shy had passed out like that, I felt my soul was going to die along with her if she had.

Mirror's and Enzo's voices on the TV forced me out of my own head and back to reality. My heart was excited and heavy to see that Enzo was out of jail. Excited because he could protect his aunt. Heavy because he would have to see what Micah had done to her. For as long as I'd known Shy, she'd never been to a hospital; and to see that nigga Micah, who thought he could play God, put her there would no doubt put Enzo into a dark place.

I listened to the reporters as they threw questions at him back to back. But it was when the reporter asked him about being an Orlando that made me perk up. I grabbed the remote attached to Shy's bed for the TV and turned up the volume just as Mirror started talking.

"Mr. Banks' birth was that of an attack on his birth mother. She was but a young girl in college when she was stalked and assaulted against her will. The attack resulted in Mr. Banks and in his mother's death as well. Sadly, it is this dark past that Mr. Banks is not proud of; however, he wanted those children in the streets of Atlanta to understand and relate with it, that he too knows the struggle. That he too knows how it is to try to survive in a world that would try to hold you back and turn you into something you wish not to be. Mr. Banks has used his past as a strength to help him be the athlete you all love and cherish. He is not a murderer or killer or any other label you wish to give. But he is a young man eager to bring a new change to Atlanta and be a mentor for the youth," Mirror stated.

"Please respect my need for privacy in this moment. I just learned of this and I wanted to explain that I am a child of Atlanta and Orlando is my blood. I am here for the people. Please don't lose faith in me. I send my prayers to those who have gone missing, who were also found murdered. I offer myself as a help to those people's families, and I know that justice will be had. God bless."

I took a deep breath and sat back in the chair. It was as if the life had been smacked out of me. I looked at Drew to see he too had been watching. I could tell by the look in his eyes and the way his chest swelled that he was waiting on my reaction. I turned my attention to Shy to see tears rolling down her cheek before she slowly opened her eyes. She hadn't been asleep as I'd thought.

I sat in stunned silence. There was nothing I could say that would make any of what I was feeling any better. Micah had been right. I'd been so busy running from Dame's ghost that I ran right back into him in a way. Enzo was an Orlando and all I could do was sit there. I was conflicted as shit on my feelings at that point. Did I still love Enzo? More than likely. I couldn't help that. I was deeply attracted to all facets of him. The good, the bad, and the downright crazy.

"Shawn and Andrew are both Orlandos," Shy's faint voice spoke up.

"I . . . I don't know what to say," I replied.

"You don't have to say anything. I hate how they came to be, but I love those boys regardless, always have, always will. Did I make some mistakes along the way? Yes, but just as I told them, I did what I had to do."

"But, how . . . What . . ." I didn't even know what to ask her.

She held her hand up then asked Drew to get her some crushed ice and water from the private facility's cafeteria. Once Drew was gone, she turned back to me. She opened her mouth and told me the story behind Enzo's and Drew's conception. When she was done, I was disgusted, appalled, hurt, and angry for her.

"Why didn't anyone do anything?" I asked her in frustration.

"He had me under lock and key. I wasn't always the fearless woman I am now. He scared me by threatening my family and those closest to me. But believe me, when I got tired of being scared and tired, Lu never got a chance to do to any other woman what he did to me."

My hand was over my mouth as tears raced down my cheek. I slowly got up, walked over to her bedside, and hugged her. Just thinking about all the shit that man had done to Shy pissed me off. I didn't think anything she told me could get worse until she told me it was Lu who had given her cancer. His dirty dick–having ass had given her HPV, which caused the ovarian cancer that was threatening to kill her. At that point all I could do was remain silent. I had no more words.

Chapter 8

Enzo

The sound of Jay-Z had me turning off my shower and reaching out for my cell. I had just gotten in my private home, close to where I had gotten my mom's secret house, and was getting the funk of several days in the slammer off my body. I was going to call and tell my birth mom that I was out, but my ass itched so I had to clean shit. My hair was curling from being wet. My face was cleanly shaved and I smelled on point. Bruises with several cuts lined my ribcage, arms, and legs. They had worked me up good, cut my lip, given me a sore jaw, but I wasn't tripping. I had gotten out and I had plans to take care of.

Hitting answer, I grabbed a towel and stepped out of the shower, steam streaming from my slick golden skin. "Talk to me."

"*Tía* is at the hospital. She got attacked and shot at by that nigga Micah, bro. Where you at?" Drew rushed out.

His voice had that scared shaking quality of a kid and it hit me on all levels. I was trying to compute what was being said. I could hear Mirror banging on my door hollering that we needed to bounce, but for some reason I was frozen in place with the steam of my shower swirling around me and off my skin.

A twinge of pain hit me in my chest. I started rubbing but couldn't make it go away. "He did what?"

Drew repeated himself. This time it was with a slightly heated tone to his voice as he asked me where I was and I just stood in a daze again. Banging sounded again, rattling the door. Eventually it had me yelling to Mirror that I was talking to Drew.

At that second, his urgent pounding stopped as I finally found my feet. "But she's good right? She can't be hurt, bro."

Drew's silence then slight sniffle let me know that wasn't the case. My baby brother cleared his throat, which let me know he wasn't about to let his tears fall while he spoke.

"Naw. Angel . . . Angel said they were leaving from visiting you when she saw they were being followed. So that old dude Jennings started doing some racing shit, handling business, but eventually they got surrounded and had to run, until she got hit. Shawn, please, I know they had you locked up, wasn't sure you were out, but you gotta come," he said.

My throat felt tight and my eyes scratchy. All types of thoughts swarmed my mind. She couldn't die. Shy couldn't leave us like the woman we thought was our real mom did. She couldn't let that nigga who abused and polluted her body, which caused the cancer, to win. She could not let that lame nigga Micah with his sick-ass ven-detta win so easy, either. Was no fucking way I'd allow it. If she died, Micah, along with every Orlando I could find, was going to meet death in the same way she experienced torture by that nigga's hand. A pound of flesh was going to be nothing once I got done, fuck the plan.

"Bro! Shawn, please; you coming, man?" Drew pleaded, shouting in my ear.

The fear, pain, and sadness in his voice brought me back to reality. I was standing with my hand on the door of my bedroom with the doorknob in my hand. I didn't realize that I had basically blacked out on my brother in that moment. Blood was rushing in my ears and I had to take several breaths before getting right on track.

I had been back in Chicago, running the streets, trying to take care of feeding Drew. In my mind, I walked in the house, dropped my backpack, sat Drew down in front of the TV to watch *PBS Kids,* and headed to my mom's room, to the woman I learned was my real aunt. Opening the door to her bedroom, I walked in just to check on her and kiss her cheek; but what I was greeted by was the strong smell of drugs, and death. Mama Sade lay in her own filth from having been lying dead for so long. My mom's once pretty face was covered in bruises; her honey brown eyes were now vacant of all life. I'd never forget that shit for the life of me and now my mom Shy was going to leave me just like Mama Sade did, except this time it was from the cancer she had been fighting against for years. I felt helpless in that moment.

"Enzo!" Drew shouted again bringing me back.

For the first time since I was a kid back in Chicago, I felt like crying, but I held that shit back for the kid who was on the other end of the phone, and the man I was trying to be.

"Sorry. I'm on my way with Mirror . . . Was getting cleaned up. I'm on my way. I promise," I murmured, dropping my hand from the doorknob and moving into my room.

I grabbed a bag with some things I knew she liked, and I listened to Drew just breathing, trying to get his own self in check before speaking up again. "Fuck is up, man? Hurry up. We need you. I need you, bro."

"I love you too, bro," I said it for him so he wouldn't feel weak. I always took on what he couldn't and I never had a problem with it. "I'm on my way," I stated again, hoping the strength in my voice would help him.

"A'ight. I love you too." With that, Drew hung up and I was out the door with Mirror trailing.

Because where my real home was was hidden and private, nothing no one knew about, and was bought under my middle name, we didn't have to do any covert driving; and getting to the hospice didn't take long for me at all. Since I was driving, I pulled up, took several breaths, then tugged on my skullcap and black fitted cap to keep a low profile. I knew this spot was a safe spot for us all, Mirror had promised that; but because I had been all on the news and still was, I couldn't trust a thing.

Once inside, we went past several halls in the medium-sized hospice. Two towering black men, we walked through that hospital as if we owned it and I knew all eyes were on us. We hopped on an elevator to go to the floor created for patients who were on the blackout list, meaning critical patients who did not want to be bothered or found. My fists were so tightly gripped at my sides that I didn't even notice my arms were bulking up, threatening to tear my shirt. When I turned the corner Angel greeted me, and for the first time since all this drama, I felt a moment of relief.

Walking her way, I kept her in my view. She was pacing back and forth outside of the quaint room my mother lay in. Her wedge Nikes squeaked on the linoleum floor as she treaded around. One arm was around her waist, and the other cupped her face. Shawty's eyes were bloodshot. She had some cuts, too. I could see that she was murmuring to herself even though her thick-coiled bushy hair was spilling around her face and shoulders.

The closer I got, and the more I could hear her, I realized that she was muttering prayers from the Bible. I remembered she said she had been a church kid before Dame took her, and it was coming out as she paced. My gaze stayed on her while various hospice staff walked past her, not even noticing who I was, which was good.

"Hey, B," I said low to get her attention.

"Shawn! You're here!" Angel glanced up then jetted my way. She hurried to me then paused, uncertain whether to hug me.

I just stood there for a moment then nodded. "It's cool. Thank you for being here to take care of her and Drew."

Shawty's whole body language changed. Her arms instantly went around me and caused me to inhale sharply with pain. I hadn't expected my body would be in so much pain after having the five-o muck me up like they did, but I swallowed and took it. Before all that happened, I would have had something snide to say but for some reason being an asshole right now wasn't a priority.

"I blew up your cell so much, and so did Drew. We were hoping you were okay once you got out," she stammered.

Angel smelled damn good, and it had my free hand holding her waist a little tighter before stepping back to see that she was holding back tears. The moment she touched me, I saw each liquid droplet fall delicately down her cheeks, which made my jaw lock tight with slight frustration. I wasn't down with the tears of a woman, not a woman who was now in my circle of family. I could see she was deeply affected, more than I thought she would be, and it had me clearing my throat and reaching out to wipe her tears.

"Yeah, Mirror had just dropped a brother off and shit. Got cleaned up then Drew hit my cell. Look, I ain't know I was an Orlando, and my bad with how I put my hands on you, okay? I see you down for real. Thanks. Are you okay?" It was hard admitting that but I had to say it again just so she could see the truth in me.

"I'm not banged up as bad as Shy, but I'm good, thanks," she muttered in a nervous tone.

My gaze went everywhere in shame and worry about my mother. In this moment I felt like a punk, so I cleared my throat, thumbed my nose, then looked back down at Angel. "Yeah, so, I need to see my aunt."

She reached up to try to wipe my face but I backed away and shook my head. I could tell by how Angel watched me that she was shocked at what I said, but she played it off. "Enzo, it's some stuff that went down. I tried to take care of it all but . . ."

Something in the tone of Angel's voice had my attention and had me feeling annoyed that this was something else I had to fix. I could tell that she was about to tell me about what went on but she was immediately interrupted. "Bianca, sweetie, why don't you give him a moment before you two have that talk. Shy is needing him before she go to surgery."

A light, almost erotic voice flowed around me. It had me taking my gaze off Angel to find the source. At my side, a light hand touched my shoulder. I would have snatched it away, but the strong presence with it had me reassessing the situation. I glanced down to notice a woman who carried my mother's eyes and who also had her shape. She also had my mother's smile, but outside of that, they looked nothing alike.

Both were beautiful, yeah, and I could see the authority and deathly quality that I had only seen two times in my life with my mother Shy. She sported a white and gold embroidered caftan that was cut low enough to see the curve of her plump and ample breasts behind treads of gold rope. Her micro twisted braids were braided upward on her head like a crown and her face was done as if she was about to model for some fashion magazine. She was a bad chick and I saw where my mother got it.

"Hello, godson. She's resting and has been calling for you and Andrew. Andrew is in the room with her now. He won't leave her side, so come on in," Anika, the woman

I knew as the African Queen and now my cousin, gently coaxed.

Even though the woman was sporting a simple caftan, I could sense the many weapons she had hidden on her. I wasn't trying to start a fight, but I knew if I did, she'd be ready with some shit. As we headed to the door, Angel's voice broke me out of my thoughts. She pressed her hand on my back and Angel moved out of my way to follow me inside. There, lying in a large bed made to look as if it were something she'd have at home, lay Shy. To her right sat Drew, holding her hand. By her feet stood a man I was slowly becoming familiar with the more we interacted with each other: Phenom. Anika smoothly left my side to stand near him, her hand sliding into his larger one, his fingers entwining with hers.

It was nice and all that they had helped my mother out, so I didn't have any smart shit to say, especially when Angel's touch on my arm had me noticing her pulling at my hand. I had been so gone that I did not realize that I was digging into my palms. Phenom gave me a nod. Dude was clean in what looked like a specially tailored suit. He had the look of murder in his eyes and I understood that emotion. We wanted Micah's head and it was going to happen real soon. I watched him guide Anika back to give me room, whispering low to Angel, and all three of them left to give Drew and me privacy with a light closing of the door.

Machines monitored Shy's progress and it pissed me off. I went for my bag, pulled out my iPod and speakers, then hit a track that was her favorite: The Roots' live version of "You Got Me," featuring Jill Scott, softly played to drown out the beeps of her monitor. It did something to me, to see her so vulnerable in this moment. The doctors explained that she had ovarian cancer, and that luckily whatever new methods she had been taking had caused the cancer to not spread any further than it had.

She also had a nasty gash in her side but the bullet had gone clean through so she was safe. The only problem was that, due to the cancer, her healing was going to take longer. Since she had relapsed from dodging bullets, they explained that they were going to go ahead with the surgery she had agreed to, a non-hysterectomy procedure that would maintain her fertility. This was going to happen to secure her health and so they would not have to work on her multiple times.

My mind reflected on the fact that cancer was eating at my mother's body and she had fought long and hard against it. I stepped to the left side of her to just watch her a moment before taking her hand and resting a hand against her short mahogany 'fro. She had just dyed it to celebrate getting better and now here she was. She looked as young as Angel did and it freaked me out. Shy had been so stressed, not taking care of herself as she should have, that the medicine wasn't counteracting the trauma the cancer was putting on her. The Orlandos had polluted her and damaged my mother. Micah tried to kill her.

"Damn, you took forever, bro. Everything good now?" Drew questioned.

I could see a multitude of emotions in just his gaze and the sound of his voice alone. My head shook and I pulled a chair up to sit while holding our mother's idle hand. "Nah, nothing is ever going to be okay, Drew man, nothing. Is she awake?"

Drew's eyes softened then darkened as he bowed his head against her arm. "Yeah. She . . . she got real bad, man. We ain't know what to do because she was hurt real bad. She started spitting hella blood, then fainted, and then started shaking."

I knew between the words he was saying, he felt scared, alone, like I did right now. My head bowed again and I felt helpless all over again. I felt like it was all my fault. If we weren't battling Micah, if that nigga had left us the fuck alone, then maybe Shy's treatments would have been going better. It was like the nigga knew no bounds. He wanted me gone before even knowing me and who I really was, but that was okay. I wanted him just as gone at that point. I wanted his face over the mantel of my condo with his blood painting the streets of ATL.

"A'ight. I'll be here until she wakes up then," I glumly responded.

"What we gonna do about that nigga?" I heard Drew ask at my side as I tried to get my mind right. My baby brother's body was tense and it was like looking at my younger self whenever someone had pissed me off.

"I'm going to smoke that nigga. Matter of fact, I'm going to start some fucking trouble after I leave here. After all this blows over you're going to stay with a set of Misfits, and keep your head in the game. Learn all you can from them, keep your nose in your books, and hold up your promise to our *tía*. Education, what you do in between that, is between her and us brothers, feel me? Just look for her." My hand rested on my brother's shoulder and I stared at him hoping he'd understand.

My baby brother shifted in his seat before responding. I knew he was practicing what we both always were taught: think before responding.

His next response threw me off: "I always will; that's our mom. But I want to help with that final kill."

"Nigga! I'll think on that 'cause I'm not trying to have you caught up. Not again. That was too fucking close, Drew. But I got you. If it's open enough, I'll slide you in to get your pound of flesh again, on my word," I said clipping my anger and trying to stay cool.

"Anyway, baby bro, you need to keep your shit smart and level. Yeah, I know. I'm the one to talk with the fucking blackouts, but that's why you gotta do and be better, bro. Soak these lessons up because more than likely, our bad blood will be gunning for you soon," I explained, hoping he was hearing some of what I said.

"Yeah? Well, fuck them niggas. They hurt what's ours, so fuck them. But I'll do what I have to for you and her." Drew's words cut off as his mind went elsewhere.

"I know, bro. Ain't shit in this life the way we wanted it to be, or needed it to be, but we make it ours. She said we are hers." Where he was coming from, I understood it deeply.

Drew let go of our mother's hand, looking away, and bit his lip in restrained anger. "That's why we gotta do whateva to protect our mom. Who's gonna be there for the shawties who get done like that, like how our *tía* was? So I'll do whatever to protect her and handle business, on my word," Drew rushed out in passion and loyalty.

Standing in that moment, I moved across the room to pull my baby brother into a hug, and then released him, with a rub of my hand on the top of his dome. "Damn, man. Aight, ain't shit else to be said about it then. You got nothing but my respect, bro. We both just got to be smart about how we handle shit with that nigga watching our every move. Which is why I'm going to leave him a fucked-up message on his doorstep."

Drew watched me as if seeing me for the first time, yet again. He reached out to hug me again, then sat back down and took Shy's hand. "What you say all the time? Oh yeah, you don't do well with flying bullets."

"Nah, I don't," I said laughing. "Niggas get killed if they try to rain lead on me, so that's what's 'bout to happen."

Shy's soft grunt let us know she was awake. Our mother opened her bloodshot eyes then gave a weak smile. "Good, now we can all plan on killing this nigga. I want you two to know, though, that I always wanted you both. It was easy to want you two regardless of how you both were created, which is why I protected you so hard."

We watched her cough and struggle in her speech but she was clear in letting us know that she had heard everything. Both Drew and I leaned forward. I moved to the other side of her and took her hand, moving the bed up so she could sit up, and a sigh of relief went through me as I sat at her side.

"You see? I'm up, so get your ass up out of here, Shawn." Shy coughed with a smile.

"Naw, I'm good, we're good. Not going anywhere until you tell me what they said you had to share," I muttered in defiance of her will.

Drew gave a light laugh, but with all seriousness in his face he said, "Ain't shit coming for you again. We're going to protect you, Mama."

"But check it, what the fuck happened, huh? Why you out there in the damn streets going G.I. Jane and shit and getting fucking hurt? That ain't cool, especially with you being sick!" I tried to stay calm but the rest of what I said came out in heated anger.

Shy shook her head. Her pale, beautiful face contorted in pain and she reached for her breathing mask as she tried to speak. "I know, Shawn. I know, baby, but I'm not going to sit there and just be a damn target. Like you, I got plans for that nigga and you need all the knowledge you can get to take that bitch-ass nigga down, do you understand me?"

I felt that familiar darkness creeping up in my mind, trying to cloud my judgment, but I let it work for me rather than against me. "I hear you, but you could have gotten killed, you and Angel. That nigga came for you. That means he's on more sneak shit. Nigga knows I'm an Orlando, the fuck you got to say to that?"

The monitors connected to my mother started going off with the rise of her stress. Her eyes darkened like mine and she fisted her blanket before she talked. "This is what I have to say: go in my bag that I always have you bring. I got some information for you, Shawn. What you see is why I suggested you step into that world you don't want, and why you need to be out there and not worry about me."

My anger took the best of me. I paced back and forth, kicked a chair in the process, and watched my brother move across the room.

Drew moved quickly to get back to holding her hand. He pulled out a thick folder and opened it. "Yo! Is that Micah?"

That name had me stopping my walk and I headed back to the bed. Interest had me leaning over to grab the folder and skim over it. My eyes widened in awareness of how deep this shit was. I realized that the woman in front of us needed to stay on this earth, because what she had gotten for me, for Drew too, was icing that could get us through this war.

"Mama Shy, how did you get this information?" I had to know. I checked my anger, leveling it to a cool simmer, and waited.

Our mother coughed, sucked up some more air. She turned her face upward our way and then smiled maliciously. "Anika out there?"

I gave a nod and she wiggled in her bed. "I hear Ahmir, too. Well, we have resources too, baby, hands deep. When you told me he was FBI, I knew who to go to, so because of that, we have a nice little gem, one I had no idea I was very familiar with. See, when I told you that it was me and my resources that helped Phenom slip into prison, I meant it. That was when I created my liaison with some law enforcement and FBI. Learn this. It's good to have law who will work for you. Not dirty motherfuckers, but real niggas and chicks who understand our life in this game and what we have to do to protect the streets from men like Dame, Dante, and now Micah."

Shy paused to take a shaky breath then continued, "When I say don't fuck with a mother, and family, I mean it. I may be sick, son, but I am still a fighter, so turn that anger into what we need to murder. Now listen to some truths and let me tell you a story about a little boy named Micah and his sister. After that, if I die, baby, know I died loving and protecting you both, but go out there and fuck that nigga up. You both are mine. Your bloodline comes from New York through me by King Kulu. What I told you, Shawn, as a kid and you, Drew, was not some gangsta shit I made up; it's truth. Remember that. Now listen as I give you more history."

What she told us changed everything in that moment. Not only was Micah not what we thought, but the beef against the Orlandos and my mom's side was too deep for words. Especially when Phenom and Anika came in with Angel following and dropped the rest of the story. The truths hidden from me and Drew, hidden from the Misfits as a whole, left me pissed, but tripped out in awe. They didn't lie.

Fury had me seeing red. Everything they said had me heated; and I needed that nigga Micah's blood on my hands. I glimpsed the people around my mother's bed, absorbed the image of her laid up in bed, bleeding and hurting, and I turned and stormed out of the room. As I was heading to my ride, I heard the sound of feet behind me.

Turning, I saw it was Angel. She gave me a worried gaze but her posture let me know that wherever I was going, she was following. Thumbing my nose in that understanding, I said nothing at all. I had no damn words. I just needed to kill that nigga and I knew I had to work out my plan right. Micah had come for my circle. He had stepped so far as to turn one of my homies against me. I needed to find out just exactly what that was.

"Let's go. I got a nigga I need to see. Two of them actually," I rumbled low.

Angel tried to keep up with my pace and I heard her softly say, "I'll hold you down."

I thought I was going through shit, but it was only a drop in the bucket compared with what the foundation had gone through. This all had me gone. It was then that I changed my plan up somewhat.

Chapter 9

Angel

"Nigga, I know you in this motherfucker so just open the door," Enzo yelled out as we stood outside of Dragon's condo.

Dragon, like most young black males, had realized too late he was blowing through his money on useless shit. So, by the time he had his daughter and realized he needed to do better, he found himself almost broke. Hence the reason he had a low-end condo instead of one that should have showed all of his hard work on the field. Still, the message Tino had relayed to me about Micah having Dragon's daughter and baby mother held hostage just so he could help to end Enzo on the field was what had me and Enzo at his door.

We could hear movement behind the door, but still Dragon didn't answer. Enzo kicked the door and then banged on it again. It was cold outside. The wind chill made me pull my hood tighter and duck my head as a gust came sweeping through. Dragon's porch light was off, but the streetlights lit up the way so we could see. The smell of fried chicken made my stomach rumble so loud that Enzo looked down at me. I shrugged and felt the pain in my shoulders from the fighting I'd done earlier.

"I'm not trying to disrespect your home, my nigga, but if you don't open it willingly then I'm coming in forcefully. Your choice," Enzo spat out.

I looked behind us when a neighbor's porch light came on and the old lady stuck her head out the door. When she saw the look on Enzo's face, she quickly closed the door and locked every lock she had on there.

I knocked on the door this time. "Dragon, I know me and you are not on the best of terms, but if Enzo kicks this door down it's going to cause more problems that we don't need. So open the damn door!"

Before I could finish my last sentence, Enzo's boot kicked forward and Dragon's door splintered in two. The place was pitch black. It was the kind of dark where you could make out the shapes of objects but you couldn't see what or who was lurking behind them in the shadows.

Enzo walked in before me. "I heard you in here, nigga. I mean, you hiding because you know it's fucked up the way you ain't been having a nigga's six in practice?" he called out with his arms wide. "That's some real fucking shit, my nigga."

Out of nowhere a big, bulky shadow came charging from the hall like a bull, tackling Enzo so they went flying over an end table that was sitting in the middle of the floor. I jumped back with a scream, picked up a golf club from a golf bag that was sitting in the corner, and rapped the man who had tackled him across the head.

"Ahhh, God. Angel, bitch, I'ma kill you," Dragon roared out as Enzo monkey-flipped him onto his back.

I went in to hit Dragon again, until Enzo jumped in front of me and stomped the nigga in his gut.

"The fuck is wrong with you, nigga?" Enzo asked his boy with so much venom in his voice that I was afraid he was going into blackout mode again.

Dragon twisted back and forth in pain again before he snarled up at his friend and jumped up. "You what's wrong with me, nigga," he growled out and threw a punch at Enzo that stumbled him.

Once Dragon had backed Enzo up he came for me. His eyes held pure hatred, but I could also see the pain in them. Blood was trickling from the back of his head over his shoulder from where I had hit him before. In that moment, as he charged at me, he really looked like a dragon breathing fire.

"Don't do it, Dragon," I yelled at him as I held the club up, ready to swing again. "I ain't . . . We ain't come here to hurt you—"

Before I could finish, the big man leaped at me and I had no choice but to swing like I was aiming for the MVP award at an MLB all-star game. I hit the man so hard that the club bent. Saliva and blood went flying everywhere as a gash on the side of his head opened up. By that time Enzo had gotten his bearings about him. He stood up and snatched his leather jacket off, and spit on the floor. I watched him charge the man he considered a friend, lift him off the floor from behind, and slam him to the floor so hard it was as if the whole building shook.

There was only one other time I'd seen Enzo fight a person he considered a friend. Back when Dame was running the block, he'd made any- and everybody in his command do things they didn't want to do. Dame had a way of convincing people that they were going to do exactly what he wanted them to do or he would find a way to make them do it. He had made Enzo kill his best friend Big Jake's grandmother. Eventually, after Dame died, Jake found out; and when he did he came for Enzo and they fought like two caged lions until it was a draw with Enzo falling on his sword. Enzo told Jake that he could kill him for the affront, but Jake had declined. Instead, Jake took a boot to his ribs and face.

Now, Enzo stood over Dragon, hitting him with fists to the face, one after the other, until his boy could no longer fight back.

"Nigga, I came to talk to you," Enzo barked out then kicked Dragon in his ribs. "Came to lend you a fucking helping hand in getting ya fam back and you gon' attack me, nigga? All you had to do was come to me and tell me that nigga had you by the balls."

Enzo was in a rage. So much so that spittle was flying from his mouth. I wanted to believe that he was so angry because on top of Micah going after his friends, he had gone after Shy. But to be honest, I didn't know.

"You . . . you gotta get the fuck away from me, Enzo." Dragon barely got those words out as he coughed and spit up blood. "Get the fuck away from me," the man yelled out. "You bad luck, nigga. Since I met you and this bitch y'all been bad luck for a nigga," Dragon roared and tried to kicked at Enzo's feet.

I didn't know if the man had tears in his eyes from the ass whooping Enzo had just laid on him or if he was hurting because Micah had his family.

"This motherfucker got my baby mama and my seed," Dragon yelled again. "And it's all because of you, nigga!"

"This shit ain't got nothing to do with me and more so with that nigga chasing ghosts. I didn't know he had your fam until somebody told me, nigga. So for you to come at me like I'm the enemy is bullshit," Enzo countered as he glared down at him.

For a long while all Dragon did was lie still on the floor as he gazed up at the ceiling; then out of the blue he mumbled, "He got my fam, man, and I don't know where they at. Ain't shit I can do," he belted out. "And I don't know what they doing to them, man, and all I can do is sit and wait on this nigga to say move."

I had to turn away from the man when he bellowed out in frustration and banged the back of his closed fist on the floor. The soundtrack to our lives sounded in the background. *I knew that old lady was going to call the cops,* I thought.

"I came to help," Enzo finally said. "I'll help you get your fam back." Enzo kneeled and laid a hand on Dragon's chest. "Just let me know you ain't in on his bullshit. Give me your word that you got my back and I'll get your fam back."

I listened as they talked a bit more and then I rushed to the window and looked in the distance. Those flashing blue and red cherries were getting closer.

"Enzo?"

He snapped his head in my direction. "What, Bianca?"

"We have to go."

He nodded once then looked back down at Dragon. "We didn't have to do this, but since you took it there, it is what it is. We good or what?"

Dragon nodded and then Enzo helped him up from the floor. "Yeah, man. Get the fuck up outta here. Go out through the back—"

Enzo snatched up his leather jacket and cut him off. "Yeah, yeah, I remember. All those ho parties we threw I haven't forgotten, nigga."

Dragon tried to chuckle, but the hit I'd given him had his face swollen already.

"Hey, look, I'm sorry about the . . . golf club."

I tried to apologize, but Dragon wasn't hearing it. "Fuck you, Angel. You'd do that shit again for the sake of this nigga. You know you ain't shit," he said.

But when he nodded and smiled a lopsided smile, I knew he and I were good. Enzo and I disappeared through the back and faded into the night.

Dressed in all black, Enzo and I sat outside of a chicken and waffle restaurant. We hadn't said too much to one another on the drive over. My heart was on overdrive. Enzo was unreadable. I didn't know what he was thinking.

When he came into his aunt's hospice room, I expected him to be belligerent, ready to turn the hospice upside down about the woman I now knew to be his mother being targeted by Micah and his warped obsession. But Enzo hadn't reacted the way I expected. In fact, he really hadn't reacted at all. That surprised me, being that we had just gone to Dragon's house and pretty much laid down the law.

"So you're just going to be this calm after Micah pretty much tried to murder Shy in cold blood?" I asked him as we sat there. I just wanted to know if we were going to go after Micah for Shy like we had just gone at Dragon. I didn't understand why we weren't going to call that nigga out.

Enzo slowly eyed me from the corner of his eye. "Just because I'm not showing my hand doesn't mean I don't know how to play."

"Yeah, but this nigga ambushed us, Enzo. He tried to kill Shy without any fucks given of what you would do about it. You're just going to let that go?"

"Don't make me regret bringing you with me," he said calmly.

"We're sitting outside a chicken and waffle joint so forgive me if I have to question the method to your madness right now," I quipped.

"Don't question shit about me until you see the full picture. You're coming at me like—"

"Like you need to do something about this nigga trying you. It's one thing when he was coming after you when we just thought he was trying to fill Dame's seat. It's another now that we know it's personal. And it's personal shit on his end that has nothing, nothing, to do with you, but because of who your father is. You ain't mad enough for me."

Enzo tilted his head then mumbled something under his breath as he turned to glare at me. "Mad enough for you? What the fuck is mad enough for you, Angel? I just had to pretty much get in a nigga's ass who I consider a homie because of Micah. This nigga only after you because he thinks you can mention the wrong thing at the wrong time and end his little façade. Once he kills you, he's done with you. You're out of his fucking hair. This nigga is aiming for my family. For me, my li'l bro, for my gotdamned mother. This shit is deeper than me showing you my anger on the fucking surface. My life and the life of that woman lying in the hospital bed depend on it. You must be out of your fucking mind to tell me I'm not mad enough for you. Fuck you, Angel. Fuck you for making me want to choke the shit out of you right now."

The more he spoke, the deeper the baritone in his voice got. He touched the spot on his jaw where Dragon had hammered him. I saw those storm clouds brewing behind his eyes, and flashbacks of the last time I'd pissed him off that bad came to memory. Enzo's left hand gripped the steering wheel so hard that I could see the white of his knuckles.

"I'm just trying to figure out—"

I started to talk, but he jumped out of the car and slammed the door. Wanting to get my point across to him, I hopped out behind him.

"Shawn, wait," I called out behind him.

He kept walking like he hadn't heard me. His broad back in the leather jacket he wore made him walk with a purpose. Only he could walk with such determination and swagger that it stood out the way it did. The gait that he carried from his posture was enough to make any woman swoon. I rushed up behind him and grabbed his hand to stop him before he walked into the restaurant.

"Please, wait," I said to him. "Look, I'm sorry. I'm not trying to upset you, I promise. I just want this all to be over and I guess in my haste I'm forgetting that you always approach certain things methodically. This isn't just about me and I'm sorry."

For a long while he just stared down at me like he was fighting with the urge to put his hands on me again. Something inside of me still feared Enzo's anger because I knew he could go from zero to sixty in a matter of seconds. But all he did was grunt and walk to the entrance of the restaurant. When he got to the door he held it open while still remaining silent. I sighed, slid my hands in my hoodie pockets, and walked in ahead of him.

Once inside, Enzo led us to the back of the establishment where a lone booth sat. I went to sit on the opposite side of the table but he stopped me.

"Naw, shawty. Sit over here. Slide in," he ordered me before he slid into the booth after me.

People stared and whispered. One little boy screamed at his mother that Enzo was in the place. I sat quietly while he took photos with his fans while wondering why the fuck we were there. I was expecting a waiter to come to the table, but when the owner and the cook came out to personally ask Enzo what he wanted, I knew more than his NFL fame was at play. Once all the hoopla had died down and we'd ordered our meals, Enzo looked at me.

"While you were so busy trying to tell a nigga how mad he should be, I bet you never took the time to notice we were being followed again," he spat out.

My instincts immediately went into overdrive. I started to look around as paranoia set in.

"There is always a method to my madness, Bianca. Never question me or doubt me the way you did. That can make a nigga already testy a whole lot of edgy. If you rolling me, telling me you gon' hold me down, then you don't do shit like that. Not when a nigga trying his hardest"—his fist banged on the table once, shaking the silverware—"to show you a different side of him."

Part of me wanted to be scared of the way he'd just come at me because as he talked, he snarled a bit and spoke through clenched teeth. But the other half of me, the side that had always been drawn to and attracted to Enzo's not-so-sane side, wanted to see what it would feel like in that moment to have him fuck me again while he was that angry. I didn't have time to dwell on my wet pussy or to respond to what he'd said. The cook had come back out with the food and another fan ran up wanting a photo with Enzo.

The chime on the door of the restaurant sounded and the smile Enzo had on his face when he was talking to the little boy faded. I looked behind us just by happenstance and frowned when I saw the police from earlier that day walking in. He was in street clothes and looked nothing like the officer I'd seen earlier that day. He casually strolled in with both hands in his pockets, locs swinging as he strolled through with a walk similar to Enzo's.

When he stopped just behind the booth we were sitting in, I looked from him to Enzo, and then back to him.

"What's going on?" I asked Enzo.

"Fuego, you going to photobomb this shit or just stand there?" Enzo asked with a smirk, ignoring my question all together.

"Cuz, I'll just stand and wait until you're done. You have some people who want to meet you," Fuego explained while looking around.

"Ain't happening. They'll have to come in here and order some shit and we all can break bread over waffles, how about that shit?" Enzo leveraged.

Fuego chuckled then walked around and gave a large order as he pointed to our table near the back of the restaurant. He gave a few women in the place a flirtatious smile that was similar to Enzo's then glanced my way with his hands folded in front of his dark jeans.

"My bad, I just relay the messages," he finally said.

Enzo stood and adjusted his leather jacket as he gave the man a cool look. His chin was slightly raised, and he scratched his pierced ear as he spoke. "You need to be more effective then. I'm not feeling the stalker shit."

A deep, rumbling laugh escaped Fuego's lips as he matched Enzo in stance and posture. There was a silent stare down before he pushed forward to talk to an elderly gentleman. Out of the corner of my eye, I could see money exchanged. It was then that the older black man yelled for everyone to leave, and he quickly turned to shut down the restaurant. People griped and complained, but Fuego simply handed ducats their way then pointed toward the door.

In my mind, I was wondering just what in hell was going on. But something else inside of me was telling me to just watch in silence. Enzo sat back down and glanced at me.

"Always a method to my madness," he grumbled.

He was still annoyed with me. I could live with that. While my heart settled in my throat, I picked up my fork and started to cut through my red velvet waffles and chicken. I picked up the syrup and lackadaisically poured it over my food.

"So, you got the family's attention and, as you see, they felt it was time to move up the reunion," Fuego explained as he came back to the table. He made a signal then thanked the waitress who set more food down on the tables we specified.

"I didn't do shit, my man, but I think you all would be interested in finding out who did," he casually replied, moving to sit down and grabbing his knife and fork.

Enzo had ordered a plate of red velvet waffles and chicken on the side as well. I learned from cooking for him before that he hated for some foods to touch, and I was assuming chicken and waffles touching was one of them.

"A'ight, you got my attention with that one," Fuego expressed.

My legs started to shake, which caused them to brush against Enzo's legs. He pushed his hand underneath the table and pressed it down on my leg.

"Stop. I told you I needed you to be my Bonnie. I need you to start acting like it right now. Chill out. Relax. Let me handle this and then we can be done and we can leave," he said to me without even looking over at me.

So even though I nodded and settled back into my seat, he didn't see me. Enzo continued to eat his food with a bored expression on his face. The chime on the door alerted us to someone coming in. I looked up and directly into the eyes of old world evil. I didn't have to wonder if the man was an Orlando. Just judging by the way he walked like he owned the world, I could tell. Everything about him screamed that Dame had come from his bloodline. From the cropped perfect waves of salt-and-pepper hair on his head to the gray beard that adorned his face, it was like looking at an older version of Dame.

My palms started to sweat as he stared me down just the way I was doing to him. His upper lip twitched like he was annoyed that I thought I was bold enough to look him in his eyes. I couldn't help it. I didn't know how to feel looking into the eyes of the man who had helped to create hell on earth. I knew one thing for sure, though: if Micah was under the impression that Shawn was the only Orlando he had to worry about then he was sadly mistaken.

Chapter 10

Enzo

If you didn't know shit, then you ain't see shit; and if you ain't see shit, then you didn't know shit. That was the motto of the game that I was trying to get into Angel's head while I told her to chill. We sat in a run-of-the-mill soul food chicken and waffles joint. This was the type of place where you knew the food was on point, even though the place looked like a decrepit asshole. My hand dropped away from Angel's shaking leg I could smell the fear coming from her, and it had me on edge. Though she now was realizing what we were dealing with, she needed to understand that in this world just a hint of fear could cause all hell to jump off. Niggas and bitches in this game were like a wolf, shark, or bull: once they caught that sample of red, it was a done deal.

My hand dropped away from Angel's lush thigh. I continued to eat my food with a bored expression on my face, igging the nigga hovering over us. Fuego had stepped out of the way to get the food he had ordered and then eventually set his tray down opposite Angel and me. He still hovered and I continued to eat. I said nothing while I studied our new guest from the side of my eye. That was when the sound of clicking heels stopped directly behind Fuego and a feminine whisper started. Everything was starting to feel like I was in a zoo and it had me feeling itchy and more annoyed. However, through it all, I just licked my syrup-coated fingers then snatched up a chicken leg and bit into it.

"Hello, Shawn. It is a blessing to finally meet you," said a calm yet hard-edged female voice.

My eyebrow quirked and I gave a curt nod while continuing to eat.

"Sit, *mami,* it's rude to stand over someone as they enjoy their meal. You know better," a deep, accented voice rumbled next to her.

The woman before me had a medium build. She had dark auburn hair and was dressed in a simple jumper with a business jacket on. Her low-cut nails showed that she was a fighter and the calluses on her index finger let me know she pumped a lot of steel, as in Glocks. She slid in quietly across from Angel and me. Angel's hand found its way on my thigh and I knew it was her signal that she recognized this broad. Without even glancing up her way, I noticed the broad give me a strange smile that was dipped in malice and sex. It had me mentally asking, who the fuck was this pale bitch?

The elder mirror of the nigga who sired me, who I wished were here to be gutted and lit on fire, coolly slid into the booth while unbuttoning his blazer and pushing it behind him with flair. He sat back in a slight lean and studied me with pride. It was only when he glanced at Angel in disgust that I mentally ticked off another reason to kill dude.

"I'm Lilith Orlando, and this man next to me is your grandfather, the one and only Caltrone Orlando. We have been looking for you and your brother for a long time now," she happily stated.

The way she spoke was as if she had won some major award and she was geeked on adrenaline with a glassy expression in her eyes. Shit was creepy and strange, especially with how close she sat to the man who slid in next to her. Reaching for my cup of pop, I took a deep gulp and set it down in thought. *Looking for me? Yeah the fuck right.*

These motherfuckers musta had me bent all the way out. They ain't know shit about me until recently so they were playing thirsty, but I would take it. It only helped me with my plans with this war. Wiping my mouth with my napkin, I arrogantly glanced up at the man who I knew shit about.

It was then, in that moment, that I stared into the pit of hell, into eyes that matched my own, and it had me sitting up straight. The nigga was an older version of Dame and Dante but with a different look to him. He sported cropped salt-and-pepper hair, with a gray beard that ran along his jaw. This dude didn't look old in the least bit. If anything, he looked in his late thirties or forties. But I knew, due to the way he sat as if he were a god, that he was older than his looks.

As I assessed him, I knew shit was only going to get more interesting from there on out, especially when Caltrone extended his hand to me and gave a smile that felt like a real grandfather's. "It makes me proud to finally be in the presence of my grandson, *mi sangria.* Yes, Lu was not worth *mierda,* but he picked the woman to give him proper children correctly. Not like his first choice. She was a disgust and produced mutts that only disappointed me like their father. But you and your brother? *Sí,* absolutely perfecto. Yes, today is a good day and we have much to discuss, *niño.* Much."

My hand tentatively reached out to touch his. Both of our palms matched in a tight grasp. I said nothing as my mind began to calculate how to get the fuck out of this shit without harm to my true family. Micah was going to burn in hell for putting me on this path for sure.

We both dropped our hands and studied each other, Caltrone with a devilish smirk and me showing no emotion but a bored, stoic grin. Silence played between us. I was tripping off of how he called us perfect, as if we were some creation of his to claim as pets, and it pissed me off on another level but I kept it cool.

"Shawn, you called for us to meet you and we are here. Whatever you need from us, we are here. Loyalty and blood is our motto and our way of life," the woman named Lilith directed my way.

There was this undertone in her voice that had me envisioning my fork in her throat, but I brushed it off, and kept my eyes on the man who would be called my grandfather. "A rat has escaped from Dame's kingdom and is currently attempting to take what was burned down and build it back up. But in order to do that, like the old days in Egypt when pharaohs wanted to practice their rule, he wants to erase anyone associated with, or who is direct blood of, Orlando."

Leaning back, I copped Angel from the side of my eye. She was using me as a means to hide from the psychopathic stare of the man in front of us. Realizing that, I kept myself angled enough so she could feel protected as I reached for my cup and took another drink, this time crunching slowly on ice.

Caltrone's pupils seemed to darken. He leaned to the side to whisper to Lilith before sitting back and watching me.

"And tell us how this affects you," Lilith said, her eyes also narrowing in fringed contempt.

Disrespectful bitches really made my palms itch. Her throat was pretty enough to choke and how she kept staring she was really asking for it. Tilting my head to the side, I tried to stay cool, because I had just basically told these fuckers how it was affecting me, but I guess they needed a clearer understanding.

"I'm sure you've been watching me all this time right? Seen the news? Yeah, I can tell. Well, that's how. I dropped a name for you to latch on to and see who's playing with my world, feel me? As I'm learning, I can't do this by myself, right? I need family, right? So, I'm here. That nigga pushed me to you, so I'm saying why not give him what he wants? Time to protect the kingdom and show him what it really takes to be an Orlando." Cockiness poured from my lips and I leaned back in a smug look, quietly waiting.

Lilith glanced at Caltrone and he reached up to brush his knuckles against her face before turning my way.

"Then that entails that you come home. That you accept your birthright and be the king you were bred to be, Shawn. Are you really wanting that?" Lilith cooed.

She gave a seductive gaze my way and giggled when Caltrone reached up to hold the back of her neck then dropped his hand again.

Feeling sick in my stomach, I studied this chick hard. She was very familiar to me. From the way she watched me to the way she smiled, and the slight movements she made. My mind held on to what was ticking me off about why she seemed familiar and I shifted forward.

"This is why this is going down. You want me back, I'm here. I get to keep playing the game and I'll represent this family to the fullest. You want Atlanta back in your hands then I'll give that to you, but know I come with bullets. That nigga is gunning for me and I just felt as if you all needed to know who was pulling at the family's strings since he's *federali*," I explained.

"Good. Caltrone?" Lilith asked.

Caltrone glanced away in thought then leaned forward. "I've been waiting on you, *niño*. You will take my place, as it should be. We will speak again. As far as that dirty thorn . . ."

The man who was my grandfather clenched his fist and his nostrils flared. He seemed to grow in size with his constrained anger and it had me frowning. Eyes dark like soot gazed at me and it had me seeing myself for the first time in years. Evil was throughout this man. There was no love in him, except a twisted kind that was formed around control of everyone around him.

He gave a menacing laugh and smirked. "We'll give you the tools to pluck him from your side, but as a show of loyalty, I want his skin as a coat."

Chuckling low, I reached in my jacket and pulled out a thin box. I dropped it on the table and flashed my teeth. "Oh shit, yeah? Like that?"

I watched Caltrone motion for Lilith to open the box. In guided caution, she reached out, slid the thin box her way, then opened it up. A perfect O formed across her face and she handed the box to Caltrone then glanced my way.

"Oh, you are definitely of our blood. What a sweet prize," she praised.

A sneer ran across my face and I sucked my teeth in pride, but it was Caltrone's eerie laugh that set off the fear of God in my spine. I wouldn't show it, but this nigga made my skin crawl and I wanted to off him and his bitch by his side; but I couldn't. Not yet, but all in due time.

"I want more, but this, this right here, shows why you are of my blood. Yes, this will be good for now," he said in elated joy.

He reached into his pocket and pulled out a card, tossing it. "Program this number in your cell phone. I advise you to call that number immediately; otherwise, we will have another discussion of a different sort."

My brow quirked and I took the card. The old man stood and brushed off his coat. "Continue your liaison with your cousin. Fuego will give you your gold and whatever else you need. The family will be pleased to have their seeds back; until then, make sure that you do not disappoint me as my son and his mutts did. I thought I had a star in Dante, but alas, a different sort of pussy became his downfall. Make sure that doesn't happen to you. For now you give me great pride. He bred well." He gazed down his nose at Angel in disgust and with a question in his eyes then walked away.

"Lilith, come," Caltrone ordered.

She slinked out of the booth then winked. "Blood sustains, and niggas get scaled, teach him that, Shawn. See you soon."

Fuego gave a nod my way with his hands in his pockets and strolled out. The sound of bells chimed again, and I sat in stark quiet, not breathing until I could hear the car pull off. I pulled out my burner, and added the number in it by dialing it and I waited.

"Good, you understand the importance of structure. As you leave, you will find a packet under your car, on your side. Take it: it is gifts, money, passports, and land deeds. As for Micah, we intend to have a nice talk with him as well. Me and you will talk soon; all of us will." With that, the line went dead and I dropped the phone on the table.

My heart started thumping a mile a minute and the sensation of Angel's hand on mine had me jerking her way.

"You're hurting me," she whispered then looked down.

I followed her gaze. Tears were rimming her bloodshot eyes. Her chest was rising up and down in strained fear and anxiousness. It was then that I realized that as I was talking I was literally squeezing her thigh to the point of my nails cutting into her.

Quickly letting go, I exhaled and shook my head. "We gotta bounce, but we'll wait and do the usual."

We slid out of the booth and headed to the car. I kept her back from the car and walked forward. Thumbing my ringed nose, I ran my tongue over my gums then sucked my teeth before crouching low to slide my hand under the driver side of the car.

"Check it: I'm dropping this car off at the compound. I'm not fucking with it no more," I grumbled; then I pulled when I felt the cushy feel of the package in my hand.

Standing back up, I opened it up and heard Angel's voice. "What is it? And are you thinking the car is bugged?"

My eyebrow quirked while I checked her out from the side of my eye. Angel was rubbing her arm and I went back to glancing through the packet. Pulling out stacks of money, I tossed a thick note her way. "Catch; and yeah. You're thinking like a criminal now."

She snatched it and thumbed it like a boss bitch. Shaking my head, I pointed at the car. "Get in. I need to think."

I watched Angel walk with authority as she counted the dough. We both hopped into the ride then drove and wound our way through the streets of ATL. Doing our usual, we made sure we weren't being tracked and followed. The heaviness in my chest had me sighing and I rested my arm on the back of the seat as I drove, combing my fingers in Angel's hair in thought.

"So where are we going to go now?" Angel asked.

Damn, she was always asking questions. I noticed that she shifted in her seat watching me while holding the envelope and looking through it again.

"Someplace. Chill on what you say in here. I'm still not trusting shit," I snapped at her while we drove; then I ran a hand down my face. "I'm tired, my bad."

From there we drove in silence until I got close to a chop shop the Misfits hipped me up to. Taking a turn, the sound of Angel unbuckling her seat belt had me glancing at her to see what was up and had me slowing down.

"You see some . . ." Before I could finish, Angel slid close to me, dropped her hands, and slipped them into my jeans. I opened my mouth to pop off but her hand had me feeling so good that I just let her do what she do. It was only when she dropped her head and slipped me into her mouth as I drove that she set shit off.

"Fuck, B. The hell are you . . . I mean, fuck!" I stammered then groaned. I gripped the steering wheel hard.

Slick, slippery heat closed in around me, causing my shaft to swell in her mouth until she gulped and slurped me. She worked her mouth so good that it had me driving slow with a lean. The dominant in me wanted to take control, but how she worked her tongue around the tip of my piercing and me, I frankly didn't want her to stop.

A low chuckle came from me, and I looked for a spot for me pull over as she handled business. Her head bobbed up and down and my hand dropped into her thick, long hair as she moaned and squirmed on the side of me. Still driving for a quick spot to park behind an abandoned building, the palm of my hand slid down her back to grip her lush ass in a kneading motion. I caressed then cupped her from behind just to see if she'd press her pussy against my hand, which she did. My strokes continued and her sucks got harder until I hit the brakes and let her do what she do.

Anxiousness made my sacs tighten and become heavy. I gripped her shoulder to pull her back then stuffed my dick back in my pants. Shawty stared at me with wide eyes and it had my dick hurting to get inside of her.

"Why'd you stop me?" she asked while panting on her knees, her thighs rubbing together in need.

I could literally smell the budding sex between us and it had me pushing out of the car in a frustrated grunt. Checking her out of my peripheral, I could see her about to climb out, which had me turning around. In two strides, I leaned back into the car, snatched her by her leg to push her on her back and pull her hard toward the edge of the car. Her gasp made me smirk and I pulled off her shoes then bottoms, spreading her legs far enough for me to drop down and kiss her swollen pearl. The sound of her gasp, then seeing her jerking hands reach out to grab the steering wheel, hitting the horn in the process, had me dipping my tongue ring deep into her moist, silky haven.

"Damn it, Enzo," Angel squeaked out.

My cocky chuckle vibrated through her body adding more pressure to the game as I leaned back to dip two fingers in and out of her to play with her pretty kitty. As she arched and slapped her hand against the car seat, I leaned up to use my other hand so that I could pull her tank down to expose her honeysuckle breasts. Palming one velvet plush tit, I showed her how my tongue could work against her taut nipple and I sucked and tugged making her cream over my stroking fingers.

The heat between us continued to grow as I sucked, fingered, and took Angel on a high in my ride. She tugged on me begging for the dick, and I reached into my pants to pull out my wallet and grab a condom. Pulling back, I ripped open the gold wrapper and rolled it on with urgency. Noticing how she watched me hold my dick, I made it jump with my hand and she gave me a lusty laugh then motioned for me to come to her.

Licking my lips, I reached out again to pull at her legs and settled her on my dick. Slipping into her heat,

I positioned her so she could wrap her legs around my waist. I pulled her out of the car, moved to the side, and pressed her against the side of the car. Riding in and out of her, her nails scored my back as she held on tight. I could feel her teasing my ear then biting down, which had me thrusting harder into her.

"Bite harder, B," I growled, needing that sting of pain.

She gave me what I needed when she pushed up my shirt to get at my skin and dig her nails in my back. I hissed and I heard her moan, "Just wanted you to not stress."

Her voice hitched and I slipped out, and dropped her to her feet. "Oh, yeah? Then turn around and poke that ass out."

Syrupy honey slipped down her thighs and had me reaching out to cup her, slip my fingers back into her, to pull out, and slide them in my mouth. The moment I did that, she turned around so fast that it had me chuckling.

I watched her arch her back perfectly. I then slipped deep into that pussy again, strumming her pretty pearl until we both came in relaxing release that we both needed. Afterward, we got dressed, I cleaned out my ride, and we swapped it for a new one so we could head to my private place then call my mom to check up on her.

Chapter 11

Angel

"Angel?"

I was somewhere. Wasn't sure where. I was in a foggy haze. I tried to talk, but couldn't.

"Bianca, shawty, wake up."

I could hear Enzo's voice, but for the life of me I couldn't open my eyes. For the first time in weeks, I was finally able to sleep like I had no worries. I moaned out as someone shook my legs. Just that slight movement made me remember how it felt to have Enzo between them. I heard a chuckle somewhere in the distance. My legs spread and my hands slipped between my legs with the intent of relieving some of the pressure from wanting to feel Enzo inside of me again. Instead, I got what felt like a rod of steel inside of me. My eyes shot open and I gasped, seeing and feeling Enzo inside of me.

"You awake now?" he arrogantly asked me as he gave me a long stroke to kill me, and then a short stroke to bring me back to life.

My eyes fluttered rapidly, back arched, and I stuttered in response. I really didn't know what that response was. The feel of Enzo's lips on mine stopped me from talking as my nails dug into his side. He hissed at the pain and went deeper. I tore my mouth away from his so that I could let him hear the pleasurable pain he had me in. I loved that shit. So much so that I sank my teeth into his neck and bit down as hard as I could, knowing it would give him that high of pain he needed.

Two hours later, I found myself seated next to Enzo. We sat parked in a covered parking deck. "Why are we here?" I asked him.

"Because I don't feel like playing this cat and mouse game with this nigga anymore. I'm fucking tired. So, what we about to do is give this nigga what he wants," he said as he turned to look at me.

I could tell by the look in his eyes that I wasn't about to like what he was about to say. Something in the way he grabbed the steering wheel and then sighed told me that.

"And what's that?" I asked.

As soon as I asked the question, screeching tires made me turn my head. Two black vans came swerving around. I snapped my head back around and looked at Enzo. I panicked with the way he looked at me. There was something in his eyes that dared me to question him.

He grabbed my hand and squeezed tight. "When I get out of this car, get in the driver's seat and run. Do you hear me, B? Nod once," he commanded.

"But—"

"Don't ask me shit," he snapped at me. "Everything we did this morning was for a reason."

My mind flashed back to the trip to see Mirror and the conversation the three of us had with Shy that morning.

"Shawn . . ."

"Trust me. Go."

This time he didn't give me time to respond. He grabbed a black bag from the back seat and stepped out of the car. He turned to look at me one last time then quirked a brow as if telling me to get the hell on. I trusted him, so if he told me to leave then I needed to do it.

Although I was hell bent on being defiant, I knew that his life and livelihood hung in the balance.

As soon as I turned the corner to go down a level on the parking deck, I heard gunfire. I was so busy looking behind me that when I crashed head-on into the black van in front of me, I never saw it coming.

For the next several hours my world was black. I didn't know where I was or who I was for a second for that matter. It felt as if the weight of the world was weighing me down.

My eyelids fluttered open just as it felt like a hammer was beating me in the head. The room was dark, but there were flecks of light coming from a small window in the room. The smell of burnt charcoal and rust assaulted my senses. I could smell the mold and mildew that had overtaken the place.

I tried to move my arms, and then realized they were tied behind my back. I was naked and tied to a chair. I felt fear trickling up my spine and it made my eyes water in frustration. Tried moving my hands to see if the rope had any leeway.

"Hello?" I called out only to be answered by silence.

I kept looking around until my eyes adjusted. I was in a room. There was bloody rope hanging from the ceiling. The smells of urine and defecation were all around me.

"Can anybody hear me?" I yelled out again.

At that moment, I was no longer Angel from the hood. No longer was I Angel trying to escape the Trap. I was once again that scared, frightened fourteen-year-old little girl Dame had kidnapped from her grandmother. I wanted to cry, wanted to cower under the looming threat of Micah having captured both me and Enzo.

"Nobody can hear you, bitch, and even if they did, who's going to come running into an abandoned house to help a whore?" a female voice said to me.

I looked toward the door in the room to see the outline of a woman. I couldn't see her face because there wasn't light on the side of the room where she was.

"So you're the famous Angel," another female voice rang out.

Her I could see. She walked into the room to get a closer look at me. For a second I thought my mind was playing tricks on me. She looked identical to a Misfit. The only thing that slowed down the whisper of betrayal was the fact that I could tell this woman was older. While she looked like an old friend, I could tell that she wasn't.

"Who are you?" I asked her, trying to keep my eyes on her as she circled me.

"The woman who's trying to figure out why Micah is so obsessed with you and your little boyfriend," she answered.

"Why do you care?" I asked then looked back toward the door where the other woman stood.

As soon as she stepped forward, I knew who she was. My eyes narrowed and I was sure they turned to slits. She flipped on the light switch on the wall. The onslaught of brightness in the room forced me to close my eyes. I could feel them standing over me as I hung my head. I slowly blinked my eyes to try to stave off the glare of the lights.

"I don't really. As far as I know he just wants you and Mr. Prime Time Enzo behind bars," the woman who looked like Gina said to me.

I gave a light chuckle. "Oh, is that what he told you?" I asked in a taunt knowing she would take the bait.

I could hear one of them suck their teeth. I assumed it was Dominique, the wannabe Misfit, since it was she who spoke up next.

"Nah, I think he wants this bitch dead," she quipped. "She knows too much."

I finally looked up into the face of the women Micah had worked his spell on. Dominique stood in skinny jeans that hugged her very minimal hips. The leather shoes she had on reminded me of army boots and the shirt that covered her C-cup breasts seemed to be too small. She had a few curves, but not as many as the woman who stood beside her. Her outfit wasn't as juvenile. She was dressed to snare a man in her Venus trap with the purple body suit, thigh-high black red bottom heels, and the leather jacket that tapered to her slim waist. She was made like an African goddess.

I gave a low laugh. "Like, for the life of me, I can't see why you would align yourself with the likes of Micah. I mean you have a perfectly good—"

Before I could finish, that yellow bitch smacked me so hard across the face that I saw flashes of me and Enzo from the night before. I screamed out and tried to lash out at her only to be reminded by the ties on my wrists that I was still stuck to a chair.

I scowled up at her, pissed as a wet cat. "Untie my hands and let's see you pull that shit, bitch," I dared her.

I didn't like the girl. Didn't like the fact that she was a treacherous cunt. For three weeks after Enzo and I had our last physical altercation, I had stayed with the Misfits. That whole time I walked on eggshells around that bitch. I told Ray-Ray that I didn't trust that ho. While Trigga, Big Jake, and the rest of the Misfits knew exactly what I was talking about, Ray-Ray and Speedy seemed to give her the benefit of the doubt. I mean, I couldn't blame Ray-Ray. After all, she had been best friends with the girl for most of her life. With Speedy, I could tell he was deep in his feelings for the girl, but the bitch was a traitor. I prayed when they killed her that she died as painfully as they could make it.

"Shut the fuck up," she yelled at me.

"You all big and bad with my hands tied, ho. Let me catch my fade in a square up," I lashed back out at her.

She smirked and then laid a hand on her slender hip with an exaggerated head tilt. "Bitch, I know you can't fight. I remember all the little jokes and stories that nigga Trigga and Big Jake cracked on you about it."

"You wanna take that bet and remove these ropes from my hands though?"

"Okay, silly little girls. Enough of the ring around the roses," the other woman cut in. She rolled her eyes to the ceiling and then cast a glance at us like we were little children squabbling over toys.

"Who you calling a silly little girl?" Dominique responded as if she had been offended by the woman's offhand comment.

"You and the little Angel over there. We don't have time for you two to be fighting over simple shit."

"You're the one who came in here to talk to her when Micah said not to."

The woman shrugged. "I wanted to see the woman he mumbled about in his sleep at night."

Dominique's head jerked. "How the fuck you know what he's mumbling in his sleep?"

The woman smiled like she knew something Dominique didn't. "How do you think?"

For a brief moment both women stood there and stared one another down.

I had to laugh. "Seriously, you two hoes are really about to beef over this nigga Micah? I mean the dick was okay but it ain't shit to fight over. You broads are basic."

This time it was the woman who looked like Gina who smacked the color from my face. "You think just because you've been taught how to please a man in a whorehouse that you're hot shit, huh? Yeah, Micah told me all the stories about how nasty you were," she then said. "He told me you have a sick fetish for sucking dick and swallowing babies, too."

My lips twitched as I looked up at her. "Yeah? Did he tell you how he made Gina do the same thing? Did he tell you he used to fuck both of us when we were just sixteen? Did that nigga tell you he was a child molester?" I yelled.

It finally hit me why the older woman looked so familiar to me. She was Gina's mother. Had to be. I could have been wrong, but based on the stories Gina once told me and the eerie way the woman's eyes seemed to convey the jealousy she had for her daughter, I knew I was right.

Dominique laughed. "So, it's true. Micah told me about all you hoes," she said as she cackled. "You, the old ho who won't leave him alone." She pointed to the woman. "And you, the young ho who won't keep your legs or your mouth shut," she finished, pointing to me. "I don't get bitches like you."

I could see I had tipped the scales in my favor and I was going to run with it. "And I don't get why your dumb ass is even here. You've betrayed the wrong people. Trigga is going to—"

Before I could finish, her boot to my face rattled my brains.

"Fuck that retarded nigga too. For the life of me I can't see what the fuck Ray-Ray sees in that wannabe thug. Nigga walks around like he's the be-all and end-all. Like he can just quote some shit another nigga said and be king of something. Then again, Ray-Ray has always been in love with stupid niggas. Bitch thought her daddy was just like the best mafucker walking the planet. But I know something she don't know," Dominique sang as she circled me.

When she got behind me, she smacked me in the back of the head and I spit the blood from my mouth her kick to the face had given me.

"While her mama was busy sucking every other nigga's dick she could find, I was fucking her daddy," the bitch boasted.

"I guess a pimp will always recognize a prime breed ho when he sees one," I taunted.

My reward was an open-handed smack to the side of my face from behind. If Enzo had taught me anything, it was the longer you kept your enemy talking, the more they could bury themselves. Just the thought of what could have been happening to him saddened me. All I remembered were gunshots and then my car crashing. I didn't know how long I'd been gone or where I was.

"Shut the fuck up," she yelled at me. "He may have known a ho when he saw one, that's for sure. Why else would the dumb motherfucker give his daughter over to a nigga like Dame?" Dominique was laughing like she was just as demented as that nigga Micah. "But you know what? And I'm going to tell you this because you won't live to tell about it. I'm the reason Dame knew who stole his shit. That's right, it was me. I was spending the night at Ray-Ray's house the night those stupid parents of hers came home high off the lick they'd just hit. Ray-Ray was asleep and I'd gone to take a piss. I heard everything. Dumb asses. I knew Dame would pay top dollar for the information and he did. And, I got to fuck one of the tops dogs of ATL's underworld."

I couldn't believe what I was hearing. "Bitch, you sold your best friend's parents out for a few dollars and some dick? You the lowest kinda ho-ass bitch the hood can have. What kind of fuck shit is this?" *In the end you can't even trust yourself.* No truer had Enzo's words ever rung than they had in that moment.

"It wasn't about the money or the dick, although both were damn good," she started.

"Bitch, I've fucked Dame plenty of times and that dick ain't used for pleasure unless he wanted it to be; and, just by looking at you, I can tell he fucked you like the monkey bitch you are."

What I'd said was true. That nigga Dame didn't use his dick for pleasure unless he felt you were worth it. There was only one time Dame used his dick to make sure I felt pleasure and I used that shit to my advantage. I didn't work for a whole week because I made sure he remembered it. Even still, when he felt he was done with me he went right back to using his dick as a weapon to make sure I knew my place. So I knew without a doubt that he didn't give the treacherous bitch in front of me any pleasure.

It seemed as if the more I gave her the version of the truth she didn't want to hear, the angrier she became. That bitch kicked over the chair I was sitting in, with a loud yell as she did so. I hit the wet wooden floor hard. The chair scooted across the floor a bit and I could feel the splinters in my face.

"You're wasting time trying to fight this girl about dumb shit," the other woman finally spoke up. "Micah is going to fuck you up if you mess something up before he gets back and gets to interrogate this little girl."

The fact that she used the word "interrogate" told me she knew more about Micah than Dominique.

Make a nigga keep talking and he'll reveal his hand without you even having to ask. Enzo was all in my fucking head so I held on to the hope that he was still alive. That he was okay.

"He's going to kill you too, you know," I said as the burning sensations in my side and face intensified.

She knew who I was talking about, because she kneeled down to look me in the eyes. "No, he won't. I know too much," she arrogantly said.

Although there was a smile on her face and she stroked my head as if she was a caring mother, I didn't trust a bitch who would put her own daughter out on the streets.

"Why do you think he wants to kill me?" I asked. I couldn't stop the tears rolling down my cheeks. I wasn't crying, but I wanted her to think I was.

"Because you chose to run with a little boy, a criminal who he wants off the street."

"Is that what he told you? And you believe it? He wants me dead because I know too much, just like you do. I know where the bodies are hidden. I know the criminals he's looking into. I know too much! I know about his sexual assault against underage girls, including your daughter."

I had never been slapped, kicked, and punched so many times in less than ten minutes than I was locked in that abandoned house with two women who both felt they had something to prove. The older woman slapped my face then stood and kicked me so hard in my chest, I felt as if it caved in. I would have sworn to God she had crushed my chest cavity with the way fire had started to gather in my chest. I coughed and gagged when her thick-soled boot connected with my stomach. Obviously she hated to hear that Micah had screwed her daughter. I didn't understand the secret to her anger, because I knew she didn't give a fuck about Gina.

For the next several minutes I lay there while they beat and kicked me to their hearts' desire. All the while neither of them paid attention to the fact that my hands were coming unraveled, nor were they paying attention to the rod I had picked up in my hand. Once they were satisfied with the damage that had been done to me, they stood back and admired their handy work. Internally, I laughed. It hurt too much to laugh outwardly. They'd worked me over.

"That's enough. We don't want to kill the bitch before Micah has a chance to," Gina's mom told Dominique.

"Nobody would miss this broad if we did," she responded. "She's just a stripping whore."

I let them get their insults in until I was sure my hands were undone and I had a good grasp on the stick-like object.

"You forgot one thing," I said to them, pretending as if I was too hurt to speak any louder. "I'm a stripper, so I do my best work while naked."

Before they could grasp the concept of what I was saying, I brought the stick around like I was going for that MVP in an MLB all-star game again and knocked Gina's mom's legs from under her. I didn't have a whole lot of in-between time so when she fell, I kicked Dominique's legs, hopped up, and brought the stick down on Gina's mom's head. Her screams and yells serenaded me until the knock upside her head silenced her. I silently prayed that Gina wouldn't hold it against me and then moved my attention back to the Ciara-looking bitch trying to get back on her feet.

My chest hurt, titties ached, and whole damn face was on fire. I was going to hit that bitch in the back of the head and just be done. But I wanted her to see me coming. So I stood there, naked as the day I was born, and waited for that ho to turn around.

"Square up, bitch," I demanded of her. She held her hands up and backed away, but I wouldn't let her get away that easily. "Naw, bitch, you talked big shit when I was tied up and couldn't fight back," I goaded her.

That lanky bitch took a fighter's stance and I went in on her. No, I wasn't the best fighter, but I had been trained by the best, a group of Hood Misfits and a nigga named Enzo whose mama was an African Queen. I let that bitch Dominique have it. I dropped the rod and a flurry of punches ate away at her face as my foot connected with her pussy. *That one was for Gina and Ray-Ray. Sour pussy bitch.* She scratched at my face and tried to grab my hair, but I was the better aggressor. I mopped the floor with that bitch then picked up the rod to finish what I'd started. I beat her until she was unconscious.

I felt like I had won a marathon; and, for good measure, I walked back over to Gina's mom as she moaned out on the floor, and I beat that bitch some more too. The African Queens had taught me about sisterhood and the cold-blooded bitches on the floor knew about none of that.

A slow round of applause had me snapping around, stick up at the ready, until I saw the woman coming around the corner.

"How . . . What . . . How did you find me?" I asked her.

"The phone Shawn gave you has a tracker. When I'd heard nothing from either of you after several hours, I had to invade your privacy," she answered.

"You were here this whole time?"

She shook her head. "No, but I've been here long enough to know that the decision we all made this morning was the right one."

I couldn't even say anything else. She looked me over and then looked behind her. I shouldn't have been surprised to see Mirror there with her. He didn't look at my naked body for too long. Just pulled his long trench coat off and handed it to me.

I felt a bit of hope and for the first time I realized I was cold and shivering.

"You look like a bloody madwoman, but I now see why the decision was made," Mirror told me.

I was sure I did look possessed or something. Blood dripped from my lips, ears, and nose. Felt like some of my ribs had been cracked, and any time I coughed my insides went ablaze. Still, all I could think about was Enzo.

"Shawn?" I asked.

"What about him?" Shy asked me as she walked over to wrap an arm around me.

"Where is he? If there is a tracker on our phones—"

"On your phone," she corrected me. "He knew there was a possibility that Micah would try some underhanded shit. So only your phone has a tracker."

"So where the fuck is he?" I asked in a panic.

"Shawn is about his father's business."

I was confused. His father was dead and, furthermore, Enzo didn't want anything to do with the man. "Huh?"

"He met with his grandfather for a reason. He told me this morning that he was tired of looking over his shoulder. He's doing something about it. Now, you come home so we can get you healed up and then we turn you in to the police."

Chapter 12

Shy

They say strength is determined by character. I say it is that, but it is also perseverance. I currently stood in a small, damp, dingy, and rancid-smelling room, with two THOTs sprawled out near my feet. Behind me was my protector and supporter, and to the right of me was a young princess on her way to being a queen. Angel had worked over the two women before me and had shown them the ass they were eager to see. It amused me and gave me a small amount of joy. A scowl danced on my face while I stared down with knitted brows at the broads who were assisting in bringing pain to my son and those in his world.

It was disgusting to see these two disrespect the very core that made up a woman. There was no unity between the pair; I had heard that as I rounded the corner. These bitches were only out for themselves and that was a recipe for discord, distinction, and disaster. Which to me was a dishonor. However, I understood kismet and karma and right now, though it was a little out of order, everything was happening for a reason.

Kneeling down, I took my cell phone and took a picture of each woman. I sent it directly by a secure, protected method to a man I knew would have use for this. I also sent a text to another man I detested with every inch of me. These two skeetrats would serve a bigger purpose and help in the overall game. So, I traced each one's face, and snatched the crown of the older one and slammed her head down hard on the concrete floor repeatedly, pausing only to check her pulse and see if she had been knocked out. Shifting to the side, I did the same with the younger trick and stood up slowly with a wipe of my hands on their bodies.

An immense pain ricocheted throughout my body with each breath I took. Shards of piercing agony ripped through me and had me slightly dizzy. It had me gripping the wall before me as a momentary anchor then turning to stare directly into the eyes of my protection. Back at the hospice, I was presented with no choice but to go through the surgery to correct the cancer that was eating away at my body. There was no sure way to determine right now if it all had been cleared out, but I had faith that the follow-up test would show something positive. If not, I was content right now in walking through the medium of death, especially since I had bailed out on my recovery time. I did not have time to be laid up, not with my sons needing my support and resources.

"If you do not tell me that you are okay, we will have a bloody problem," Mirror muttered low near my side.

A faint smile played at the corners of my lips. I wanted to touch him, but too many eyes and ears were around us. "I'm okay. Can you take Angel out of here? But not far. You two need to be close enough to listen but far enough to be hidden."

Mirror raised a brow while thumbing his nose and glancing up and down at me. I swore he gave a grunt, and it made me chuckle; however, he backed away and nodded in respect.

"Trust me, you can put all the makeup on you to change your looks, but I'd rather keep you totally hidden so you can work how you do," I explained.

Mirror adjusted his hood and shades. He sported a black houndstooth scarf that wrapped around his mouth and nose, and an all-black outfit that fit the curves of his muscled frame perfectly. At his side was a long silver chain that connected to the black Rottweiler he had brought with him to torment his prey. "I trust you, especially your mind. What would you have me do with these two righteous cunts?"

Observing the dog sitting in wait at Mirror's feet, I watched her ears perk up and I noticed Angel watching from the doorway. "String them up. Strip them to their underwear. Unlike them, I get no pleasure from seeing pussy unless it's done artfully. And check their clothes for trackers. Angel, honey, pick whatever pieces of clothes of theirs that you can fit into and go with Mirror. You both need to move fast. I have a mini meeting to take care of, and then we are handling business as discussed."

I turned on my heels and picked up the chair Angel had just previously sat in. Unwrapping my shawl, I set it down on the chair, then took a seat myself, observing Mirror do his thing while Angel quickly pulled on clothes and took the young girl's boots. She gave a flash of a smirk and glanced around as if looking for something, but instead settled for stomping them both.

"Stupid, ratchet, sour pussy, following-ass bitches!" she hissed out with each stomp then stumbled backward.

Mirror's chuckle surrounded us. He caught Angel before she fell, then settled her to the side to quickly tie each one's mouth, then finish hoisting each female by their arms to the chains hanging in the ceiling behind me. "Don't worry, Angel love. Females like that don't last long and never get what they really want, which is power to rule over the men they so-called want."

My smile warmed even more at Mirror's words. He looked my way then picked Angel up. "I'll find a quiet spot for us. Keep Martha at yuh side; she'll protect you."

Angel pushed to see over Mirror's shoulder and she watched me. "Will you be okay?"

"Whatever happens, happens. They will never break me, and if they try I'll be beyond ready." My hands rested in my lap.

As I crossed my leg, I watched Angel. The concern in her face was disheartening but understandable. She had no idea what I was planning.

"Who is coming?"

The gun that rested in my purse was not enough protection in my opinion; however, since Martha was here I figured she'd be an additional resource. "The father of the devil. The true one who is Satan."

Angel began to shift in Mirror's hold. "You can't meet him alone!"

My hand raised and I shook my head. "Trust me, I will be safe. Just be near, listen, and learn. It's a method to my madness, honey, and these two will be wonderful gifts in the cause."

"If he hurts you . . ." Mirror grumbled low. He looked over his shoulder to watch me for a moment; then he walked out. "We'll be your shadows. Make this meeting go fast and in your favor."

Watching him leave, I bowed my head then mentally prayed while I silently mouthed, "For my sons, for my lost family, and for Grandpa Kulu, I will. On my word, for us all, I will."

My wait did not last long. The sound of both women slowly waking up made my day. I figured they would wonder who I might be, but I did not care. They could not see my face from my head shayla that shielded the side of my face. The rest of me was in the familiar dark purple jumpsuit that attached to my shayla I wore just to keep my appearance modified from those who would try to identify me. My nude-painted nails strummed my knee and the sounds of muffled screams started.

Rolling my eyes with a sigh, I slightly titled my head and put on a British accent. "Oh, do shut up, you two. Do not scream now. You both are bad bitches, about this life, correct? Then hang in and enjoy what you learn. Besides, you both might enjoy who you are about to meet. I know the young THOT will."

At that moment, Martha's ears twitched, and the sound of two sets of heels on pavement let me know my guests were here. I stayed seated, and then I dropped my hood. My hair was laid like Erica Campbell from Mary Mary. I had a new, silky, soft, crinkled, long wig tailored to be dramatic with its gold, jeweled headband to symbolize my African Queen affiliation and also give the man who stood in the doorway something to fawn over.

Caltrone Orlando suavely walked in. His gaze did not leave me, though I knew he saw the two women hanging on both sides of me. The sound of high heels shifting to the left of Caltrone had me smiling in joy yet again, as I noticed the young woman Enzo had detailed in our previous meeting. Allowing them to walk in and access the area, I quietly waited.

The woman I learned was calling herself Lilith muttered harshly, "This *punta* had a guard dog? Who the fuck does she think she is?"

My head shook slowly the moment that broad said those words. I did not even have to count in my head before the sound of Caltrone's massive hand meeting the side of that woman's face echoed around me. I studied him as he quickly turned in a way that kept his movements guarded from view. In some strange way he was being respectful and keeping me from seeing him choking that bitch up. The only reason I knew the woman was being choked was because I was intimately familiar with the practice and I could hear her sharp, jagged intake of breath.

Caltrone's voice ebbed out in cold and smoothly restrained anger. "You will show her respect. She is the woman whose name I allowed you to borrow. You will behave accordingly, *comprende?*"

"Of course, *papi,* forgive me," the woman whimpered, then moaned.

In that moment, my stomach clenched tightly in familiar angst from old memories at the display between the sickening pair. I wanted to scream. Wanted to pump bullets into the both of them, but all I could do was sit in stalled silence as the familiar sensation of bars closing around me threatened to return. I needed calming peace, and balance, so I moved my hand to pet Martha, and waited for them to move the hell on.

"Good. Now let us sit," Caltrone commanded. He led the woman forward while assessing me.

"Beautiful Iya, it has been a long time overdue, *mami.* I've missed your presence," Caltrone drawled.

He took two steps forward, gave a slight bow to take my hand, and turned it to kiss my wrist. His light pupils simmered in that familiar gaze I remembered Lu used to hold for me. I watched this man, as if he owned the place, sit in the chair Mirror found right before they came; then he rested his ankle over his knee.

That woman moved to stand behind him and she rested her hands on his shoulders. Her pale face was ruddy and the smack left her with a handprint against the side of her face as well as one around her neck. My heart went out to this woman, even though madness had clearly claimed her. A weary smile settled across my face. Already, I was ready to leave this private meeting.

However, I had to maintain the image that I was an equal player in this battle. "King Caltrone. The feeling is equally returned."

That woman gave a slight scoff as she watched with squinting eyes. I glanced up at her and just smiled while stroking Martha's warm head.

"Do excuse me, beautiful queen. Before you is Lilith Orlando. I'm sure you are familiar with the role she plays, the one you abandoned?" Caltrone snidely responded.

He reached into his jacket then smoothly pulled out a gold cigar case I remembered from my past. He snapped it open, pulled out a thick cigar; I was very familiar with the scent in my past dealings with him. He rolled it between his fingers, glanced up at Lilith, and slipped the cigar between his teeth to bite the tip off and spit it to the side of him. Shifting up to hold the cigar between his fingers, he waited for Lilith to light it and I sat in patience watching this man work.

"Ms. Banks, we assume that you called this meeting to discuss your nephew?" Lilith coldly stated.

It wasn't a question, but more an observation. With how her tone relayed it, it had me grinding my teeth in disdain and insult. I made way to respond but was interrupted by Caltrone.

He took several puffs then used his cigar holding hand to motion behind me. "However, before that, who are these two delightful creatures? Was this a gift of solidarity, Iya?"

Displaying a slight smile, I tilted my head to watch the women behind me. "Yes, it is—"

He gave a slight chuckle as he interrupted me again. "I am very pleased because it only reminds me of how much I've missed your unique gift of gore."

Every movement the man made was calculated and I knew them all. He was casting seduction my way but he also was silently challenging me. To see how much I had changed. Part of me deeply enjoyed it, because I was no longer afraid of what he could do to me. I knew he had separate plans for my sons, but he also had his own plans for me, plans I recalled long ago the moment Lu died.

I felt Caltrone's eyes settle on my plush ruby red lips. Like them all, he had a weakness for pussy, but he was better with controlling his primal needs verses his work. His control was one of many things that made him different from the other Orlandos. However, he was just as insane and masochistic as they were.

However, I played the game by licking my lips, softly laughing, and shifting my language to Spanish. "King Caltrone . . . and Lilith, is it? As you are seeing, he is coming into his bloodline, which was unfortunately leaked to all of Atlanta."

I calmly opened my purse, pulling out my specially designed cigarette holder for my ganja. Connecting it and then adding my blunt to it, I lit up and took a slow puff at the same time as Caltrone.

Lilith gave a sour smirk with her own tilt of her head while smoothing her hands over Caltron's shoulders. "Humph. We've already heard about this man who leaked out family business. This is what Shawn came to his family about."

Taking a slow drag from my ganja, I kept my cool and gave a slight giggle. "But of course he came to his family after being forced to before his time, Lilith. However, it was I who led his way to his grandfather while you stood stalking in the shadows, ineffectively I might add."

A slick smile spread across my face the moment she dropped her hands and almost came my way. I cleared my throat and shifted my legs to cross them again. "As you see, the women behind me are associated with that man. As a gesture of us coming home into the fold, I wanted to gift them to you, to do whatever you wished, at whatever time you wished."

The man before me gave a broad smile. I could tell he was enjoying the banter between Lilith and me. This was apparent by the lust that shone in his eyes and the slight way he smoothed his hands down his leg. I knew the secret language of his body movements and, at the moment, he was aroused. The flicker of the devil in him made its slight appearance then disappeared the moment he opened his mouth.

"I'm amused by the gesture, *bella,* and pleased. This will do. The enemy's *puntas* in our hands? *Muy bien,* very good." He allowed the smoke of his cigar to wisp between his lips while amusingly studying me.

Lilith placed her hands back on his shoulder and gave another huff. "What's the point of this meeting then? We have them; now what funny little plans do you have? I doubt you really have us in your best interest since you have kept your sons hidden from us."

Annoyance flashed in my mind, but I held my composure. *So they didn't take the bait I set long ago that Enzo and Drew were my nephews? Interesting.* I made way to respond but Caltrone's growl garnered my silence.

"You speak too freely, Lilith. Iya, what naughty little games do you have for us? Lilith is correct in her assessment."

My thumb tapped my cigarette holder and I tried to keep from popping off as I sat in front of a madman. "I assumed these two women could return to their master and discuss with him how they were captured. Then you could relay a message through them to him? As I know you both know, family business is already occurring as we speak. I believed that you both would enjoy the early spoils . . ."

I noticed Lilith leaning down to whisper into Caltrone's ear. His eyes darkened then he gave a slow, contemplative smile. He then relaxed his posture while he spoke to her in hushed tones. I could tell by whatever he was saying that she was not happy at all. However, she adjusted herself to rigidly smooth a hand down her clothes. "Caltrone is a proud grandfather and is pleased that you have decided to stand by your word and show your loyalty to us."

Caltrone smirked then nodded. "*Sí*, your tenacity and loyalty to your sons only shows how much of an asset you are to this family. You birthed two strapping boys, and successfully hid that fact from us until Lu shared his mind with me before he died. It was very surprising in the most to learn that, but a welcomed gift nonetheless."

I watched the man I loathed leaned forward to steeple his fingers against his lips while he blew plumes of smoke around us in thought.

"Caltrone believes that even in your diminishing light, you are incredible. Had Prince Lu not made that last visit to take care of your sister, we wouldn't have known they were blood," she explained.

It sounded as if she hated saying even that, and it made me chuckle in my mind.

"*Sí*, you and your sister were very resourceful. It was a shame how even I couldn't control my son's behavior in those last days. He disgraced me and this family and also lost those I cherished. Had he not died you could have given us more grandchildren." Caltrone's darkening eyes hovered over my mouth and dropped over my chest; then he smirked.

That irking sickness crept into my throat. I didn't want to think about birthing that monster any more innocent children. I meant that with the core of me.

I casually waved a hand around and gave a sweet smile. "King Caltrone, I am honored; however, I am too old now, and in punishment for my behavior, your son took that from me. Although, you and he did push me to my choice in hiding my sons. I knew Lu would have killed them and never told you of their existence."

A brief spark of acknowledgment shone in his eyes, knowing I spoke the truth. He gave a light, gruff growl and said nothing. Flicking his hand, he motioned for Lilith to sit on his lap, which she did with sickening eagerness. Lilith menacingly smiled my way, and Martha started growling low, which caused me to smile in malice.

"Shh, good girl," I whispered.

A light suck of the teeth sounded, which had me staring her way. "What do you want of Caltrone?"

"He knows," I simply responded before casting a bored gaze. "I was given an agreement to be left alone to my own devices. To live my life how I wanted. You and your family were obligated in alerting me of your return. You did not, so you breached contract. I know for a fact that this is not how we do things, correct, Lilith?"

Sharp heat bore into my face. Lilith knew I spoke truth in my words. She was shocked that I was bold enough to address Caltrone in this matter; I could tell it in her gaze.

"Yes, that is true. However, with our business being in the air—"

Waving a hand in the air, I cut her off: "That isn't my problem. As the first, Lilith, I still have rights and still require the utmost respect as a member of this family. My bed was chosen for me, King Caltrone, don't forget, so I have stake in this too. The world is yours, Caltrone, but I have a right to it as well, as was agreed when you named me the Queen of DOA when Lu died."

Caltrone scowled then gave a panty-dropping smile. He said nothing, just nodded at Lilith to continue.

Her evil face gazed at me in shock. I could tell she was shocked and it amused me to drop such gems in front of everyone. "Well . . . Well . . ." Lilith shot up as she stammered. She pointed her finger in heated anger. "I would put a bullet in your damn head, but he won't allow it! I . . . am . . . Lilith! You left your place, bitch. You will respect the king and me!"

Coolly untwisting my cigarette holder, I snuffed out the smoked blunt, tucked the holder away, then gave a light laugh. Slowly standing, I wrapped Martha's chain around my hand and also placed my purse in that hand.

I gave a light chuckle. I watched bitch from my peripheral fuming, and I glanced at the two bodies behind me before hauling off and backhanding Lilith. I turned in the same motion, smoothed a hand down my dress, and got joy at seeing her fall backward.

"Cute," I softly muttered, and nodded toward Caltrone. "You may be new pussy, and a new Lilith, but I will always be the queen, because from my womb came kings. Now . . ."

Lightly smiling at Caltrone, he held out his hand and I kissed the ring nestled there. Choices were playing in my mind. I had to play my role and lead the nigga into the tar.

Caltrone's booming voice sounded in wicked calmness that caused a chill to shift down my body. "Do not touch what is mine, Lilith." She got ready to speak up again and the unsaid, "Why?" hung in the air as he continued: "She is a queen as I am king. Respect the order. Now, Iya dear, before you go: one more time or I will crush your windpipe. What do you want?"

I kept my back to Lilith. I knew she was going to come for me and I was fine with that. Unfazed by his threat, I showed him the madness in my own eyes, which caused him to smile then nod. "I want Micah Tems dead. I want you to give my son all the access he deserves, and not distract him from the illusion he has built around him. Will you do that?"

Caltrone's brush against my arm gave me the chills as he spoke. "He is ready to be a prince. That is a given. All that is mine will be his. No game on my end but no games on your end, Iya. *Comprende?* You're mine as are your sons. I've waited too long for this and we have much to do. Taking out that roach will be nothing. He actually bores me and I am not amused at him snatching for my throne. Don't you agree, Lilith?"

Caltrone held out his hand and waited for the woman to slide her hand into his. He walked her around him and sat her on his lap again, leaning up to kiss the side of her neck.

"*Sí*, he is a problem. Maybe I'll visit him," Lilith suggested with a wicked gleam in her eyes. She turned to slide her arms around his neck, and the women began their screams again at the mention of Micah's name.

Pleased, I stood by the door and watched the devil and his new bitch. "Good. I have one more suggestion then. Your other grandson had a love for something called the Underground. I happen to know some of what occurred down there. How about we introduce them to some of that then politely leave Micah a calling card?"

Lilith gazed at Caltrone as if mentally begging to be the one to give the pain. He ran his fingers over her back and smiled. The low rumble he made had Lilith swaying in satisfaction. Caltrone kept his eyes on me and I noticed the visible bulge in his pants.

"Oh, how I've missed your evil, Iya. Lu never understood how to use you, but I did. Welcome back to the *familia, bella,* and we will definitely have fun with these two," he cajoled.

"Enjoy. Oh, and don't kill them. Keep them viable; it makes the games better." I left it at that and guided Martha out with me.

I squared my shoulders then walked out like the queen I was with the door closing behind me. I slowly strolled away with a quiet sickness ebbing in my body. I saw Mirror and Angel resting in the shadows. I nodded their way and saw the shock in their eyes. I thought disgust would be there, but instead it was respect. As we headed to the car, joy bubbled up in me at the sharp screams behind us. Those two bitches were going to get theirs and were learning a valuable lesson: don't fuck with my son or his true family.

Two down for now and one more to go.

Chapter 13

Enzo

Gunplay was my seduction and I was moving through the garage with a purpose. In my mind, Angel was set and safe behind me. I had a goal and a purpose that needed my full attention, which was why I dug into the black bag, an actual backpack, hanging on the side of my arm and pulled out a grenade. Niggas were on the left and right of me. I stomped and kicked the faces of those who fell in front of me as if I was playing football.

Skulls cracked and necks snapped while I positioned myself to get closer. Micah's hands were thick with roaches who were working his will. I knew that each and every one of them needed to be taught a lesson. I used my teeth to pull the clip, and then tossed the grenade in front of me. I made sure not to leave any DNA by spitting the clip out and putting it in my backpack.

A loud force shifted the garage, causing it to tremble, once my baby exploded in the car it flew into. Bodies burned and the smell of cooked flesh with that of gas had my nostrils flaring while I stalked that van. I signaled to my left. Fuego stepped from the garage stairway and moved to stand in front of the van that was trying to get away. He shot off several rounds to hit the driver, and I covered the back, shooting out the tires.

A snarl came from me causing me to flash my teeth as I shouted then ducked behind a pillar. "Get what we came to get, nigga."

Several other cars were coming our way, filling up the garage, making it feel like we were on the battlefield in Afghanistan. I had heard the stories from some of the men my mom would have us sit with at the VA hospital as kids, men who taught me military maneuvers as favors out of love for her. Thinking back on it, I had to give her respect. She had been training us for the day this all may happen and I was thankful for that shit.

Salty wetness dripped down my face as I reloaded. I let my gloved hands wipe away at the sweat that was running into my vision and adjusted the mouth mask I sported. Yeah, I wanted Micah to know it was me, and through the chaos that was ensuing, I knew he would know that it was, but on some real shit I still had to make sure I kept my identity safe, which was why I had on a ski mask. A nigga running through the streets—no, scrap that—a well-known athlete running through the streets playing super fucking man was bound to be noticed. I needed to be Enzo from the Trap. Enzo no one really checked for, except to do the occasional transportation of hoes, drugs, weapons, and even bodies. A nigga who dabbled in the underground only because the boss man demanded it. I had to be that nigga. Had to be calm and collected and not know shit.

So that was what I was doing, because if I got caught, with the fact that I already had the cops on me, I needed to make sure my story lined up in a way that didn't get me on death row or give me life. Pressing my shoulder against that same pillar, I glanced to see Dragon slam the door of the black van and nod my way. He ushered a tattered and disheveled woman and her child away, then stepped back into view. He pointed the tubular projectile that rested on his broad shoulder at the limo that was attempting to get away.

I chuckled then gave a sharp whistle. In that same moment, Dragon let off a missile that jetted into the limo and blew that bitch up. I smiled under my mask then moved away from the pillar.

Fuego sprinted my way and ran a hand over his brow. "A'ight, the area is clear. Your boy just handed out some serious thunder. What now, fam?"

Glancing at Dragon, I pointed; then he nodded again and disappeared after his family. No lie, I was tired. We just murdered many of Micah's goons but that nigga was nowhere to be found.

"Did anyone run from the limo?" I asked, glancing around.

"Naw, man. We trailed that shit and I know he didn't switch out, so he must not have even been in there," Fuego explained while holding up his cell to his ear.

My jaw clenched tight in thought. This nigga was always one step ahead. Always running like the bitch he was and with the heat of the flames of the vehicles burning behind us, I knew we needed to flush him out.

Crossing my arms over my chest, I scowled. "What you hear?"

Fuego's irises darkened in annoyance and he ran a frustrated hand over his head. "Word is that nigga is at the stadium. He's holding a press conference about y'all's upcoming game toward the Super Bowl."

I dropped my hands in thought, pacing. My mom had told me that her resources had learned that Micah was doing a transfer. So, I knew that ever since we all went ham on him, he was now surrounding himself with the best. We needed her to get to the root of where Micah worked, the FBI, hell even the CIA. If she could go that deep, then exposing him was just going to be icing.

"A'ight, we need to take down his crib and leave him with nothing but his condo. That way we can start pushing the cage around him, feel me?" I explained.

I reached up to thumb my nose, glancing around to make sure the area was straight. I knew police and probably Feds would be on their way soon, because that was how that shit was done. But I wanted to time that because it meant Micah was watching and my message had been sent. The cousin and me then sprinted to a safe spot where our cars where.

Fuego began going in on his cell, spitting out orders, before hanging up and turning my way. "A'ight, fam, whatever you need we got."

Taking that nigga's hand in a clasp, we both nodded as I assessed him thinking about that dude's POV in all of this. "Thanks, man. One thing though: what do you get out of all this shit?"

Fuego gave a shrug then a familiar smirk. "Keeps me out of Gramp's madness in trying to create a family of devils, and brings me some interesting fun in my boring life as a cop, fam. Like I said we all ain't insane, just maybe a little crazy, *comprende?*"

His words made me slightly smirk and chuckle. With Fuego I knew I needed him to stay exactly in the role I needed him in. If he was truly about that loyalty shit and just doing this to keep the devil off of him, then I was down with that. I knew that I would never trust that nigga totally. However, he could serve my purpose in this game and life. Although it was going to take a lot more than blood and his actions to get me to accept him.

"A'ight, man, get back to what you do to keep the eyes off me and directly on that nigga Micah, then . . ." I explained, stopping midsentence to point my Glock at the shadow walking toward us.

In that moment, Dragon stepped out into view. He had a big scarf wrapped around his face with a black skullcap. How he was shifting back and forth, I knew he needed to talk to me in private. So I motioned for Fuego to step off and explained to him that I would call him for the next orders, then thanked him again.

Fuego headed out and I holstered my Glock, then dropped my hands as I stood wide-legged with an arrogant gaze. "What up?"

"Thank you, man," was all Dragon said.

My arms crossed, I gave a slight nod of my head then stepped forward. "All you gotta do is trust in me. You had my back at one point, and if you had given me the chance, I woulda had yours on the fucking spot, nigga. Now all this shit had to go down just to get your fam, damn."

Dragon looked away for a moment with a pained expression. I could tell he was in his emotions. It had me wanting to punch him for losing faith in me and almost had me pressing my gun to his skull.

"I know, man, but you ain't got a family. You don't have a kid and wife to worry about being raped, beat up, drugged up, or some other shit. I do. So I had to do what I had to do, nigga: survival," he explained.

His words had me feeling some type of way. It had me stepping a little closer in a heated manner as I fisted my hands. "Don't assume what you don't understand, nigga. I got family. My life's been turnt up because of family. So yeah, nigga, I know what it means to sacrifice, but the thing about me, nigga, is I'm the fucking fittest. Everyone around me I make sure are survivors and don't do dumb shit like you did by siding with the wrong nigga. It's game to this, and you fucked up game, but shit, now you know better, don't cha?"

My sour laughter echoed around us. I glanced away then shrugged.

"Look, yeah, you're right, and I'm sorry 'bout that, but we got my family and we took down a lot of your enemies. I'm just saying, thank you," Dragon said.

Shrugging again, I headed to my ride and tossed my bag into it. "Take them to where we spoke on, and keep them out of harm's way until I'm done handling business."

"I'll help you, man. I mean it," Dragon interrupted, stopping me from getting in my ride.

Turning my head, my eyes cut him with restrained anger. "If you help me, I need your true loyalty, nigga. No fake shit, no siding with my enemies, because then you become my enemy and I will kill you on the fucking spot, homie. No love lost."

On some real shit, I ain't have time for this nigga soap shit going on. Nigga catching feelings and getting all soft was annoying me. I got what he was saying, I was living it right now, but there was no fucking way I'd let that nigga Micah break me down like he did Dragon. Yeah, I saw the old killer on the field in that man, but fuck it! That nigga was broken down. He needed to get back to the monster he was, a monster I knew who could hold me down in this empire building shit.

I watched that nigga open and close his fist. He bowed his head as if in thought then glanced up at me. "I'll be your security, man."

Chuckling, I shook my head while leaning on the door of my car. "Last time someone with my blood trusted in a second hand and security, that left him burning up."

"I mean fuck it, homie. I ain't to be trusted; not in your case, but in that nigga Micah's case. He took from me, hurt my family, and then tried to have me turn on friends? Naw. In the street, I know that would have me eating a bullet. I'd rather be on some honor shit with you and die than on some pussy shit with Micah, ya know?" Dragon growled.

It was as if the old him was coming back and it gave me pride.

"Listen, man, I know you gotta do some shit you don't want to and I know niggas are gunning for you. I have my family to protect too and I feel like on some real shit, man, I feel you are fam. We come from the same place, and I don't trust a lot of people but . . . yeah," he explained, stepping closer.

In reality, I had no one I trusted on my side besides my family. My boys Trigga and Jake were doing their own thing and building their shit. I had to do the same in order to survive so I had to think strategically. Bringing Dragon in could help bring him up in money and act as my protection in the NFL world. Like I taught Angel and Drew, sometimes a nigga can't even trust his own self. So, I studied Dragon, and made my choice. *I'll trust him as long as his actions prove to me that he can be in my fam, then I'll bring him in as a whole, just like I had to do with Angel.*

"A'ight, you just blew up some rides, man, and didn't flinch 'bout it, a'ight." I offered Dragon my hand then pulled him into a shoulder bump while studying his expression with a blank expression on my own face. "But check it. You ever try to stab me, or successfully stab me in the back, check your throat first because I'll cut that shit before you ever can touch me. This is life and death, no games."

Dragon shook his head. We did our old handshake and he gave a smirk in understanding. "I feel you. Ya don't even have to ever question me like that, but a nigga understands it, man. You saved my kid and wife. I'll be down for life even if that means my death," he reassured me.

Still thinking, I smirked. "A'ight; hopefully it won't be that way. I'll take care of you so you can protect your fam because that's what we do. Just manage your finances better, nigga, and don't blow through that shit."

Dragon gave me a genuine laugh then rubbed his chin. "A'ight, man. Like I said, I'm ready. What you need?"

Digging in my pocket, I called Fuego and put him on speaker. "Nigga, you're going to help out Fuego."

I could see that Dragon felt unsure about that, knowing how I felt about the Orlandos, but I quirked my eyebrow, hoping he understood the code, then nodded.

"What you need me to do with the homie?" he asked.

My posture shifted to lean against the car. I chuckled then went into my plan. "Fuego is going to pay a visit to Micah's residences. Y'all going to go through that whole shit and wipe it clean; then I want that shit to burn down in a clean fire, no trace, got it?"

"Yeah, got it," both said in unison.

"Plan is to leave him with only his condo. No big mansion, nothing. I want to find out where that nigga really operates and lays his head. So keep an eye on his crew, too. That means check Uncle Phil and Deebo too," I continued.

Both laughed, and I shifted to stand. "Good. Let's keep this feeling of giving going. If you see anyone worth snatching on his team, then snatch 'em. Dragon, you and me gotta play the role like you don't know shit. That means the little hit he got on me, keep that shit going. Egg it up, a'ight? Use your resources to our advantage."

Dragon gave a low chuckle that sounded as if a rumbling storm was in his throat. He gave me a salute and I gave it back to him.

"A'ight. I'll keep my family out of eye's length, too," he suggested.

My hand tapped the top of my car then I chuckled. "Yeah, do that."

A fist shifted into my view. I pounded it and Dragon turned. "Bet, game time then. I got your back."

I said nothing after that, just watched him. Already I was planning a backup plan, just in case both niggas fucked me over. Couldn't trust those who showed consistent weakness. Gotta make them prove it, and then truly decide what's the real deal. That was my motto.

Sliding in my ride, I heard Fuego ask, "So you bringing him in the team?"

Starting my car, I quietly thought on it, and then pulled off. "Yup. Set him up nice and keep his family safe. I don't fuck around with that trafficking shit, so don't expect the new DOA to be about that unless it's some grimy bitches I'd rather shit on than trust, feel me?"

"Just checking, fam. I'll report back with what we snatch," Fuego said then hung up.

I turned a corner as I exited the backside of the garage and then my ride came to a screeching halt. Revving up my engine, I glanced around. See, I knew that since we'd set off rocket launchers and grenades we should have heard sirens somewhere, but no. I chuckled. Wasn't shit funny, but I chuckled anyway. The fact that there wasn't a police siren anywhere let me know that Micah's FBI status was at work. I looked up and saw Micah in my rearview. He came around the corner like he'd been watching me the whole time.

A smirk played across my face. The cutting edge of the voice of the nigga who sired me roared in my mind: *"Kill that nigga! This kingdom ain't his!"*

Yeah, I was hearing voices. Had been hearing the man who'd sired me for quite some time. I ignored it until today. I didn't need the constant reminder I'd come from the bloodline of sadistic killers. I didn't need the reminder that the sins of the father were cast upon the son, a big reason why Micah was after a nigga so hard.

I pulled to the side and exited my ride. "Enjoy the fireworks, nigga?" I taunted him.

Micah ran both hands down the front of his blazer, the shine of his leather shoes glinting my way. "Imagine my delight when I get the call that you just snatched up my grand prize. You know I had to come down and see how true that shit was, and to put a bullet in your head."

Chuckling, I stood my ground then pulled out my Glock, sending bullets his way. "You first, nigga," I yelled at him.

We both ran toward each other. Micah ducked then zigzagged from my bullets, but was able to rush me. The gun in my hand went flying over the side of another car. My fist connected to his face before he sent his foot into my leg causing me to drop to a knee. The back of his fist connected to my face again but my uppercut sent him falling on his back.

Strain from his blows had me pushing up slowly and heading his way. That was when that nigga used something to cut me, slicing through my arms, and then he gave me a stab in my side. Pain shattered through me, but adrenaline kept me going. I took in my surroundings just to make sure no niggas were creeping up on me, because the setup was too easy for that to happen. I rushed forward. Micah rolled out of my way.

I followed as he ran to avoid my attack. Micah's laugher sounded around me and I gritted my teeth, while wiping at my face.

"Bet you didn't expect this shit, and now I'm going to have my prize: an Orlando rotting in prison," Micah gloated. "No, scrap that; you attacked me so I get to watch you die as I gut you, bitch," Micah snarled coming at me on my side.

I realized I'd chased that nigga into an empty warehouse. The scent of musky mold, water, and other unidentifiable smells surrounded me. Behind us, there were boulders of broken concrete from bare wall beams. Various poles of twisted iron, pipes, glass, and other sharp objects protruded from many spots in this place.

As I took in my surroundings, I turned and felt a blade slice through my mask, cut at my jaw, and almost slam into my shoulder. Pushing out, I snatched at his arm, twisted it, almost breaking bone so he could drop the knife; then I slammed him down to the floor. Dust clouded around us and I slammed him down again. That sound of sirens grew closer signaling that I had to get out of here.

"Kill me and I still won!" Micah hissed out.

A calming sensation flowed through me as I made that nigga eat dust. I pressed my knee into the back of his neck, and then I took that same blade and slammed it into the middle of his shoulder blades. I twisted it and he hollered. The sound of me crushing his face into the dirt gave me the utmost pleasure in the moment. I couldn't just kill Micah, although I wanted to. Everything in me screamed to just off that nigga right then and there. But I was smarter than that. I knew there was a live investigation going on and my name was at the center of it. If I simply killed this nigga, everything would point my way. I couldn't risk that. Couldn't risk going to prison and leaving my brother behind. Couldn't leave Shy behind while she was sick like she was. So I had to play with my prey. Toy with this nigga until I found the right time to take him out.

"They gotta catch me first. Until another day, nigga. I have a present too sweet for you. Can't kill you just yet and I got a game to win, so holla at'cha," I muttered against his ear. That nigga squealed like a pig in a pot of boiling water and it made me laugh. "Ahh. Ah, nigga. Ah, you just hit a note higher than Mariah Carey, bitch. Damn I love it when you scream."

Micah squirmed trying to get his footing, but I reached for the other blade he had, stuck that shit right through the back of his hand and then twisted. I chuckled as that nigga twisted and screamed. His face held a look that said the pain he was in was too much to handle.

"Thank you for coming out to see the show. If you hadn't then we wouldn't be enjoying this dance between us, yeah? Anyway, homie, I got you right where I wanted," I said, smacking his head. I pulled out a small object from the side of my ski mask.

"The fuck is that?" he garbled against the dirt.

"Oh, shit, just a little evidence, Mr. *Federalie*. A little show and tell of me defending myself against you. A camera. Say cheese." I showed it to him then chuckled before slamming his head against an iron pipe.

Brushing my gloves off, I tucked the camera I had back in its place. Voices were multiplying in magnitude outside. It wasn't my time to be caught up so I had to bounce. Micah was a fucking thorn that just wouldn't stop being a prick. He was a foul cancer and, with time, I knew we could snuff his ass out. That was why I also was enjoying the pain I was giving him. Everything was a process. Everything was going down with reason. Me getting caught now would mess that up.

"Until we meet again, niggarali," I said, kicking Micah in his ribs then bouncing.

I quietly made my way out of the big building then sprinted away finding my ride. Relief had me letting out a huge sigh then cranking up some music. I drove away then headed to my safe house to handle the wounds that were leaking all over the place. Damn I couldn't wait for him to see his house in nothing but ash.

Making it to my safe house, I headed upstairs, stripped out of my clothes, and turned to glance in the mirror at my wounds. My eyes scanned over my tats, my abs, and the cuts and bruises against my golden brown skin.

He had cut me good, but where his blade hit my jaw, I knew that my beard would hide the scar it would leave. I guessed I had to walk away with some reminder of him. Wasn't shit I was tripping off because I planned upon paying him back tenfold.

Stepping into the shower to clean the blood and dirt away, I enjoyed the sensation of the heated water washing out my pains; then the sound of Jay-Z popping off let me know I had a call.

Grimacing in pain, I reached for the cell then hit speaker. "Yeah?"

"Hurry up and meet us at the house, honey; we have a lot to talk about. Angel was snatched but it worked in our favor," Shy urged in my ear.

As I quickly laced up my black Timbs, wrapped my waist with bandaging, then pulled on my shirt, I asked, "Is she hurt?"

"No, baby, she's good. Healing up so she can go turn herself in. Did Micah come out and play?" my mother asked, with a slight tone of amusement in her voice.

"Yes, ma'am, as planned. Wasn't sure if he was going to do it but he did eventually. Fucked me up real good but I got him like we set up," I explained while quickly heading out to my ride.

"Good. I love you, and come home safely. I want to see the wounds so we can heal you up better, okay?" she demanded, which had me chuckling.

"Yes, ma'am, on my way. Love you back." I hung up.

Speeding away, I took the back roads. My body ached and my jaw was tender. Parts of me were raw and dripping and it annoyed me. I hoped that nigga was enjoying the knife in his back because I had more where that came from. To kill Micah would be too easy. I really wanted that nigga to suffer now that I thought about it. I wanted him to suffer the same way he was trying to make me suffer. I was tired of the cat and mouse because this shit needed to come to a head, immediately. Tapping my hand on the steering wheel, I silently hoped that the next phase would get us moving faster and bring all his skeletons out.

Chapter 14

Angel

I hadn't expected any of what had happened to go down the way it did. It felt like Micah had chased me and Enzo to the end of the earth. The game he was playing seemed like a revolving door. Shit reminded me of an episode of *Tom and Jerry* and I was over it long before it started. Still, the game I was in had no time for whiners. In the Trap, that kind of weakness would be your downfall. So you had to suck that shit up and keep it moving.

Shy had told me the best thing to do would be to turn myself in. Beat Micah at his own game, she had said. I couldn't front like I wasn't scared shitless because I was. I didn't want to be anywhere near a jail. For some reason just the thought of being locked behind bars reminded me of being locked away in Dame's mansion. On second thought, shit, if I had survived Dame's world then maybe I could survive prison.

I was so nervous that my pussy had started sweat. Felt as if the boy shorts I had on were too tight. The fact that I was battered and bruised from my time with two bum bitches only solidified my appearance as a victim. I didn't know how Shy's plan would work or if it would work, but I trusted her. Still, what I didn't expect was for my ride to be Caltrone Orlando and his pet bitch, Lilith. The man didn't like me, as was apparent by the disdain on his face when Shy had told him who I'd become to her and Enzo.

We'd met at a safe house so Caltrone wouldn't know where Shy laid her head. As I walked out to the car, he stood there with a cigar in his hands while he casually talked to his driver. Shy was behind me and I had to admit that she played her part well. If you didn't know any better you would think she fit right in as the queen of DOA. I couldn't wrap my mind around how deep the evil of the Orlandos ran. The son, Lu, had been obsessed with Shy, but it seemed as if the father was too. It made me wonder what kind of power the women of the African Queens had over the Orlandos. I said that because Dame had been smitten with Anika. It had been so obvious back when Dame was alive that Anika had that nigga by his balls whenever she was around. He wouldn't dare utter a disrespectful word to her. Wouldn't even smack the shit out of one of us when she was around.

Shy must have felt my discomfort because she laid a hand on my back and said to me, "It's okay, Bianca. I wouldn't send you if it wasn't. Tap into that inner queen you're destined to be and handle this nigga."

I glanced at her over my shoulder. Anytime the street in her came out it always baffled and surprised me. The African Queens were women of many faces. I turned to look at the woman who had become the only mother I'd known.

"I don't want to ride with them, Shy. I'll do what you asked of me, but can't Mirror take me or something?" I asked out of nervousness and, quite frankly, fear.

"No. We have to beat Caltrone at his own game. You have to show him that you're worthy to stand next to Shawn. I know it sounds crazy, and it is. But these men have great disdain for women who show any kind of weakness. It takes a powerful queen to bring an Orlando to his knees. Understand? You can even show him that you're afraid, but do it in a sense that leaves this motherfucker trying to guess just who you are. Do it so that when he looks at you he sees something, the same thing he sees in me. And as sick and disgusted as you may be, keep in mind that he's considered the sane Orlando. As we both know, that ain't saying much."

I studied her for a long while. Although she stood regally, I could see the fatigue in her eyes. I'd come to know her well enough to see when she was trying to hide her pain. She should have been somewhere laid up in recovery, but not Shy. She wouldn't hear of it, wouldn't rest until her sons were safe. I turned back to look at the man. Even in old age he was a head-turning, panty-dropping male chauvinist asshole. While his smirk may have been painted on by God Himself, the malevolent intent behind it was anything but godly.

I forced myself to walk forward. All I had on was a thin sundress and a pair of flats that strapped around my ankles. So while the woman standing beside Caltrone was dressed in everything designer from her head to her feet, my threads came from Goodwill and the difference was apparent. Still, that didn't faze me and neither did the properly trained attack dog at Caltrone's side.

I made my way to the man in the most docile of manners. Didn't make any sudden movements, but I wouldn't break eye contact with him. I wouldn't let his ominous gaze force me to look at the ground. Dame had done that to me enough. I wouldn't give Caltrone that kind of power over me. I walked to stand in front of him. Took the hand with the Orlando crescent ring on it, and then placed my lips gently against it. My whole face went cold, my body went rigid, but I played my part.

"It's an honor to be in your presence," I told him.

Bile was rising to my throat and I felt the incessant need to vomit, but I didn't. I cast a glance back in his direction as I stepped around the bitch in his snare and slid into the car. It didn't take me long to figure out which side of the black-on-black Hummer he sat on. On one side there was water, cognac, and cigars. Lilith was such a lap dog that he could tell her to bark and she would. So it was clear that she sat on his left side. I moved to the right and waited for him.

I smiled at the man when he took his seat next to me. His muscular thighs brushed against mine and, surprisingly, I didn't flinch. As soon as Lilith saw where I'd sat she bristled. I smirked.

"You bitches are beside yourselves," she grumbled.

Caltrone looked away uninterested. I only giggled as the driver got into the truck and pulled off, which seemed to annoy the both of them.

He asked, "What's funny?"

I smiled seductively, just the way his other grandson had taught me. "Queen Iya told me you had a bitch of a guard dog. I didn't think she meant one standing on two legs," I casually replied.

Caltrone only grunted and cast a sidelong glance at Lilith who looked like she was ready to jump across the seat at me. Her catlike eyes had turned to slits and I could see the murderous intent in them. The red cat suit she had on contoured to her petite, shapely hips and thighs and her black stiletto pumps looked as if she used them as weapons more often than not.

"What is your purpose for tagging behind my grandson like a bitch in heat yourself? We know nothing of your pedigree, what stock you come from. You could be a simple mutt. Mutts have never worked out well within our faction," he scolded.

I glanced at Lilith then back to him. "I could be a lot of things, but what I'm not is disloyal," I said, remembering Shy had told me the Orlandos were big on loyalty.

"How do you know Shy—"

Caltrone turned to look at her as if she had committed an offense by calling Shy her street name. Lilith cowered and then started her question over.

"How do you know . . . Queen Iya," she spit out through clenched teeth. "How do you know she isn't setting you up just to get her son off scot-free?"

I didn't answer her question; in fact, I didn't even look at her as she asked the question. I kept my eyes on the man who mattered. "Haven't you trained your pet not to interrupt when royalty is speaking?" I asked him.

I didn't know if I had offended the man. Judging by the way he kept flexing his hands, I couldn't tell if he wanted to punch me or the mutt sitting beside him. The rest of the ride was silent. If he wasn't speaking low and in code to Lilith, he was studying me and I could tell that, just as Shy had said, he didn't know what to make of me.

When we pulled up to the precinct, my heart jumped into my throat. I looked around at the circular brick building, intimidated by all the police presence there. My attention was thwarted when Caltrone leaned forward and gripped my knee with so much force and pressure that it took everything that made me a woman not to flinch in pain.

"The only reason I wanted you to ride in my presence to this precinct is because I'm trying to do things Queen Iya's way. But, rest assured, if you fuck this up, what my grandson may have done to you while you were his whore will be nothing compared to what I will do to you. *Comprende?*"

"Clearly," was how I answered.

And although I wanted to cry out at the grip on my knee, it was in that moment that I saw where Enzo got his crazy. Caltrone's light eyes had darkened and then returned to their light-colored essence all in one sitting. I saw where Dame's madness was inherited from as well. Both had gotten it honestly.

When I walked into the precinct, my first mind was to turn around and run out. But I'd given my word. So my word would be what I would stand on.

"Can I help you, honey? You lost?" a female officer behind the desk asked me. She looked young and the bulletproof vest she had on made it appear as if she lifted weights for fun. Her sun-kissed skin gave her a tropical look.

"I'm looking for . . . I need to report a crime," I told her. I had my hair pulled back into a ponytail and my dress fit a little loose. The shoes on my feet looked as if they were years old and I looked unkempt, as was the plan.

The look of concern that immediately flashed across her face let me know that I'd gotten her attention. "Come this way," she said as she laid a gentle hand on my shoulder. She led me over to a sitting area and made a hand signal to another officer as she sat next to me. "What kind of crime?"

"My name is Bianca Smith and I was kidnapped when I was fourteen."

"Excuse me?" she said as her eyes widened and she leaned forward to get a better look at me.

"I was . . . My grandmother . . ." I intentionally stammered and stuttered my words to appear more out of the loop than I really was.

"Slow down. Slow down, sweetie. It's okay. There is no need to be scared anymore. Slow down and tell me what you're trying to say," she coaxed me.

I wiped the tears away from my face. True enough, what I was about to do was all a farce to bring down Micah; still, it was the emotional truth for me.

"Damien Orlando kidnapped me when I was fourteen from Garden Walk Boulevard in Riverdale, Georgia."

As soon as I mentioned Dame's name, the woman's eyes got wide as saucers. She jumped up and grabbed my arm, dragging me to her captain's office. I looked on as other officers watched us wondering why such urgency seemed to be in the officer's stride as she dragged me along. Once the captain heard my story, the whole precinct was in an uproar. She wanted names, dates, times, places. Any- and everything I could remember, she wanted it.

"Why are you just now coming to tell us this? Damien Orlando has been dead for a little over a year now," the captain, a pale-faced woman with blond eyebrows and brown stringy hair, asked me.

"Because the FBI has, well, Micah Tems with the FBI has been keeping me tied to him so I could still do Dame's bidding," I told her innocently.

"Say what now?" she asked as she stood over me. I could tell that she knew the name and she must have known a little bit more with the way she was casting the skeptical glance at me.

"Micah Tems, he's FBI—"

"And you know this how?" she cut me off.

"When Dame was alive, Micah purchased me from him—"

"Purchased you? As in bought you like you were some kind of product?" another officer cut me off this time to ask. His name was Lieutenant Duffy, a balding black man who looked as if his face had a run-in with nails that left holes in his face.

I nodded. "Yeah, that's because me and the other girls were product. I was fourteen when he took me, but there were girls younger than me sometimes in the house. But Micah, Micah was Dame's inside man. That's why it was so easy for him to fly under the radar of the FBI."

"And how do you know all this?" Captain Roland asked again as she took notes and kept her recorder in her hand.

"On the days Micah would be able to make good on his purchase, he would take me to the hotel with him and I would overhear him on the phone speaking to his people in the FBI. I saw files and everything on stuff that I wasn't supposed to see."

"So, if all this is true, and Micah has still been keeping you under lock and key, how did you get away today? How did you get here?"

"I was able to go out. I'm a Bounce Girl for the Nightwings, but only as a cover. Micah makes me sell pussy to the NFL players and such. I figured I needed to come in and report what I'd seen this morning."

"There's more?"

"Yeah, Micah had this woman and little girl he was threatening to sell . . ." As I talked, the woman was listening intently. I could see that she was either believing me or just knew that if what I was saying turned out to be true then she was on her way to another promotion.

"And where are they now?" Lieutenant Duffy asked.

"Who?"

"The girl and the woman."

I shrugged. "I don't know the address, but I can tell you how to get there."

"Duffy, get somebody over at the GBI on the phone so we can see if they can share anything with us about undercover operations going on. If the FBI is in my county then the GBI would have more about it," Captain Roland ordered. She looked back at me. "Get comfortable, honey, you're going to be here for a while."

On the outside I was crying, feigning the poor, innocent victim. In reality, I should have been crying for real, but my circumstances had numbed me. Inwardly, I was smiling at the easiness of it all. For over four hours they kept me in that precinct. I was questioned, fingerprinted, everything under the sun until they identified me through the National Center for Missing and Exploited Children. I looked at my photos and for the first time, real tears cascaded down my face. My grandmother had looked for me. She'd done all she could until she couldn't anymore.

The way I cried in that room only made my story about Micah more believable and even though I was beyond emotional, I had to get a hold of myself. Everything was all good until two detectives walked into the room. Judging by the way they both glared at me when the captain walked out, I could tell they were Micah's henchmen. Not to mention, Enzo had described them to me in great detail. They did look like Deebo and Uncle Phil.

"Since you thought it would be fun to come in here and stir shit up, you just dug your boyfriend into a deeper hole," Deebo said as he eyed my braless chest.

Uncle Phil smiled like the Cheshire cat. "Ha-ha," he taunted. "We're going to make it so you have to testify against the son of a bitch. So thank you for coming in here and signing his life over to the federal penitentiary."

I didn't flinch or recoil when both of them stood on either side of me and taunted me with threats of me testifying against Enzo and him going to prison. Deebo slammed his hand down on the table in front of me. "I bet you didn't see that coming, did you?"

"You really think Special Agent Tems didn't think this far ahead? And who do you think a judge is going to believe? A detective with over ten years of service under his belt or a two-bit junky whore?" Uncle Phil blasted as he sprayed the right side of my face with a flurry of spittle.

"You know, I'm going to need all of you to come up with a better way of insulting me than calling me a whore. I know what I used to be and I own it because I did what I had to do to survive." I spoke in a state of calm.

I sat regally, back straightened, arms under the table on my lap, and eyes straight ahead. Uncle Phil reacted like a viper, striking out to snatch me by my throat and forcing me to look up at him. His eagerness was short-lived.

"I'm going to need you to take your hands off my client." I didn't need to see the face to know who the voice belonged to.

Mirror slammed the door behind him and I heard the lock click. Deebo backed away and Uncle Phil slowly let my neck go.

"She isn't being charged with anything, so why the lawyer?" Deebo asked.

"We were just trying to refrain the potential witness from harming herself," Uncle Phil lied.

"Bullshit," Mirror damn near growled low in his throat. "Please leave me so that I may have a moment with my client," he demanded.

"I see the mighty Enzo sent in reinforcements for the little lady," Uncle Phil continued as Deebo sized Mirror up.

Mirror didn't break a sweat; in fact, he seemed a bit bored.

Deebo spoke up. "Let him know Little Red Riding Whore over here is going to be his downfall when the DA puts her on the stand."

Mirror set his leather briefcase down and folded his muscled arms over his broad chest. "On the stand for what?" he asked.

"I'm sure when the charges are brought against him the state will subpoena her to take the stand. That's how it goes in the States, my man."

Uncle Phil chuckled. "I'm sure they do the same thing in the UK, no?" he asked, putting on a fake accent.

Mirror wasn't amused. "Good luck with that," he told them.

"Oh, there will be no luck needed on our parts."

"Sure there will. You can't force a woman to testify against her husband," he informed them.

Then and only then did I turn my eyes on each of the men in the room. A slow smile crept onto my face.

Deebo's head jerked back as if he had been slapped. "Wait, what?"

"You heard me. You can't force this woman to testify against her husband. In criminal cases, a husband and wife can't be compelled to be called as a witness against the other, in cases such as the one you're threatening Mr. Banks with. Now, if you will excuse me, I need a moment with my client."

The looks on both of their faces were incredulous to say the least. I chuckled to myself thinking of how Shy would leave no stone unturned. She told me from the moment she thought of the idea that she was going to go by any means necessary to make sure her sons were safe. She carefully thought of every angle that Micah would try. She covered every base. Enzo wasn't too keen on marrying me at all and especially not for the sake of his freedom. But me, I had something to prove so, after careful consideration, I agreed with little to no fight.

Whether I wanted to admit it or not, there was no blood relation between me and Shy and although I knew her to be a woman of her word, I knew that if push came to shove, I would be the oddball out. I wasn't an African Queen. Hadn't established myself to be anything other than a girl who happened to be brought into the mess Micah had made. Had Micah not brought Enzo and me back together, we probably wouldn't have ever made an attempt to even be caught in the same room together. I would have been okay with that.

But after all that had happened, I needed to build
my place somewhere in the world. I needed to build a
strong foundation. Thinking of how my grandmother
had actually searched for me in her last days still had my
eyes watery, but my work had been done. After ensuring
I wasn't being brought up on any charges, Mirror walked
me out of the police precinct and back to the meeting
place. I could hear Enzo's voice down the hall. I knew
Caltrone was there judging by the deep rumble of his
voice. I walked into the room of the venue for Shy's safe
house and changed clothes. I pulled off the tattered sundress and worn shoes. Traded them in for my signature
skinny jeans, wedge sneakers, a thin polo-style shirt, and
a hoodie.

I looked up when the door opened to see Shy walk in.
She held her arms out to me. Once I walked over to her
embrace, she placed a kiss on the center of my forehead.

"You did well," she told me. "Thank you."

"No thanks needed."

"Oh, trust me, there is. You didn't have to do any of
what I asked of you and, at the risk of your own freedom,
you did it without thought. I know Shawn fought like
hell for you two not to be legally married, but it had to be
done."

I chuckled, kind of bashfully. "No worries. I'm sure
after Micah is in the grave Enzo will rectify all of that and
the marriage will be annulled in no time."

"You think so?"

I shrugged. "If I've learned anything about Shawn it's
that he doesn't like to have his hand forced at anything,
even if it is by you."

Shy laughed lightly. "I would say you know him well."

"Just a li'l bit," I said.

She hugged me and kissed my forehead again before
we walked out of the room together. We talked a bit as

we walked down the hall. She told me the story of Br'er Rabbit and I had to laugh at how close Enzo and Micah's story was to the legend. When we walked into the room, all eyes turned to us. Enzo was sitting near who I'd come to know as his cousin Fuego. Lilith sat on the left of Caltrone.

"I see you were able to do that simple task, Angel, is it?" Lilith spoke up.

That bitch always had something snide to say and it was starting to work my nerves. Caltrone openly studied me and then grunted as he puffed on his cigar. I ignored him as I took a seat next to Enzo, wondering why I was in the room. I could feel Enzo looking me over. My face still bore some of the scrapes and bruises from my escapade with Gina's mom and Dominique.

"You good?" he asked me.

I nodded once. "I'm great."

"So, Gramps, we're here," Fuego stated. "What's on your mind?" he asked his grandfather.

Before Caltrone could even start to talk, I stood to leave. Lilith jumped up and blocked my path. "How rude of you to have the audacity to walk out when the king is about to talk," she snapped.

I could tell she wanted a fight. Was itching to start one with me since she was really pissed at Caltrone's infatuation with Shy. But she knew if she even looked at Shy the wrong way Caltrone would end her, so I was her next best choice. Even Enzo had tilted his head as he watched me.

"And how rude of you to sit around while grown folk are talking," I countered.

Enzo stood. "Yo, Angel, what's up? You breaking out on me."

I turned to look the young man who I'd grown to love in his eyes. I could see the storm cloud brewing behind them. I said to him, "If I don't know shit, I can't say shit."

Out of the corner of my eye, I saw Shy smile. There was no need for me to be in that room for whatever it was they were about to discuss. Enzo had taught me well. The less I knew, the safer I was. The less I knew, the less I would have to tell. It would be just my luck that that sneaky bitch Lilith would leak some shit just to have the finger pointed at me because I was the oddball out. I shoved her out of my way and left the room.

Chapter 15

Micah

My ears perked up when I looked at the door leading to my home office. By rote, I stuck my hand into the drawer that held my badge, but realized Enzo had taken it with him and I no longer had a badge. I'd been suspended from the agency pending investigation. Just that quick, my life had become something I hadn't expected. I'd been accused of being one of the criminals I'd pursued. True enough, I'd done some shady shit in my time as an undercover officer, but it was all in the name of justice.

Nothing I'd done hadn't been to avenge my family in the long run. The list I had on Enzo was long. Even had footage of him torturing people in the basement. *What? Thought I would just be undercover and not keep recording what went down while in Dame's employment? Fuck outta here.* I was still an agent before I was anything else. I wasn't the fucking criminal. I was the victim, the avenger of . . .

My thoughts escaped me as I thought back over all the years of my hard work. On my desk was a picture of Caltrone Orlando walking the streets of Atlanta. He stood there in his tailored suit, one hand in his pocket and another up to his mouth puffing on the illegal cigar in plain sight. The anger that festered in me reared its ugly head again. Countless men and women I'd put behind bars in the name of the Orlandos. Lu Orlando had been my first big fish from the Orlandos. Had put his ass away and then the nigga got offed in prison. He'd ruined that part of my satisfaction of having that nigga locked away.

"Special Agent Tems," someone called out to me as they opened the door to my apartment, the only thing Enzo hadn't burned to the ground.

The son of a bitch was proficient, I could say that.

I knew the man without even having to see his face. I knew I'd be having a conversation with him sooner or later. I just didn't know how close he was to the situation. He was my superior, one at the very top of the FBI food chain.

The man took a seat in front of my desk. He crossed his ankle over his thigh as he watched me closely. "How did we find ourselves here, Special Agent Tems? How did the man I specifically put on the job of taking the Orlandos down end up in the same position he was supposed to put them in? What happened, Micah? How did we end up here?"

I shrugged. "Sir, to be honest, I don't even know why I'm here. All I've ever done was what you asked me to do. I got in. I got in deep."

The man's cold gaze took me in as he spoke nonchalantly. "Yet, Damien and Dante Orlando rest in hell instead of rotting in prison."

"There were variables there that I didn't see coming, sir."

"Obviously. I thought when I picked you for the job, you'd keep a level head, Tems. Was I wrong?"

"No, sir."

"Bullshit."

"I can still do the job, sir."

"You fucked up."

"It can be fixed."

"You fucked up, Micah. You fucked up and went after the wrong kid."

"He's an Orlando."

"Do you know just how many other Orlandos you could have gone after, Tems? Do you know how many men and women in the Orlando organization you could have gone after and taken down?"

"Yeah, but this kid, this kid is Lu Orlando's son. I see in him what we saw in Caltrone Orlando. The kid has potential to take over DOA and take it to the next level. I was trying to prevent that. Trying to prevent another reign of terror," I explained.

"You sit here, brought up on the same charges you accuse him of, slurring your words, being accused of the most heinous crimes, and you talk about preventing another reign of terror?" my superior asked me.

He sat straight up, spine stiff as he talked to me man to man. There was no direct indication of what was to come by the tone of his voice. I respected the man sitting in front of me. Years of training under his wing got me to the level in the agency I was at. One day I hoped to be at the level he was. My superior was so high in the FBI food chain that some people didn't even know he existed.

He pulled the folder from underneath his arm. "All this time and I thought the Orlandos were the criminals. This shit in this folder, Tems, I can't pull you back from it. I've got power, but not that much power. Bianca Smith, what she's accused you of alone is enough to bury you in the federal prison system. The raid on your apartment this morning, all the evidence to support what she has accused you of pretty much put the last nail in your coffin. I put you on this case, not to go after a boy who had no idea who he was before you came along. Now that he knows who he is, I do say you've created a monster." My superior stood and then casually slid his hands into his pockets. "And now, now, I have to take down my grandson because you just had to wake a sleeping giant."

What he'd just said hit me like a ton of bricks. I jumped up from the desk chair. "Wait, what the fuck? What?"

"You should have left him alone, Micah. You forced my hand before it was time."

"Sir, with all due respect, I don't understand."

"Now, because of your actions, I have to ask not what if I have to take my grandson down, but when. Good day, Tems. I came to hand you your official termination papers," he said as he strolled out of my office.

I stumbled behind my desk, fell, and then pulled myself up to run behind him.

"Sir, I don't get . . . I'm not understanding what you're saying to me right now," I yelled behind him.

He turned to me as he walked out of the door. Looked at me with something akin to annoyance in his eyes. "What's understood needs no understanding. Half a truth is often a great lie, Tems. You'll realize that too late."

Chapter 16

Enzo

I hadn't expected to also get married. Shit was so unexpected that I'd almost blacked out on Shy for even suggesting it. Shit had me seeing red, ready to go to prison for killing Micah and just say fuck all the rest of this shit. I mean the bullshit had me . . . accepting what I had to do and becoming a married man. Fuck my life.

I knew I had to shoulder some shit, but I wasn't expecting it. I was twenty-one and a married man. Fuck that nigga Micah for real. I really didn't know what to do with a wife. I knew the shit was for show but it was still real nonetheless.

Shit, yeah, an annulment could go down, but I bet if the impromptu wedding helped me like Mirror and my mom explained that it would, then the DA would still be looking to see if this shit was legit. So, I really couldn't annul a damn thing. Like B and I had to be in this for a minute until the dust settled and what the fuck did I do with that? What the fuck did she do with it?

My gaze locked on the thin red cord on my wrist, symbolizing Bianca's quickie marriage to me. A quiet ache attacked my stomach in the moment. I felt like I was trapping her and ruining her life. Felt like we were taking each other's freedom away, all to save my ass, and save my family. A dull ache started in the back of my head. I noticed Angel getting up to leave and her and that broad Lilith going at it.

I wasn't sure why I did it but I pushed back and shouted at her, as that ache in my mind spread and I felt that creeping blackness overtaking me. Maybe I was feeling possessive because I didn't want her to get hurt again, I really didn't know. But, if she was going to be down for this family then she fucking needed to be here and be by my side, fuck the rest. She really had to start coming into her fold and taking on some boss bitch shit, because I could not have a chick at my side who wasn't as strong as me. It would make everything cave in for me and have the old demon coming at me funky.

However, when she spit that code at me I let her go do her and sat back down. I knew I was tripping. My mind was feeling fractured. I was feeling tired and feeling like Atlas with the weight of the world on my shoulders.

All my plans for me were to just get in the NFL and make that money to provide for my family. Since the year of Dame's death, my life went from being contracted to the devil to turning into a spiral of other shit that I could not control. I felt like I was grasping at straws, trying to make shit fit to protect my family as I scrambled around and cut niggas' throats. The streets were flowing with blood by my hands and I sat listening as Caltrone offered me a throne surrounded in a sea of that shit.

Stress had me fisting my hands. I swore I could see that nigga Dame with our sperm donor watching me with a smile. I didn't want any of this shit, but I had to play the eager prince. Had to get in deep to secure the safety of everyone at the sacrifice of myself. This life wasn't how I wanted it, and I wished I could have been some normal cat, doing normal shit, but . . . whatever. It was what it was. The world's tiniest violin could stop now, because I had to play this game for the ultimate revenge.

So my gaze focused on my mother who sat regally, daintily sipping a cup of tea while looking over the edge of it with an amused smirk and secret sidelong stare. It was as if she was not only casting shade but also absorbing everything being said in the room. When, honestly, I knew she was. Taking her cue to me, I then focused on the door that Angel exited from and a wicked smile flashed across my face.

"Hey, yo, thought I'd interrupt but, yeah, when a bitch got too much bark, or she starts running foul, then it's time for that bitch to be brought down. I don't trust rabid bitches with my dick, let alone my Glock. Might be wise to snuff that shit out before she starts trying to take over what is mine."

I tapped the end of my blunt on the table as I spoke that understanding to my grandfather. My gaze stayed locked on that Lilith bitch. She knew not to ever cut her eyes at me, or mumble a thing, or it would be the end of her. That was why I slid back in my chair with a wide, cocky smile.

Lilith's seething could be felt all across the room. Her nails scraped the table before her then her lips formed a thin line. She turned in her seat to Caltrone. She glared at him, as if he were going to do something; then she slammed her palm on the table before her. Realizing he wasn't going to do a thing, she sat back in her chair and thumbed her nose.

Caltrone's deep, rumbling chuckle had others laughing as he tsked. "Duly noted, my grandson, very smart words."

Tilting my head in a respectful nod, I rubbed my jaw and continued listening as Caltrone's hands discussed the welfare of the southern region. Mad talk started popping off around me about the remaining drug lords in the A and the new blood that was rising up. Supposedly, it was a new group of kids who were in the field of stealing cars, and techno thief, which had them bringing in mad dough to the Trap. I said nothing while I listened. I knew about the kids. Had worked, and still did work, closely with them through getting new rides, various devices, and erasing my history to keep Micah off my back.

There was no way in hell that I would speak on my affiliation with them. Or say that it was Trigga and Jake who set that new crew up on their feet by recruiting them to their chop shop. Like me, the Eraserheads were linked to ENGA and their loyalty was to that as they did their own thing. Fucking with them was like fucking with me, so I was glad that their activities wasn't anything Caltrone was interested in because they were not fucking with the dope game. So the old heads moved on to other topics, and it all came to a halt the moment that Caltrone held his hand up.

"Let us get to the real meat of this meeting. As we all know, I pride this family on its blood and loyalty. That is what keeps us on the top and the weak on the bottom and with the return of my long-lost grandsons, the Orlando line can continue to flourish," Caltrone gloated.

All I knew in that moment was that I just wished I were on the field. That I was playing ball and that was it. This shit was for the birds. I was straight up in a *Scarface* movie and the shit was lame. All we needed was mounds of that dust around us, and we'd be popping.

Caltrone stood, then smoothed his suit, then walked my way. His large hand reached out to clasp my shoulder as he stared down at me in pride. "Today, I make it known that my heir is here. Shawn Orlando will take my place as regent of our clan!"

A cocky smirk played on my lips. I leaned back and moved my shoulder from his grasp then reached for my cup, took a sip, and set it back down.

"Once that nigga is taken care of and once my cover in the game is cleared up, I'll decide what I'm going to do then; otherwise, the world is still yours, Gramps."

I didn't even look at him when I said it. I just glanced around the room, noticing Fuego's slight chuckle; then I turned my gaze on my grandfather while rubbing the side of my jaw where Micah cut me.

He watched me with slight heat in his eyes. A darkness I was familiar with myself set stones in my stomach but, I was by far not about to let this nigga punk me. So, I shifted in my chair and gave him the same gaze back. No fear, no emotion, just darkness.

A grin spread across Caltrone's face while he studied me. He clapped his hands together and turned to the family. "He is one of us, is he not?" Collective *yes*es spread across the room and he turned back my way. "Agreed. You need to have your kingdom cleared so that you can bring our power back into Atlanta the correct way."

I nodded in agreement. A part of me wanted to spit out in defiance, as he did when taking out my grandfather then having his son claim my mother as the ultimate insult to the Kulu Empire. But I kept that in my mind. I needed to play the loyal prince, soon-to-be regent, and I needed to make them work for my favor.

"Exactly. With Micah's home now ashes and his shit now on blast, yo, the rest of the battle should come easy, right? With the power of the Orlandos?"

Caltrone gave an amused chuckle. He snapped his collar then turned on his heel to sit back down. "This is why I am confident that you and your brother, once he comes of age, will raise this family up for another generation and keep us strong."

Like that, everyone raised their glasses and toasted me. We ate, we smoked, we drank, then we all parted ways. I knew I had another meeting to go to that my mother had set up. This one involved the Queens, Phenom, and the Misfits.

***

"You make up ya mind, homie?" I heard Jake ask me across the table.

We all sat around a simple family-style table. Unlike the meeting with the Orlandos, where it was about money, style, power, and intimidation, at this meeting we sat around each other like we were at Grandma's house. Which we were. We decided to hide in plain sight and hit up the old neighborhood, the old house where ENGA came into growth, my old house with the dining room table Jake's grandmother used to own.

My hand slid up to my face as I glanced at that dude. Phenom was watching me with a light smile on his face while Anika whispered in his ear. My mom was in the kitchen with Angel. Drew rolled out with food in his mouth chopping and yapping while being followed by a little girl sporting bright colors who was digging into her plate.

There was no doubt, when I looked at her, that she was of my blood. I knew why I had ignored it before, because I didn't want shit to do with the Orlandos, still didn't. But when Trigga pulled me to the side and explained it, I accepted it. She and I were alike on more than a blood level; we both hated the DNA that linked us, and I was down with my niece from that moment on.

I realized that Jake and Trig were waiting on my response. All the Misfits were there. I noticed Diamond had gotten up to help my mom and Angel, while Baby G quietly spoke with Anika, who had sat down again and laid a hand on her belly. Everything felt right. I was glad that broad Dominique wasn't anywhere around. Was reassured she knew nothing of this secret meeting, so I glanced up at Jake.

The chains attached to my jeans made noise while I shifted in my seat. "I told that nigga that I was thinking on it. That I wasn't making a choice until Micah was put down."

"A'ight, so what's your real choice?" Jake asked again.

He knew I was in my dome and it had me chuckling. "I'm ENGA for life. Most importantly with that knowledge I was given, I'm Kulu Tribe and DOA. So my choice is simple, once this shit clears up. A nigga will step onto the throne as king and take it down from the inside. Clean it out and, if we have to once the Orlandos are wiped out, reunite the clans like it used to be and keep it that way, no distinction."

Silence fell around me while I watched everyone at the table fall into thought. "When you do this, you'll have to take on that mantle of evil, you know that? So you say you down now, but from history, we saw what evil did to a good man. That evil flourished and turned into a cancer that spread like a plague, until it took out everyone in the main family back in New York. That's our history, nephew. I call you nephew because I see you as family, so what say you?" Phenom calmly explained.

The man before me spoke to me with respect, as if I was an equal. There was no intimidation at all, just honesty and trust. For me, that act alone was a vast difference from what I went through with Caltrone. I knew that, without being forced to fear this cat, he could very well end me, but I also knew he saw everyone at this table as equal and I respected that.

His words made me nervous and had me rubbing the back of my neck. I didn't want to fuck this up. Didn't want to bring a blood war to my family. I wanted nothing to do with any type of blood war that meant repeating history, so I wanted to make sure my words, my intent, and my heart were true to the cause.

"I heard y'all's history, the truths you all have shared. Shit, I know it's a lot y'all haven't shared and probably need to, but I know we are the new generation coming up. All of us got put into this 'cause of the beef. None of us really wanted this life, except for maybe my man Trigga, but that was because of survival," I explained.

Trigga gave a cold smirk and nodded. "True."

A chuckle came from me, as I shrugged. "I ain't him. I'm me and how I dedicated my life shit, I'm about that 'get what I can get' to keep my family safe, period. So shit, yo, I'm saying. This blood in me, I hate it, but I got another set of DNA, too, the kind I got mad respect for. In my part in this, I know I'm going to go mad and play the role to the fullest, but I got purpose to that madness and you all are my fam. So I'm going to get what I get, to keep my family. 'Cause, from the cradle, I see now that the foundation was set up to protect me and my brother and that shit is insane, but respected. I ain't turning my back on what my mom decided at my birth and I ain't turning my back on y'all. I got a brand DOA on me, but ENGA is resting tatted near a nigga's heart undetected."

I lifted my shirt to show the tattoo where the letters were embedded. How it was written it literally had to be pointed out by me to find, and that's how I liked it.

"So yeah, so a nigga gonna be a kingpin now. Kinda fucked up and funny but, like Don Corleone said, 'Friendship is everything. Friendship is more than talent. It is more than the government. It is almost the equal of family,' and you all are both, feel me?"

Phenom tented his fingers together and tapped his fingers against his mouth. "He also said, 'Many young men started down a false path to their true destiny. Time and fortune usually set them aright.' We'll play the game to the T. Our businesses only will cross when in taking down our common enemies. That keeps you safe and us safe from our true plan. This circle is all that needs to know. No new niggas need to know shit, ain't that right, Moseif?"

Speedy thumbed his nose and nodded. "Never opened my mouth on family business; ain't going to start today just because I get proper head. On ma word, bruv, cha know, blood is bond."

How he said that made me laugh hard. Yeah, him and me had a moment and I still was watching him closely because of that shit with Dominque. But watching closely was different from not trusting and, honestly, I trusted this cat. So, there was no beef. I'd just do what I had to do if he crossed me wrong again and call it even.

"Bet, no new friends. Y'all will know who I got around me is my inner circle because they'll be around me. But in this, like my niece, Trig's daughter, shit, we'll all be ghosts." A smirk flashed across my face and I noticed Ghost watching.

Something in her eyes let me know she was going to have many stories to tell and birth many warriors. She was just as lethal as we all were and she was only a kid. That was saying a lot and was kinda dope, though I felt with her like I felt with Drew: she needed to be a kid first. None of us here got that, but at least she and Drew could get a little bit of it.

It was then that Anika spoke up as she held her cup. "At this table is the original faction, how Papa Kulu had created it. We'll honor his spirit, the true nature of this syndicate, which was to uplift the hood and take out the evil by any means necessary. Since we are quoting *The Godfather*, '. . . society imposes insults that must be borne, comforted by the knowledge that in this world there comes a time when the most humble of men, if he keeps his eyes open, can take his revenge on the most powerful.' That is the foundation of this. We take out those who harm our people, our communities, and do this by getting our hands dirty. Indigo has been spreading through the streets and it has taken down several crime bosses and political elite."

My mother smoothly took over for Anika. She gracefully stood and moved to rest a hand on my shoulder while she addressed us all. The sweet smell of her perfume gave me reassurance in the passing of the torch. "Soon Caltrone will hip you up to this, Shawn. It will be your duty to find out the source of Indigo. Of course, we all know who is the creator, but he does not. And by presenting him with a different set of thugs as a scapegoat, people who actually are aligned with him, we will effectively begin not only taking out the bitches and niggas in the street who are about that thug life, but also break away from Caltrone's foundation.

"But, first, we have to continue in this act and game. Handle Micah. Keep his eyes off you, but also away from Phenom and these Misfits. I'm pretty sure once we chop the head off the snake, another will arise in the FBI, but that is why we have eyes and resources to try to keep us as safe as possible," Shy continued while she headed to sit next to Mirror, who sat at Phenom's right.

Trigga's deep mumble drew my attention. "Knowledge of self allows us to lead the savages to their destiny, be it chaos and death, or enlightenment."

I remembered him saying that back in the streets. It was one of the things that I repeated to myself daily when on the football field or killing niggas.

"This is why we must show and prove. Then gain the knowledge in order to control the chaos that has been created so that we can unlock the keys to this reality and let everyone know the universal truth of that nigga's existence. The same goes with the Orlandos," Shy added, with Phenom, Anika, and Mirror nodding in unison.

"I remember you spitting that, Mom, and repeating it with Trig and Jake. It was my anchor. That is why the proof is being dropped as we meet. Micah has lost his home. Nigga is probably heated over that shit. Not only that but, the big shit of it all, B got that nigga by the throat with her confession. So, shit, the blocks are falling and that nigga is 'bout to be gunning harder with murderous intent in his mind. I'm already ready for it and I'll do what I have to do. If I get taken out, the next phase goes into effect." My fingers rubbed against the thin cut on my jaw and my gaze settled on Angel as she sat next to me while I was in my dome.

"B stands up in my place and runs shit as queen. I mean, damn, it's expected, right? She's my wife. Oh, yeah, guess we gotta start the media rounds, too, about this secret wedding. Already got Dy on it. Got to make this look as legit as possible, right?"

My mother gave a slight chuckle. Angel's fork stopped midway to her mouth. Pieces of chicken with greens fell on her plate. Then I shrugged. "Interesting thing though, once they see she's the survivor of being trafficked, that's going to bring more attention my way. We'll have to spin that shit and handle it too."

Everyone gave a nod of agreement. My hand ran over my face. Everything was out on the table and settled; I now had to settle crap between Angel and me. So I pushed up from the table and headed to the hallway. "We need to talk, B."

"If I may say this quickly. Ladies in this room and to our young princess Ghost, remember all of this. Ladies, we are the gatekeepers. We keep the truth, and hold it to our hearts in order to protect our dynasty. Let no nigga or bitch control the universe that we created. We fight at the sides of our men but we elevate ourselves in elevating them. Remember this," Shy passionately stated.

Anika moved to stand by my mother, their hands linking together. "Learn how to be generals in a war room, and provide the necessary tools to cut the throat of your and your king's or prince's enemy. These men should do the same for you. We queens and princesses will speak in the next room, after Enzo and Angel have their discussion."

Angel glanced around the table. Her honey brown face was scarlet red, and her pretty lashes fluttered in embarrassment; then she looked my way. In that moment, both Ray-Ray and Baby G giggled.

"You's married now," Baby G teased.

Jake's bear of a laugh sounded and he flashed me the thumbs-up. "Nigga already strapped down, who's next?"

The sound of a slap followed, and with it I heard Jake mutter, "Ow!"

"What that nigga always say? Don't know shit, can't say shit. Shut up, Big Jake," Trigga spit out laughing hard.

"Mate, it really is a lotta female in the crew, bloody hell," Speedy added then gave his famous kooky laugh.

With that, I led Angel to the back room so we could talk about this shit. I could tell she was nervous, so was I, but there was also something else I wasn't sure about. The sound of the chains attached to my jeans was our only form of speech. I opened the door for her, and let her step in, with me following right behind her. Life was a funny bitch, but a bitch nonetheless.

Chapter 17

Angel

For a second, Enzo and I just stood in the room, silent. I had a lot to say. Wasn't afraid to say it, but I was trying to figure out the right way to say it. I didn't know what he was thinking just by gazing at his features. Still, I was shocked that he talked about us telling the world we were married. I thought for sure his first order of business would be to get it annulled by any means necessary. I folded my arms across my chest as we both just stood gazing out of the window, staring at everything and nothing at all.

The room looked as if it had been used for an office. The walls were off-white, the floor was wood grain, and there was a lone desk with a chair in the left corner. There was a closet with its door ajar, but other than that the room wasn't much to look at.

"Can we talk? I mean, can I say some things to you without overstepping my boundaries and without you feeling some type of way about me afterward?" I finally asked him.

He smelled good. I figured if ever a king had a fragrance, the scent Enzo wore would be it. He was stressed. I could see the weight of the world sitting on his shoulders and part of me wanted to relieve some of the pressure. I would if he allowed me to. We hadn't had a moment's peace until that very moment and it was welcomed.

As he slowly turned his head and gazed, somewhat disenchanted, down at me, I got lost in the hypnosis of his eyes.

He licked his lips once and then took a deep breath before responding: "Say what you need to say."

"Is this really what you want?" I asked him.

"Being married? No—"

I cut him off by waving my hand. "No, I mean do you really want to jump headfirst into an age-old war between two factions that have been fighting long before we were born?"

His eyes darkened a bit. "I don't follow."

"You're so anti-DOA and anti-Orlando and I don't want you to lose yourself trying to prove yourself to be better than them. Truth be told, you only know one side of the story." I quickly held my hands up when I saw his mood change right before my eyes. "Look, I know what that monster did to your mother and aunt and, for that, you have the right to hate him, even in his death. Still, he's part of you. Whether you like it or not, you're your father's son. He's in you and plenty of people have felt that. All we've heard is the good of the Kulu Tribe and the bad of DOA. Just like all of DOA aren't heartless, evil monstrosities, there can be no way all of the Kulu Tribe are good people."

He backed away from me a bit and folded his arms across his chest. His upper lip twitched as he stared me down. "So you team DOA now? After all that nigga Dame did to you, you're defending the men and women who bred him?"

"Shawn, no. I'm saying I don't want you to get so dead set on being anti-DOA/anti-Orlando that you forget who you are," I said emphatically, speaking with my hands to get my point across. "Don't get lost in a war that's never going to end. Don't get me wrong, I have mad respect for every elder in the room up front. I love Shy like she's my own mother, but it just seems as if they all have an agenda. Are they trying to use you to kill half of what you are?"

"I'm half Orlando and half Kulu. In order to step into the role my grandfather wants me to be in, I know I'm going to have to do some evil shit. Really I'm not DOA or a Kulu King. I'm Shy's son, Queen Iya's blood, but most of all, I'm me. So no one can use me to do anything unless I choose to be used."

"I'm sorry, I'm just . . ." I sighed and turned to glance out of the window again and then back at Enzo. "I'm just saying I don't want them to try to use you to take out DOA for old shit. I mean, I don't know all of the history of bad blood. I know what Shy has told me and for all of the pain DOA has caused your families, the ones who committed and helped to commit the foul acts, need to be held responsible. Don't get me wrong, I just don't ever want you to get so caught up that you forget what your true agenda is. And that's to make sure Drew and your mother are always protected and never have to want for anything."

Enzo bit down on his bottom lip as he watched me. He stood in a wide-legged stance that made the jeans he had on stretch across the huge bulge in his pants. Even when being serious, I couldn't help but to admire that part of his male anatomy. The nigga had a dick that had to have come from kings. I shook out of my oncoming lustful haze. Shook my head to get the images of him naked out of my head and I looked back up into his eyes.

"I never wanted this to begin with, but it fell in my lap and I won't allow evil to dictate what I do with it. Shit, I won't let anybody dictate what I do with it." I nodded in understanding as he continued, "I know not everyone in DOA is bad blood. My mom, Shy, told me that much. Still, I have to see for myself and go from there. I'll keep DOA around, but I'll make it into what I want it to be and it won't be to terrorize, rape, kill, sell drugs, and ruin more black communities. Naw, I ain't here for that. I only trust the people in the room up front. So just because a nigga steps to me and mention he's a Kulu King doesn't mean I'm going to let him into my inner circle. I'll mend fences and build the bridge to this the way I want to."

"I understand. I just, you know, wanted to let you know how I was feeling. Don't want to just be tagging along with you being a yes-woman, you know? Not trying to be your Lilith. I refuse to let you jump out the window without first surveying what's on the ground below," I told him.

His eyes widened and softened a bit. I could see he was kind of surprised at my words. Shit, I'd surprised myself. I was coming into my own woman and the shit felt good. I was no longer looking to others for approval. He came back to stand beside me at the window. We went back to having the silence serenade us for a while. We could hear the laughter and cheerful taunts of the males joking about Jake becoming a father in the next few months. Enzo pulled a blunt from his pocket and passed it to me. I took it and sniffed the potent loud. I hadn't had time to partake in any vices, but it was welcomed. I put the blunt between my lips and he lit it for me. I took a long pull then held it in until my lungs couldn't take it anymore. Just like before when we had smoked together, he chuckled at me when my eyes watered and I started coughing like I had emphysema. I passed it back to him and tried to catch my breath again.

"You know what the fucked-up part about this shit with Micah is?" Enzo asked out of the blue.

"What?" I asked him as the tendrils of the smoke started to caress my face.

"That nigga was trying to avenge his family just like most of ENGA was trying to do, but he lost himself."

I nodded slowly, then said, "He became the monster he was hunting."

Enzo took a few puffs of the blunt. He looked like he was deep in thought before he responded. "Had he not tried to force me into a position I didn't want, none of this would be happening. That nigga may have been okay had he not fallen into darkness while working with Dame." He puffed and then passed me the blunt. "Had he kept his perspective, that nigga might have been okay."

"And that's where I don't want you to go. Micah is the kind of nigga I don't want you to become."

"He kind of reflects who I could be. That's one of the reasons I said I don't want history to repeat itself, B," he said and then looked at me. I smiled because I'd started to like the new nickname he gave me. "So, see here, Ms. Don't Get Lost and all that rah-rah." He smirked. "I know I have to keep perspective in this and I do pretty good. A nigga has done pretty good thus far. I know if I forget then it's all over. Then I become no better than the man who raped my mother at his leisure."

In that moment, I felt damn proud to be the one he called a wife, even if it was, technically, an arranged marriage. He'd said the words I needed to hear and I felt, in part, it was a part of my job to make sure he stayed true to his words. I wrapped an arm around his waist and was pleasantly surprised when he did the same to me. He put the blunt back to my lips and laughed when I tried to hold in the cough that came afterward. He joked about having to teach me how to handle the blunt like I handled his dick. I laughed and playfully shoved him before standing on my toes to kiss the cut on his cheek.

In that moment, we weren't Enzo and Angel; we were Shawn and Bianca, the little kids who had their lives snatched away because of demons in the flesh. It felt good just to stand in that moment of peace because we knew at any moment it would be over.

"What are you afraid of?" he asked once we got serious again.

"Losing the woman I've become. I like who she is and I want to keep her, nurture her, and make her stronger. I don't ever want to be afraid of my own shadow again. I don't ever want to be afraid to speak up for myself or defend myself again. I don't ever just want to give in or give up."

"So you still that conwoman who be taking niggas for their loot and diamonds?"

I smiled wide and nodded. "I'm just being honest. I'm going to always be that woman, but I know when to bring that part of me out and when to leave her locked away."

He didn't say anything. We were higher than a camel's pussy at that point, but it was welcomed distraction.

"What about you? What scares you?" I asked him.

He removed his arm from my waist, let me take one last hit of the blunt, and then snuffed it out. "The rape of my mother. The killing of my aunt, the woman I thought was my mother. Me running from the drug dealers when we lived in the Chi, the killers. Drew being homeless and hungry again. Trying to feed Drew and keep him warm when shit wasn't kosher back in the Chi. Those are my nightmares, B. That's what I'm afraid of."

I felt his words deep within me. That was the first time he had ever been that honest and open with me. I walked behind him and then wrapped both arms around his waist. I laid my head against his back and listened to the way his breathing changed. He'd opened up to me, but I wouldn't force him to show me the water that glazed over his eyes. I'd let him keep that to himself.

"If you ever decide to jump out the window with anything, just know I won't let you go there without taking your hand and jumping with you," was all I said to him.

I smiled warmly when he brought his hands to where mine connected, pulled them apart, and then connected his fingers between mine. I couldn't say we were in love or any of that, but I could say, without a doubt, I knew that Shawn "Enzo" Banks had my back in a way no one had ever done. We stayed in the room for about another thirty or so minutes. We didn't say too much of anything else. A few things about Micah and what was about to go down with him here and there. He didn't care for Lilith and told me as much. I kind of felt sorry for the woman and wondered exactly what had been done to her to make her behave in such a manner.

We walked out of the room to find the Misfits one man short. Phenom, Anika, Shy, and Mirror were all sitting quietly as they watched the youngsters in front of them.

"Where Speedy go?" Enzo asked.

"To see a pimp about a ho," Trigga answered.

I quirked a brow and wondered just what that meant. I looked to the table and saw straws laid about. Ray-Ray was sitting with tears in her eyes as she held a long straw that was the same length as the other ones, except for the one lying where Speedy had been sitting. Ray-Ray wiped the tears from her face, shoved away from the table, and then stormed from the room. I remembered what Dominique had told me about what she had done in that moment. She'd turned snitch on her best friend's parents and in turn helped in getting them killed. I looked to Jake as Gina stood and went after Ray-Ray. I figured I may as well tell them.

Enzo's phone rang and I could tell by the look on his face it was his grandfather, but I halted his departure for a moment. I told them what Dominique had confessed to me. After I was done Trigga left the room and headed in the direction Gina and Ray-Ray had gone.

I didn't know if he was about to tell her what I'd told them, but I could tell that the Misfits had their own agenda they had to deal with. Just by guessing, straws had been pulled between Speedy and Ray-Ray after it had been determined that Dominique had to go. What there was left to do afterward was anybody's guess. After all the Misfits had made their exit, Enzo and I were left alone.

"Now what?" I asked him.

He looked at his ringing phone again and then back down at me. "When I told you I was going to give Micah what he wanted, I meant it. The only reason I didn't let him take me before was because my gut told me not to. Maybe that was because he had found a way to capture you." He shrugged for emphasis. "I don't know. All I know is now I'm going to meet this nigga. Once and for all, we're done."

"What do you need me to do?" I asked him.

"You already know what I want and need."

I nodded and we both said in unison, "Be the boss bitch I know you can be."

"You're on your way to becoming an African Queen now, B," he said to me. "Find your place and stay there."

"I know and I will. I'm all in."

Enzo was about to say something else, until Speedy rushed back through the door. It was an "all hands on deck" moment when Phenom saw blood pouring from his mouth.

"Bloody fucking hell," Speedy yelled as he fell backward through the door and kicked it closed. "I didn't 'ave anywhere else to run," he said frantically. "Get fucking down," he yelled again.

I saw Drew and Ghost run for the bulletproof basement. Anika stood so fast she toppled the chair over behind her. She and Shy flipped the dining room table over making dishes crash to the floor. Phenom snatched an AK from the bottom of the table while Shy and Anika followed suit with their own weapons. Enzo shoved me down when bullets started to dance inside of the house. I heard Trigga yelling for Gina to get to the basement. Ray-Ray crawled in a panic to Speedy who was bleeding from bullet wounds to his stomach.

I'd never seen Enzo move the way he did as he, Jake, Trigga, and Phenom worked in tandem. Someone kicked the back door in and was met with the rounds of a shotgun from Enzo. The shit blew that nigga clear back out the door.

"Angel," Enzo called out to me.

I jumped up, grabbed the shotgun he tossed at me, and hit the deck again. While the shotty was too heavy for me to hold standing up, he had taught me a nice little trick. I positioned myself in the center of the hallway leading from the dining room to the back door, and using an overturned chair as somewhat of a shield and a perch, I lay in wait.

"Take the legs from under any motherfucker who comes through that door," Enzo said to me.

I saw Ray-Ray and Speedy firing guns at the door that had been blown off the hinges. Speedy may have been hurt, but he was still a fighter and it showed.

Phenom, Jake, and Trigga all had the windows covered. It sounded like a Fourth of July celebration. I heard a woman scream. Looked to the left of me to see Anika and Shy working a bitch over. When Shy used her gun to smack the bitch, Anika took the woman's legs from under her then brought a booted foot down into her sternum. All I heard were bones crack.

"You led a firefight to our door, Speedy," Phenom yelled. "Better be a damn good reason." Phenom was angry, that was clear by the way he snatched a hooded gunman through the broken window and pumped his back full of bullets.

"Went to do my duties with the traitor, Unk, swear down. I get to where she is and it's an ambush wai'ing for me," Speedy called out. I could tell he was in obvious pain by the way his breathing was labored.

"She set you up?" Ray-Ray asked him as if she still didn't want to believe her best friend was a snake.

Speedy looked at her and there was something unspoken that passed between them. "She set me up, blood," he told her.

"I had to be friends with two crazy niggas who don't care about dying," Jake's voice boomed.

I looked up to see Enzo and Trigga leaping through broken windows, taking the fight to the intruders. Just because I glanced around the room didn't mean I wasn't in on the foray. My shotgun was singing a tune of sweet music as I snatched limbs from the niggas trying to get in through the back door. Anika ran toward me, jumped over my head, picked up the empty shotgun Enzo had discarded and used it like a baseball bat to knock a nigga's head back who had been coming through the kitchen window.

"Iya, to the basement," Phenom demanded of Shy.

"He's right," Anika added. "This is too much for your body to handle."

"Already on my way," I heard Shy yell over the noise.

Her grunts told me she was still fighting her way down. Glanced to my right to see a body fall, then up to see Phenom flanking her until she got down to the basement.

"Everybody outside except for Speedy. Diamond, get him to the basement." Phenom yelled out another order to Ray-Ray. "Get them away from the house."

Then it made sense to me why Enzo and Trigga took the fight outside. I hopped up with the quickness. Flanked Phenom as he exited through the back door, while Anika flanked me. As soon as my eyes took in the sight, I saw a bloody Enzo. Couldn't have been his blood because the nigga was laughing while holding what looked like a machete. Where he had gotten it from was anybody's guess. In his hand was a severed head that he tossed to the side like it was nothing. Trigga stopped his run midstride and gave Enzo a look. It was something akin to "nigga, the fuck is wrong with you?" and being amused. We'd lowered their numbers but there were still more. I came out shooting first and never asking questions. When the bullets ran out in my shotty, I grabbed my Glock 19 from my waist. Who I couldn't shoot, I beat with the shotgun. Didn't matter to me how I backed you up off me, as long as I backed you up.

All the while I watched my back, I watched Enzo's too, just as he had done mine. For a second we were back to back killing niggas until he had to get a nigga off Jake's six. For as crazy as the whole thing was, some shit I still didn't expect. I didn't expect for two niggas to sneak up behind Enzo and try to take him out; no, didn't see that one coming.

"Shawn," I called out to him. "Shawn, watch out," I cried as a red laser trained on his chest.

"Awww, look, how cute. Your guardian Angel is coming to save the day, nigga," a voice taunted.

There was Micah, sneaking in from the back of another house. He had a shotgun in his hand that made mine look like a Nerf gun. There was an evil grin on his face that read like Enzo was about to be dinner. But not if I could help it. I aimed in his direction, all set to fire, before I realized my clip was empty. Another masked man had come from another direction. Enzo dodged his knife while Micah trained the shotgun on me. I took a leaping dive just before he sent the shells my way. I hit the ground hard, feeling like I'd broken something in the process.

When Micah turned his attention back to Enzo, he didn't hesitate to fire the shotgun. Enzo maneuvered the masked man he was fighting with around to use him as a human shield.

"Whew, nigga. Almost had you," Micah yelled arrogantly.

I got my bearings about me, and went to take a peek at seeing if it was safe for me to move until another blast came my way.

"Don't do it, Angel. Don't make me clip your wings, baby, even though I gave them to you."

Micah was like a madman. The way he came at us, I knew there would be a turning point. Enzo was too quiet. When he was too quiet, he was in his deadliest form. I saw a pair of boots move past me and looked up to see Phenom scoping Micah.

"A man who's always talking never finds time to hear the words not being spoken," Phenom said coolly and Micah laughed.

Micah slowly turned to the sound of the voice. "Well, I'll be damned, if it isn't the infamous . . ." He stopped himself, tilted his head, and looked at Phenom as if he wasn't sure what he was looking at. "Naw, it can't be. You wouldn't be that stupid, would you?"

"Seems like the only stupid one here is you, mate."

"Kill me with that fake-ass Brit accent, my nigga. I know all about the Kulu Kings. You motherfuckers just as bad as the Orlandos. What a prize it would be to kill two birds with one stone."

"Guess you're going to be the only bird-nigga dying today," Enzo coolly said as he stepped behind Micah.

Micah never saw the hit to the back of his head coming. It was lights out before his body hit the ground. Enzo had knocked him unconscious.

Chapter 18

Enzo

I looked down at a nigga who really should have been six feet under by now. Annoyance had me shaking my head while I took in his appearance. This nigga was slumped over with his gun in his hands, cradling it like the fuck boy he was. Micah sported all black and I wasn't sure if everyone saw it or not but an insane glint of desperation and anger that had him stinking with pitifulness wafted around him. It was really a shame how gone this nigga was, but shit, wasn't any sympathy for this nigga anymore. He lost that right, long ago, so I hop-skipped and slammed my boot on the side of his face.

I heard Angel next to me asking what I was going to do with him. That was a good question because I had many things I wanted to do to him.

"Let him hang again," came from the left of me.

Drew stood there in his hoodie with his hands fisted and heated anger in his eyes. He'd come up from the basement with my mother not too far behind him. I moved to the side, waved a hand over Micah in a gesture, and my baby bro took the offer to slam his fist into that nigga's skull. He stood up, and pulled a knife from that cat's body and sliced it across his face with a smirk. "For cutting you, bro."

"Respect, baby bro," I said with a slight smile. My hand slid up to my jaw while I straddled the void of darkness.

That was when we were suddenly covered in a rain of bullets.

"Everyone get the fuck back and under cover! Nigga got more reinforcements!" Phenom shouted out.

Both Drew and me broke apart in rapid sprints. The shots that fell had me taking Angel by the hand, who came up on my side, moving her in front of me and shielding her while we ran. I took in my surroundings, trying to get to my mother to shield her at the same time, but Drew was my saving grace. I saw him make it to our mother, who was running toward the side of a nearby house. Mirror was at her side, and both my brother and he threw their arms around her, and picked her up to move her to where she was going. Relief hit me, and both Angel and I ducked behind a car.

"Shit! That nigga is crazy," Angel panted out, pushing her hair from her face. She held her Glock in her hand and shakily reloaded it by going into her pockets and pulling out a new clip. The sound of glass shattering from meeting the force of the raining ammo aimed at us had us taking in our surroundings and trying to move without getting hit.

Carefully leaning, I looked to see where Micah was lying. Of course, the dude was gone. Anger blazed through me, but as I was moving back to duck again, I saw two familiar faces carrying Micah to a car: Officers Deebo and Uncle Phil. Heat had me fisting my hands and punching the side of the car we rested against.

"What!" Angel jumped then moved to position herself on her hands and knees.

"Get ya cell, call Fuego, and tell him to come to this block. Then when you hang up, tell the Misfits and Phenom to lay low because Fuego will be coming, a'ight?" I quickly spit out, turning to look into Angel's concerned eyes. "Don't ask me shit, just do it. I need you to be

Queen because this shit ends tonight. Go to that empty house, take out whoever the fuck you can; just watch your fucking back, ma. I'm going after Micah." I pushed up to crouch low, looking for a window of opportunity to run and make my way back to the house. I needed my whip.

The feel of Angel's hand on my shoulder had me turning toward her, where she gave me a frustrated gaze then ran off to where I pointed. The sound of gunplay sparked up again. I watched her turn and pop off several rounds before safely making it to where she quickly pulled out her cell, and began making moves.

Because she had run ahead of me, this also worked to draw attention away from me, so I pulled my cap down and jetted. I knew the block better than did the niggas who were gunning for us. Occasional flickers of people's lights going off on the block let me know which houses not to go to in order to protect the people, and which houses to go to. It was code for those of us who protected the block.

Though me and my mom hadn't lived in this area for years, it was she who made sure the block stayed clear of any crime and drama. This was African Queen territory. If any AQ needed protection, everyone here gave it willingly due to the help the Queens gave in not just keeping crime away but, in keeping the area safe for children, and keeping the schools together, as well as helping the elders who lived here get whatever they needed.

So I ran until I saw one of the empty houses where we used to stash various rides in the garages, and I pulled out a bike. Hopping on it, I copped the keys in a hidden compartment, revved it up, and circled back around. I could see the car with Deebo and Uncle Phil finally pulling off. Phenom and Anika had made them pause due to their gunfire going at them. I waved a hand, signaling that I was going after them, and then they turned to run off and disappear to go after several other of the Micah's people.

Leaning on my bike, I zipped fast. I could tell how the car swerved that they saw me. They turned to go toward another section of the block, also AQ zone, and I smirked. Pulling up on my Kawasaki, I popped a wheelie, zipped up to make them turn where I wanted them to, then whipped out my Glock and set off rounds. I watched bullets hop off their shielded car until they hit their brakes in a cul-de-sac. I revved up my bike, making it smoke and giving signals to the people in the houses around me. Anxiousness had me rolling my shoulders to crack my neck and I gripped the handles, waiting.

For me, I wouldn't have been shocked if Glocks were pointing at me right now, and, surprise, that was what happened. Both Uncle Phil and Deebo exited their ride to shoot off rounds at me. Turning my bike to the side, I hopped off then sprinted to the right of me. I felt the graze of a bullet on my bicep and right thigh. Too amped to feel the pain, I turned as I ran and squeezed off my own rounds, narrowing my eyes to focus on my enemy.

I learned how to shoot and run with good aim the moment I told my mom, Shy, about working for Dame. That day, in her anger, after getting into it with me to the point of her putting hands on me like a mother would, she dragged me out of my room, then took me to a secluded spot in the woods of ATL to show me how to protect myself. Years later, she would do the same for Drew.

Now, I was using that skill by checking my breathing as I ran, tightening my arms and squeezing with purpose. One bullet hit the middle of Uncle Phil's dome, right between the eyes; the other hit Deebo's fleshy arm. I saw Uncle Phil fall to the ground in shock on his fat-ass face. Satisfaction hit me with a smile and I turned to find protection by a house.

"You just committed yet another crime, nigga!" I heard Deebo's greasy, husky voice bark out my way.

Fire burned in my lungs as I caught my breath. I pulled out another clip from my jeans, and closed my eyes at that pain that was slowly waking through my body. Licking my chapping lips, I ran a hand down my face and quietly got up to move around the house the opposite way I came, listening for Deebo or for the car to start up. Hopping over a fence, I landed in a side alley near the first house of the cul-de-sac. Turning to run back to where my targets were, my boots skidded to a halt, as I was greeted by only my bike and the car that those niggas were in.

Pissed off, I turned to get my bike then stopped when Micah stood at the entry of the cul-de-sac. He must have come the way I did without me realizing it, which annoyed me. Looking left then right, I knew Deebo was somewhere, which soon was evident with the bullet from behind that entered my side then exited. Turning again, I saw Deebo behind me on the opposite side of their ride. A evil, contorted look was on his face and I saw his finger squeeze the trigger again.

"Shit!" spewed from me, and I ducked low, only to hear Micah's Glock go off at the same time.

Thinking quickly, I pivoted and fell vertical. This allowed Micah's bullet to meet Deebo's heart, as his bullet sliced through Micah's thigh. Holding my side to keep the blood at bay, I quickly pulled off my skullcap and tucked it into my shirt to soak up the blood.

Get up! echoed in my head, urging me to push up, which I did.

Micah sat on one knee holding his thigh, his Glock shakily pointing my way before dropping. Lights from various cars stopped near the entry of the cul-de-sac and I saw two familiar Misfits, who gave me a signal that they were still watching my back and the block. They pulled off and a second car came up, which had Fuego in it.

Slowly walking forward, I thumbed my nose then spoke through my gritted teeth, eying that kneeling nigga. "You ready to finish this, nigga?"

Micah's head snapped up as he stared at me in vengeance and indignation. "Beyond ready, nigga."

With that, he pushed forward to charge headlong into me, crashing us to the concrete. Blow after blow connected to my ribcage then face. I could feel bones breaking and knew that if I made it out of this, the healing process would be a long one. The feel of metal against my jaw had me noticing that Micah had a knife in his hand and was using the handle as additional force.

Hissing, I wished I knew some fucking martial arts moves, but I didn't so I had to work my way off of him using football moves. Letting each blow hit me, I let him feel himself and lose it in working on me until his eyes held a glassy look. Sticky, heated liquid spilled from my mouth and nose, and then I used both hands to grab his wrists, and twisted then rammed my head up into his face.

Following him as he fell backward, I caged him then slammed my own fists into him, two times. The sound of his cheekbone shattering, then his nose, made me laugh aloud. Using a third blow, my knuckles connected to his Adam's apple, making his eyes buck up then had him automatically grabbing his throat. Pushing up, I used a fourth punch to his solar plexus then snatched him by his skull to slam it on the ground.

"Niggas never listen to the clues God gives them about what to do in their lives. You should have let me stay in the dark, nigga!" I spit out before pushing up and kicking his gun to the side.

At that moment Micah, still wheezing and gasping, reached out to snatch at my ankle. I turned with force and brought my foot down on his face. His scream hit the air and he rolled to the side in a fetal position to cover himself. I steadied myself as I slightly rocked to the side and limped.

I inhaled deeply to get strength, and turned to snatch him back up. The fucked-up part about it was that I wasn't fast enough because Micah's fists came at me again, but I pulled into him, kicked out, and met his chest again. Following, Micah stumbled but greeted me with more blows.

We went at each other like two rams with horns locked, until I had him slammed up against the car using my strength to snap his spine with my hold. I squeezed then tried to turn him so I could hit him where I had stabbed him when we last fought, but he slammed his elbow into my face catching me off guard. My daze was hazy from blood lost and his blows. I saw him stumbling to get his Glock but anger had me shaking my head and reaching out for him.

"Fuck you Orlandos. Never again will you take from me!" I heard him yell.

"You're going to let this nigga get you? Fuck that! End this bitch! You played enough, son," roared in my mind.

As his Glock turned into position, I ducked low, slammed my fist into his stomach, and then reached up to grab him by his throat to lift him in the air with a body slam to the ground. All my force was in that moment, and in that blackout I took my blade from my boot, then let it slash across his throat deep enough to cut but not kill by missing the jugular. Beautiful ruby liquid splashed over the ground and me.

Micah shook, seized, and clutched at his throat in disbelief under me. His feet thrashed in his all-black clothing. Hatred filled his eyes. As he tried to snatch at me while I kneeled over him, I held out my blade to him in amusement then pulled it back.

Slowly I stood back up. Wiping off my knife, I secured it back in my boot. The sound of several feet coming my way piqued my interest. Glancing down, I took a knee then grabbed Micah by his head and started to drag him. If there were snow or dirt under us, I'd have imagined his body would be making a line behind me; instead it was his blood. I walked forward, toward the people who came at me, with purpose etched in my face.

"Fuego, call up my gramps, tell him to send me Lilith. I have something for her," I ordered while I kept walking. Micah's kicking and bleeding body continued to drag with my pull.

My mother stood ahead of me on the corner of the cul-de-sac in utter shock while she stared at me dragging Micah. She quickly moved to my side, laid a hand on my arm then whispered, "You don't have to do this. You can let him die right here."

A flicker of sadness for my mother's concern appeared on my face then disappeared in my darkness. She knew me so well.

"You know I can't. I did that enough; and you know better," I said in a low, monotone voice.

Tears shone in her loving eyes then she stepped back. She knew there was no way I could walk away now without making sure Micah was no more. The only reason it had taken me this long to off the nigga was because I needed to make sure my grandfather, Caltrone, would look after me once I did the deed. I hated to make a deal with the devil, but what had to be done, had to be done. And now that I knew Caltrone would ensure no evidence of Micah's death would be traced back to me, I could end Micah once and for all.

Quiet, I paused and stared at my mother with dark eyes. "You know I have to make sure he will never bother us again. I didn't do all this shit for nothing. I didn't go through this whole thing just so this nigga could pop up again later. He must die and I must ensure his death. I have to do this."

Licking her lips, she nodded. "I know you do, sweetheart."

I watched her walk off to meet up with Mirror. She took a quick right turn and disappeared away from the cul-de-sac. I heard Fuego rapidly talking, asking for a cleanup crew as I continued dragging Micah out of the cul-de-sac and down the neighborhood he and I had just shot up.

Fuego reached out to touch me but I jerked out of his reach and stared at him in my madness.

"I . . . Yeah, need me to help?" I heard him say. He watched me with a stoic but concerned gaze as he quirked an eyebrow.

"Naw. I got this, just follow where I go and tell Lilith where I'm at," I said then continued my dragging.

Thumbing his nose, Fuego cleared his throat and followed. "A'ight, fam."

I wanted no distractions. I knew Micah had passed out from blood loss and pain because he had stopped thrashing, and I really didn't care. Random brave people peeped from their windows to watch in shock while I walked and dragged a body down the street.

Micah represented everything this neighborhood hated. So did I; however, they knew me and knew my loyalty. So some came out to help clean up the mess that ATL police would take forever coming to clean and fix up themselves. Taking a quick right, I stopped my dragging to grab Micah and hoist him over my shoulder. The strain of his weight hit me hard but I kept on until I made it to an empty house that was just two houses in front of Shy's. Walking to the back of it, I stepped down several steps and walked into an open door.

Fluorescent lights guided me, and I went deeper into the basement of the house. Inside, I saw my mother standing by an empty steel medical table with a quiet sadness and determination to her. Mirror stood at the door, holding back Angel who watched me in shock. A hand touched my shoulder and I didn't jerk because I knew it was my baby brother's. Squaring my shoulders, I dropped Micah on the table then forcefully yanked on his arms and strapped them as if he were on a crucifix. It fit him since he felt he was a martyr hunting me.

"Enzo." I heard Angel say my name.

Shy held her hand up and, from the corner of my eye, I could see her shaking her head then motioning for everyone to follow her out of the place that used to be hers.

"Let my son work in his zone," she tenderly stated.

My mom was familiar with this place intimately. This was where she had taken the man who had tried to touch me and ended him. This was where she had brought a lot of people to silence them for my and Drew's protection. She had told me this place was mine to use the day I hung Micah up the first go-round. She explained I could hang him here better and clean up more effectively.

I listened to everyone leaving then I cleared my throat. "Angel, Lilith is coming. Keep her chill, and then I'll call you to bring her in. Yo, Drew. I'm sure Gramps will show up; entertain him with your presence, you know, how we all spoke on."

I didn't even look at them while I spoke. My eyes stayed on the concrete wall before me as I decided what to do first. I could hear both Drew and Angel walking; then I heard Angel whisper, "I got you."

Then Drew gave me a simple, slightly shaky, "Okay. I'll play that shit up."

Silence covered me in a blanket, as the door to my dungeon locked me in with my plaything. Stepping back from a bound Micah, I moved around the room and grabbed the medical kit that my mother left for me. Taking off my shirt, I cleaned my blood off and bandaged myself. I also adjusted my shirt to hang it off my hips, leaving my white stained beater exposed while I grabbed an apron. As I did so, I heard the slight movement of Micah waking up. His shallow gasps started and I turned with a smirk. My work by far wasn't done; it was just about to get better.

Chapter 19

Enzo

"I didn't cut your vocal cords so speak, nigga. What'cha gotta say for the big day that you led us to?" I said, snapping on gloves while heading back to Micah, who lay on my worktable squirming.

Micah gave me a harsh snarl then worked up enough saliva to spit on me. A bloody glob ran down my face. I wiped it off, and then walked forward to slap my spit-covered hand on his face.

"Funny."

He shook his head staring at me in an animalistic scowl before pain contorted his face and he gasped then croaked out, "Kill me and you still go to prison."

Shrugging, I took a needle full of Indigo and waved it between my fingers. "Probably, but I gives not one fuck. I'll use it to my advantage and make sure I don't do life or death, because I'm special."

Laughing, I poked him with it, pumping it in his veins. I ripped off his shirt and then turned to get an IV bag. "So let's play. I got a story for you. See, that woman I call my aunt is my mother, but I'm sure you know that, right? Anyway, she gave me this nice little bag that is full of some crap that will keep you awake and let you feel everything I do to you. This makes this shit fun for me and fun for you. Ready?"

"Fuck you, you sick bastard!" Micah raggedly hissed out. He tried to pull at his bindings, but it only made his wound at his neck bleed more. "I knew, knew, you were nothing but evil!"

Grinning, I attached the IV then slapped his veins. Walking away, I pulled out a tool, moved to stand by him, and then shrugged. Light glinted off the surface of the massive knife I held in my hand.

"I mean the mom dukes is a nurse and my work has only gotten better. Anyway, it's interesting enough that you call me evil when you done more shit than I ever have; strange, huh?" I murmured with a frown, flipping the knife back and forth.

"You can't do this!" Micah screamed.

"But I will and I am, nigga. Told you to leave me the fuck alone, but nooooo, we have to be hardheaded, which . . . Let me tell you a story," I said in joy with a smirk.

Grabbing my other tools, I pulled up a chair and worked on removing his clothes. "See, my first torture was ordered by Dame. I didn't want to do that shit, but he insisted. Said I had to because I was one of his best runners, and best players in the camp. Said if I wanted success I needed to know this shit. So, he had me work on a nigga he had kidnaped from the Latino Kings' side. Nigga was around my age at the time. I was about fifteen then. Shit, it was crazy for me. Dame had me go to his Underworld. You remember the place. I remember you fucking chicks in the joint, getting off on hurting girls in front of Dame and cutting them up. That was your thing, wasn't it?"

Sweat spilled off Micah's forehead, as his eyes rolled in his skull. The drugs wouldn't let him pass out at all. I had to remember to thank my mom.

"Yes, my Iya was the best bitch at the way she played with my toy. Only made me fuck her more. Probably is why you're here," echoed in my mind, causing me to scowl and ignore the sinister feel of it. Sharpening my

knives, I slapped his stomach and laid a blade near his groin.

"Wasn't it, nigga?" I repeated myself with cold contempt going back to my original convo.

"Ye . . . yeah, bitch! It was! Loved it!" Micah stammered.

"Thought it was. Anyway . . . I smell fire. Let me go check that shit." Getting up, I walked to where I had an iron hanger chilling on a burner. "You remember when I put that shit in your dick? Yeah, I know you do. This is going to be worse, so anyway. I had to slice this dude open using a glass Coke bottle. It was crazy, right? Had to feed that nigga his own flesh, and everything."

Moving around, I grabbed Micah's nut sacs. I pulled them like gum from the bottom of a shoe then cleanly sliced them off and walked around to put them in his screaming mouth with a bored sigh.

"So like I was saying. Made that nigga swallow that shit right, and had to walk through his shit, piss, and all of that extra shit that fell on the floor. After that, Dame was happy and geeked about my work. Praised me, and shit. Gave me extra money. But the funny thing was, I went home, and broke down in front of my mom. I didn't want to do that shit. It wasn't me. Gave me nightmares and shit, but it was my mom who helped me through it all until I got to a place where it became pleasurable for me, like now. Nigga, this is so good to me. I know you enjoy it. You practically begged for it."

"Fuck yeah, he begged for it, like the pussy he is. It has my dick hard and I'm dead," I heard a roar boasting in my mind. On some real shit, that was funny to me and made me inwardly chuckle.

"Anyway, what should I send off as a gift? See my other brother I'm told liked eating hearts. I just might give that to my grandfather, with your liver and your dick to my

Angel as a present for being a AQ. Yeah, I think I'd like that." Walking around him, I gave a slow, shaking inhale and looked down into his face. "And for me, I'll keep your brain and eyes."

"You should eat it, son. Absorb his strength!" the voice said, causing my face to contort.

"Not eating that bitch and ain't nothing about the nigga strong!" I shouted aloud then chuckled getting back in mode.

Panic flashed in Micah's eyes and he tried to pull on his straps again. At that same moment, a soft knock sounded grabbing my attention. I headed to the door opening it and sliding it on its hinges to the side. Covered in blood, I stood in the doorway to see Angel staring up at me with Lilith behind her.

Fear appeared across Angel's face while curiosity shone on Lilith's. I stepped to the side and waved them in. "Come in, bring her. Hey yo, Micah, I got someone for you!" I said in a singsong voice.

I could see the way the blood drained from Angel's face the moment she saw the blood on the floor and the small scalpels had jammed in that nigga's legs, and arms. I wanted to shake her, but I saw her do that to herself and change her expression before Lilith could see. Smirking, I kept it pushing. *Good girl.*

Humming, I walked with my hands behind my back, grabbed the brander, and put it in Angel's hands. "Since you're here, shawty, why don't you handle your business? Go for where his sacs were and take off his dick."

Angel opened her mouth to protest, but she gazed to where Lilith stood staring down her nose at her in annoyance. Lilith's arms were crossed over her chest and she seemed slightly bored.

"Bitch ain't made for this world," Lilith grumbled then huffed. "Why am I here?" Lilith gripped then dropped her hands.

Angel sucked her teeth then walked over to Micah waving her fingers at him. She ran her nails over his thighs and glared at Lilith. "Shut the hell up, bitch. You ain't bad. Anyway, hey, Micah. Having fun? Looks like it, 'cause damn you wide open."

I laughed at her words, and then smiled when she rammed the iron up his ass instead of where I said. Micah screamed. The smell of charred fleshed made my nostrils flare. A slight change in Angel's body language let me know she was disgusted but she played it off with finesse. With that, I watched Angel turn and glare at Lilith flipping her the bird. She then rolled her eyes at the woman and walked out closing the door behind her as if she were never there.

Chuckling, I waved Lilith in as she huffed, "Bitch. Anyway, again, why do you have me here?"

Quirking an eyebrow, I sighed. "You are fucking disrespectful. You know who I am."

"So? But you ain't Caltrone. No one can be him, including your weak ass," she spit out.

This Lilith was a foul bitch who felt too entitled in her damn life. She was annoying. The perks she was getting were only making her spoiled and only setting up a situation that would eventually turn sour for the Orlandos. I really had no love for this pale bitch at all. I could tell before knowing her background that she was weak broad who wasn't really as built for this world as she acted.

Smirking, I moved around the table and reached to turn Micah's face toward Lilith. "So your true thoughts are out, right? But check it, you came now didn't you?"

"Yes, because Caltrone ordered it, so what you want and why you got this nigga here?" she asked walking around with glee in her eyes. "You want me to help?"

I studied the way Lilith's whole appearance changed. She seemed to get a sick joy out of getting her hands dirty. That was no biggie for me though. "Yeah, why don't you take this knife and cut his hand off," I suggested.

Lilith happily stepped to the side of the table and ran her eyes over his body. The lights of my den washed over her illuminating her sinister looks. From her dark hair with strawberry blond highlights to the stilettos heels that I could tell she would use to kill a nigga in a minute, she had dressed for Caltrone. I could tell because she wore a pencil skirt and a form-fitting blazer that showed off her small, pert breasts. There was a level of masculine mixed with the allure of the feminine that projected her power of being a bad bitch in her attire. That had her giving off the mantel of Orlando.

Micah tugged at his wrists and was able to scratch at Lilith's hand as he sneered. Through muffled yells and grunts, I could tell he wanted her nowhere near him.

The chick I knew felt she was a queen pin just with how she carried herself leaned forward, and then smashed her hand against Micah's bulging, squished face. "Only Caltrone puts his hands on me. You ever disrespect me in such a manner again, and I won't just break your neck, but I will also pull your intestines out from your dick hole and ass. Little brother or not."

An amused jeer spread across my face. It had me rocking on the back of my heels with the display before me. The two didn't even fucking know how good this was to me. "My bad, my bad, Lilith. I'm being rude, why don't cha tell your brother sup."

Micah stared with glassy eyes, then spit and chokingly gasped. His eyes were so wide they threatened to split in the corners.

I watched Lilith give an eerie smile then lean to kiss Micah's temple. "It's good to see you again. I missed you so much, but damn if you still aren't annoying."

Patting his head, she let him go then happily walked my way. She reached out to run her fingers under my chin then sighed. "I think I really like you. I see Caltrone in you, even though you still will never be him."

Smirking I moved away from her then chuckled as I watched the horror on Micah's face intensify. "Would it fuck you up if I laid her over your body and fucked her? Bet she has a mad sexy cum face yeah?" My laughter became manic and I lifted my shoulders in a shrug then slapped the side of his face with a grin. "That's not in my plan, but yeah, it's a Tems family reunion, nigga!"

At that moment, my hands lifted in the air then with force, I slammed a sturdy pair of shears into his chest. Turning them I effectively cracked open his chest. Micah's shock and screams filled the room.

"You really did it! You've been very bad, Micah," Lilith squealed in madness.

Micah's hand reached out in his stunned shock and gripped at the tails of her blazer. It slightly shocked then amused me when this broad whipped around, then slammed her palm into Micah's face again. She gripped it with her nails digging into his flesh then lifted his head some to slam him backward with all her might into the table. The loud clang had me staring at them both in amusement as she slammed her elbow into his neck.

"I told you! Do . . . not . . . touch . . . me!" she hissed. Her eyes darted around in a crazed madness before softening and realizing who she held: her little brother.

"Damn!" was all I said though. There was no love lost between Micah and me, so the fact that he was getting his ass handed to him made things all the better.

As they had their moment I returned to my work in holding the chest shears. Scowling, I shook my head while I looked down at his bare chest. Using my hands to use the shears, I pried him open and studied his beating heart. His sharp screams bounced off the walls and had Lilith covering her ears as if she were a child.

"Yeah, ahhhh! Hurts right?" I asked in jest as I patted his chest. "You like the work, mama?"

Lilith seemed to shake herself then sneered while licking her lips like in heat. She slowly sashayed to the table touched Micah's shaking sweaty body then cooed, "Hello, little brother. I'm sorry."

My brow quirked and I was suddenly introduced to Erica Tems. I wondered did this bitch have multiple personalities. Because if she did, I couldn't blame her for it. I was hearing people too.

"I like her, son, but she's a cannon. Maybe you should fuck her; it would be good," I heard in my head.

I sighed speaking back in my mind, *no shit, Sherlock; and naw, I'm good. I don't fuck old men's pussy.*

Focusing back on the two, Erica stroked her brother's bruised face as she murmured, "Sorry."

Though Micah was in a daze, he was still very coherent. I snatched his balls from his mouth so I could hear what he was trying to say to his sister. The fight in him was strong, so much so that he was able to gruffly stammer out through his shattering pain, "No, no. I thought you died. Did this all for you."

I watched the woman who was just seconds ago this crazed, lethal, want-to-be queen pin soften and transform into a young girl. She reached out to caress Micah's face. Her gaze seemed to soften and switch into another zone while her voice sweetened. "Bodies can be found anywhere, little brother. I'm sorry you had to be deceived like that."

Water leaked from the creases of Micah's eyes. Whatever crazy was in his own mind had him staring at her as if he worshiped her. If I had loosened the straps, I could tell he would have reached up to hold her, but instead he just pulled on the straps on his wrists as he tried to get as close as he could to his big sister. "I would have searched harder had I known."

"Shhhh, it's not your fault. I got what I deserved," she said with fresh tears rolling down her face.

"No, Erica, that wasn't what you deserved. You were just a kid. A little girl who didn't know what she was doing," he pleaded. His voice was raspy from the screams and wound at his neck.

"I knew what I was doing, Micah. Just didn't think it would get our parents killed or get me in the situation I was in," she admitted.

Erica reached out to cradle her little brother's head into her arms. She told him how she had been locked away in basement alone. She'd been starved, raped, and beaten into submission. Erica told him of how they'd taken away who she was, stripped her down to only a shell of a girl.

It had taken them five years to do it, but they finally broke her down and made her do what she wanted them to do. She told them of her nightmares of having to see their father murdered in cold blood and then their mother. Micah had to tell her that their mother had survived in body but died in mind and spirit. Erica's shoulders then shook as she cried.

In that moment, he was that ten-year-old little boy looking up to his big sister. She was once again that six-teen-year-old vibrant teenage girl who'd falsely assumed she could handle the situation she'd found herself in.

"I'm so sorry, Micah," she cried in a whisper.

"Wasn't your fault," he choked out.

"I'm so sorry," she then said over and over.

There, in that brief moment I saw two little kids whom the Orlandos had turned into demons of their original selves. In the height of their emotions, that was when I put a bullet in her skull right before his eyes. The sound of that bullet going off and making contact with the flesh and bone of Erica "Lilith" Tems-Orlando left me wickedly smiling. Her astonished gaze then the sound of her body dropping to the floor had me feeling damn good.

Her ruby essence leaked to pool around her head in a halo. Her face held that of madness and peace. It was kind of poetic and I would remember it always. I smoothed a hand down my chest and strutted around the table. Thumbing my nose all humor drained out of me to be replaced by a cold, menacing darkness the moment I bent down to stare into Micah's eyes waiting for him to comprehend what just happened. This was no longer a cat-and-mouse thing. This was my world and my game. *Checkmate, bitch.*

My father's laughter sounded in my head and I licked my lips. In a deep, stony, detached voice I calmly stated, "You understanding me now, Micah?"

His own agony was locked on his contorted face in that moment until he screamed and struggled to get at me shaking the blade I had in his chest to the floor. "I will kill you!"

I was amazed at the fleeting power a person always showed in their last attempt to live. Too bad the emotion behind was lost on me. That was inspired me to stand up then exhale grabbing a scalpel. "Yeah, you understand me now."

With that, I slammed my blade down his scalp, ripped the flesh open to expose his brain; then I reached out to rip his heart out. Watching his face in those moments, I laid it on his stomach then leaned back to pull his brain out. I worked how I said I would. Dismembering him in quiet solidarity. Until I had nothing but pieces of Micah, blood, and silence. After dissolving the rest of this trash, Caltrone would be getting two gifts: parts of Micah with that of his sister, as well as a piece of my darkness.

Chapter 20

Angel

"Please don't let him take me," the woman pleaded as tears of fear rolled down her face.

Her beautiful chocolate face was covered in welts and bruises. She was almost naked. The purple cat suit she'd had on was ripped to shreds, almost. I could see the bruises on her thighs. Felt the pain in her body each time she tried to move. Just hours before, she didn't know what it meant to be a woman in her position. She was a doctor, a well-known one with more than one OBGYN office in the Metro Atlanta area. And now she had been reduced to nothing more than a sobbing echo of a woman.

I felt sorry for her. Pitied her because I knew she would now know what her daughter endured, but only she would get the same pain at the source of evil. Gina's mom held a pleading look in her eyes and, for a moment, I remembered, and flashed back to Gina's first trip to the basement. I felt myself getting sick. The things that had been done to Gina should have killed most women. In a sense, I guess it had killed her; mentally she had been murdered.

"The fact that you would even fix your mouth to ask me to save you is comical," Shy told the woman who lay at Caltrone's feet. "I just watched what you did to Angel. Know what you did to your daughter. There is this little thing called karma, Candace. That's your name, isn't it?

Why would any woman of your stature choose to get in bed with Micah? Choose to do his dirty work? I don't understand it nor do I care. There is nothing I can do for you at this point. You've made your bed and now you must lie in it."

The woman screamed and pleaded as Shy turned to walk away. "No, please, please don't leave me. He said if you just told him to let me go, he would. I . . . I don't want to go back with him, please," Candace cried.

I saw a side of Shy I'd never seen before in that moment. A woman all about sisterhood flicked her wrist and kept walking. "Not my problem," she yelled over her shoulder.

Candace knew she was pretty much fucked. She looked up at me from the trunk of the car. I saw my best friend. Saw Gina's face staring up at me and it bothered me.

"Be careful who you kill and be even more careful of who you leave alive."

Enzo's words played over and over in my head. Candace's thick thighs were bruised. Nose had dried-up blood caked in the crevices of it. Her thick, luscious lips had been bloodied and were swollen. Paper cuts lined her breasts and one could only assume Caltrone had allowed Lilith to play before she'd gone to see Enzo. But no matter how hard I tried to see the woman Candace was, all I could remember was the way Gina had been treated in that basement. It was for that very reason I spit in her face then slammed the trunk closed.

It was over. Finally, it was over. At least that was what I was hoping as I waited for Enzo. It had been hours and we hadn't heard a word from him. Nothing. So I waited. Waited where I knew no one would look for him. I prayed silently as I waited. Didn't know what else to do. After bringing Lilith to him as he'd instructed, I hopped in the car and got Shy home. Mirror had demanded it when she had almost lost her footing because she'd been too weak to stand. There, we waited on Enzo. I just needed him to call me or text or something. But all we got was the hum of the central heating system and silence.

That was why I sat outside of a sprawling mansion in Alpharetta, Georgia. I needed to see a man about his grandson. I hopped out of the car dressed like I was one of those La Bella Donnas who married into the mob. I'd seen the way Shy had dressed when she'd gone to see the man. I made note of it as I dressed that morning. I probably could have afforded to buy the red bottoms and designer clothes if I had used the money Enzo had given me before, but I wanted to use my own money so Target, Walmart, and Macy's were all I could afford. Still, I made that shit look like it was designer everything.

I knew that what I was about to do would probably cost me more than money in the end. It would probably cost me my soul, but I had to do it. Had to ensure that what happened to Micah didn't fall back on Enzo. I mean, I knew Shy and the Kings had pull, but whether we liked it or not, the Orlandos still ran ATL. They were all in the prison system, in the governor's mansion, the mayor's office, the police office. They had their shit on point. Hidden in plain sight and you would never know it.

The wind was blowing so hard that it threatened to knock me on my ass as I waited at the door. There was no sun. Just dark and gloom seemed to hang overhead. Maybe that was a sign that I should have left, but I'd come too far to turn back.

Two armed men opened the door for me. It didn't take a rocket scientist to see that they were Orlandos. Those men had a look about them. One gave a lopsided grin as he ogled my body while the other respectfully, surprisingly, asked me to step inside.

"The old man is in the dining room waiting on you. Angel, right?" the respectful one asked.

Before I answered him, I moved to the side so his partner in crime wouldn't be behind me. Didn't trust him. My heels clicked against the Italian marble flooring as I moved and then looked up at the man. Both looked like their skin had been kissed by the sun. The respectful one had a Cuban accent that would make most women moist; it only made my flesh crawl. They were five feet eleven and six feet in height. The one talking to me had a bald head with a goatee that had been razor shaped to perfection. Eyes so black it looked like he could see right through you. There was a scar that ran from his left ear all the way around to the right. I didn't want to know how he'd gotten it.

The one obviously focused on my ass had a low-cut fade with deep waves. Coffee brown beady eyes that annoyed me instantly. He had a baby face with grown folk teeth. Not to say that he was ugly; he just wasn't my type of hype. Both men were dressed in black pants with red dress shirts.

"Yeah, I'm Angel," I finally answered.

"Gotta pat you down for weapons, little lady," the other one said.

I wanted to put up a fight, but I knew if I did I risked getting kicked out. So I spread my arms and pretty much allowed the goon to molest me. He took his time, went way too slow as he ran his hands up and down my sides. The high-waist skirt and button-down shirt I had on basically tapered to my shape so there was no way he thought I had a gun on me. When he stood in front of me and ran his hands over and under my breasts, I smacked the shit out that nigga. I hit him so hard that his respectful comrade chuckled and then stepped in front of me.

"That's enough, Mark," the other one told him.

Mark looked at me like he wanted to lay hands on me.

"You feeling froggy then leap, nigga," I dared him. There may have not been a gun on me, but there was a weapon somewhere.

"*Puta de mierda*," he growled low, calling me a fucking bitch. He bucked at me like he was going to come for me, but with the respectful one standing between us, he couldn't get to me. I'd already slid my hand into my purse, ready to defend myself. I was scared as shit, but I wouldn't let him know it.

"Frederick, what's the holdup?" Caltrone called from the dining room.

"We're coming. Had a little situation," he yelled back. Frederick shook his head as he whistled and laughed low while Mark continued to call me bitches under his breath. Frederick made Mark walk in front of me and he walked behind me as they led me to the area where Caltrone was waiting for me. He was sitting at the head of an elaborately decorated table. A feast was set out before him. Although the man was a menace to society, he was very well put together. I was sure he knew I was there. Still, he continued to cut into his steak and eat like I wasn't. Part of me wanted to look around the place and take in my surroundings, but the other half of me just wanted to get in and get out as quickly as I could.

"Come, have a seat, Angel. Break bread with your husband's grandfather," Caltrone said without turning to look at me.

I already knew the drill. As a woman, I had to kiss his ring again. It was another way for him to slight me being a woman. Another way for him to keep women in their place. I took his hand then kissed the Orlando crest before sitting to the right of him. I'd noticed before that his hands were soft, but the calluses there told that he didn't mind getting his hands dirty. I sat in silence as he ordered Frederick to have the cook bring me out a plate.

I wasn't hungry, but knew he was prolonging my visit because he could. Control was what he lived on. I saw where Enzo got it from.

I half expected Lilith to stroll in. Lilith had been Caltrone's mouthpiece. He'd trained her so perfectly that she knew when to speak and when not to speak. She could carry on a whole conversation for him as if he wasn't in the room. But she wasn't there and I could only speculate what Enzo was doing or had done to her. I brought my attention back to the enigma in front of me. Caltrone never looked up at me; his eyes never even looked in my general direction. The only thing I could hear was his silverware hitting the plate at times and my nerves jumping around the place. I was so nervous that I accidently knocked over the glass of wine in front of me.

"Shit," I mumbled to myself.

Caltrone stopped eating and looked over at spill; not me, but the spill. "Clean it up," he said in a low monotone.

"What?" I asked.

"Clean it up. Now."

My mind flashed back to Dame. That nigga had OCD. There was never a dirty room in his mansion. Not even a crumb had touched the floor. If so, that nigga would flip. I didn't want a repeat of that, being that the man in front of me was probably the originator of all the evil that ran through the Orlando men. Luckily for me, I didn't have to do too much cleaning. Frederick called out to someone in Spanish in the kitchen. A young woman came out with cleaning supplies. She cleaned the mess I'd made so fast it was like it had never happened. I thanked her. She nodded and then quickly exited the room. Caltrone turned back to his food and started to eat.

"Why are you here?" he finally asked me. "Need me to do what this time?"

"This thing with Micah, I need to make sure that none of it leads back to Enzo. For the past few weeks he's been all in the news for alleged charges of guns and drugs. If Micah comes up missing, I don't want Enzo's name anywhere near it."

"And how do you figure I can help you with that?"

I inhaled then exhaled as I squirmed around in my seat. Caltrone was a mind fucker. He liked to make you state the obvious just to keep you where he wanted you.

"He doesn't mind sitting in jail, but I do. All his life all he wanted to do was play football, make it to the NFL, get to the Super Bowl, and take care of his family. If he goes to jail for any reason at this point he'll miss that opportunity because of some shit he wanted no part of anyway."

Caltrone's fork stopped midway to his mouth. "Was that an insult to the Orlando name?"

"If that was how you took it."

He gripped the fork in his hand a way that let me know he was having thoughts of shanking me with it. "What you will not do is insult this family," he snarled.

"I'm only responsible for what I say, not for what you comprehend. I didn't come here to be disrespectful or to get into a piss slinging match with you. I came to keep Enzo out of jail."

"Not going to happen."

"Why?" I asked. "You came in telling Shawn that if he needs anything he can call on you and now you say no?"

Caltrone's eyes narrowed as he looked down his nose at me. Chills settled into my spine and goose bumps rose on my flesh. "I told him he could, not you." Caltrone laid his fork down, casually wiped at his mouth with the cloth napkin that had his initial inscribed on it, and then turned to look at me.

"So, I don't have the right to speak for him?"

"Maybe in the outside world you can, but not with me."

"And just why the hell not? I'm his wife."

"By force, not by choice."

"It doesn't matter."

"So you say."

"Does this mean you're going to help?"

"Only if you do something for me."

I got a bit uncomfortable and squirmed around in my seat. The man was an Orlando so agreeing to do him a favor could have me signing my soul away to the devil. "Something like what?" I nervously asked.

"I need a one on one with my grandson," he said casually.

That confused me as he could speak to Enzo anytime he wanted. I shrugged. "You can talk to Enzo whenever."

"I have more than one grandson, Angel. I mean the one they're intentionally keeping away from me."

"Andrew?"

He nodded once. "Andrew."

I shook my head. Shy would never allow for that to happen. That was why Drew hadn't spoken to him the way Enzo had asked before. Shy knew Caltrone had a way with words and the last thing she needed was for him to be in Drew's ear. No matter how smart we all knew he was, Drew still had a lot of growing up to do.

"Shy wouldn't—"

"Do you want me to help Shawn or not?"

"So you won't help him—"

"Bring me Andrew."

"Why?"

Caltrone looked at me with a smile so sinister it chilled me. Actually, saying it chilled me would have been an understatement. "Because he's impressionable," he had the gall to answer. "Let's be honest, here. The Kulu Tribe has painted me as the devil, no? And in many senses, I am, *sí*. However, there are always three sides to a story: their side, my side, and the truth. The truth of the matter is I've done some evil shit, *mami*. I've taken out every Tribe king I intended to. I've never bitten a dog that didn't bite me first. I always bite the dog that bit me and that will never change. Ask yourself how two men went from best friends to arch nemeses. Ask yourself why the blood spilled between our two factions runs so deep. See, the thing with the Kulu Tribe is that they like to make themselves the exception to the rule. I kill and I'm the devil. They kill and it's justified. Doesn't matter your reason for killing somebody, you're still a killer, no?"

He paused, took a sip of the blood red wine sitting in front of him, and then continued talking. "Tell my grandson to never make himself the exception to the rule, *mami*. They've poisoned him with their half truths and whole lies. Ask him, how could Kulu King Phenom, Queen Anika, or any of them tell the whole truth when they don't know the origin of this beef between two grown men, huh?"

Caltrone was passionate in the way he spoke. If one didn't know any better they would say the old man showed a hint of emotion. I didn't say anything because I didn't know what to say. I would allow him to keep talking as long as he got his mind off of me bringing Drew to see him.

"So," he continued, "they can paint me any way they want to. I own every fucking evil deed I did. Feel no kind of way about it, because I own my shit." He spoke emphatically as he used two fingers to tap his chest. "One day I'm going to die. All my sins will come back to haunt me and I'll be waiting for death with open arms because it will be no more than I deserve. Until then, my aim is to tell my grandsons the whole story, the whole truth, *sí?* So do we have a deal or no?"

I took a deep breath, and felt my heart sinking. "I couldn't betray Shy's trust—"

He cut me off again. "Does Queen Iya know you're here?"

I moved my gaze away from his piercing one and then looked at the floor before back up to him. "No," I murmured.

"Of course she doesn't. Tell me this, Angel, if I help you, what's in it for me? I know for a fact that Shawn didn't send you to me. I can tell he doesn't want anything to do with me. No matter how much he tolerates me, he's been poisoned by his other side of the family against me. I see the Kulu Tribe all through him."

"What's that got to do with anything?" I asked.

"If he knew you were here, what would he do to you, Bianca Smith . . . Orlando?"

My eye twitched when he added his moniker on to my last name. I shuddered to think what Enzo or Shy would think knowing I'd gone behind their backs and tried to barter a deal with the devil.

"He would probably be pissed, never trust me again. Would probably lay hands on me." I shrugged for emphasis. "Doesn't matter to me though. I'll do whatever—"

"Be careful what you say in my presence," Caltrone cut in. "Saying you'll do whatever for Shawn would be walking into the lion's den." His smirk was disturbing as he watched me. "I am who I am."

I didn't know how to respond to that so I didn't. The elder Orlando sat at the head of the table like he was a true king as he studied me. There was something in his eyes I couldn't read, but I knew I didn't like it. Caltrone had a poker face that was just as deadly as his bark and his bite. After a while, he picked up his fork again and began to eat.

"So, will you help me or not?" I asked, a bit frustrated.

"That depends on if you will help me, Angel. I do nothing for free. If you fuck me, I fuck you."

The way he looked at me after he said that made me uneasy. I felt the need to get the hell up out of there. I decided to follow my first instinct. I pushed my chair back then turned to walk out. Frederick and Mark blocked my exit.

"Sit down," Caltrone calmly demanded of me.

Even though piss was damn near running down my leg at the thought of being defiant to the man, I stood my ground. "Not if you're not going to help me. I didn't come here for bullshit. I came to talk business and if you don't want to do that then there is no reason for me to stay here."

Caltrone stood up so quickly that I stumbled over my feet trying to back away from him. I backed into Frederick, who felt like a brick wall behind me. The old man closed the distance between me and him swiftly. His lips were turned down like I stunk to him as his eyes narrowed to slits. Flashes of the times Dame had laid slaps and punches across my face had me visibly shaken. I took a deep breath and swallowed, finally seeing that Dame's temper came honest. Caltrone was a lot taller, way more menacing when he was standing directly over you, glowering as he did so.

"I said sit down," he demanded through clenched teeth. "No one leaves this place alive unless I say so. Don't make me lose my grandson; I just got him. You mean nothing to me and I will kill you if you disrespect me in my home again. Understand, *sí?*"

There was something in me that made me want to tell him to fuck himself. Something grew in me that had my gripping my purse, ready to draw my weapon and end my life while ending Caltrone's. Then I remembered how incensed Dame would get when one of the girls would fight back against him. I remembered the way he seemed to be turned on by it and in turn he would go harder at them, whether it was with sex or knocking one of us the fuck out. I remembered how Shy told me Lu liked to make her scream for him. Said it seemed to only feed him, make him worse. Add those thoughts to the fact that no one knew where I was and I knew I was fucked. There would be no way I could win that fight.

As bad as I wanted to fight the old man, I had no desire to see, first hand, where Dame and his father had gotten their rage and aggression.

I glanced at Mark to see him watching with a slick smirk on his face. I could tell he would have given any-thing to witness me feel the old man's wrath. I picked my pride up and slowly walked back to my chair. My whole body stiffened when he moved behind me and placed his big hands on my shoulders.

"I don't do anything for free. Even if he is my grandson. I need reciprocity."

My breath hitched and I swallowed, finally accepting the fact that I was in over my head. I may have wanted to be Shy, may have even thought I was going to be on her level one day. But, the fact of the matter was only Shy, a true Lilith, could negotiate with the devil. I was no Lilith. Just a fool who'd fallen into a pit of vipers.

"Bring me Andrew," he demanded again, "and I'll clean up the mess behind Micah. Then you tell Shawn that he owes me. He owes me because of his wife. Make sure you tell him that, too."

I didn't know what else to say after that. It was simple. If I wanted Caltrone to help me then I had to find a way to do what he asked. There would be no ifs, ands, or buts about it. I agreed and felt that, in the long haul, it would be the biggest mistake I'd ever made.

***

Hours later, I jumped awake when I heard the door of the condo open. It had been almost twenty-four hours since I'd seen the man who stepped over the threshold. He had on a trench coat, hands in his pockets, as he walked forward and scowled at me.

"What are you doing here?" he asked me.

"Waiting for you."

"Why?"

"Because I wanted to. Where you been?"

"Working the graveyard shift," he replied.

"Is it done?" I asked him cautiously.

He didn't answer. Tossed me a gift box wrapped in a blood red bow. I opened it curiously. I blinked slowly as I looked down into the box. Blood soaked the bottom with male genitalia that I was sure belonged to Micah. I thought I would be disgusted. Instead, I smiled. I smiled and then I rushed over to hug the man who'd been forced to marry me. Micah had stolen the little bit of humanity I'd had left. So fuck him. I hoped that in death he was in hell with Dame and I prayed they were burning together.

I kissed Enzo long and hard, just to show him that I appreciated what he'd done. "Thank you," I whispered to him as I pulled back and looked into his eyes.

He didn't say anything, just smirked. In that moment, I saw the evil that sat just beneath the surface. There were two sides to the man I could finally admit I loved. And I loved both sides equally. He'd promised me that there would always be a balance, a methodical ratification to his madness. I believed him. Stood by him. Trusted him.

"I need to tell you something," I told him as he moved to the kitchen where I'd lined the floor with plastic just in case he'd come to me needing to get rid of evidence.

He tossed the trench coat and I could see he was still covered in blood. "Tell me," he said as he stripped down to his bare minimums.

"I went to see your grandfather."

He stopped moving around and gazed down at me. "And?"

"And he says you owe him."

"For what?"

"I asked him to make sure your name and Micah's disappearance didn't show up in the same sentence on any news outlet."

Enzo scratched his five o'clock shadow. "Why did you do that?"

I shrugged, feeling a bit nervous. "I wanted to make sure you were covered on all fronts. Better safe than sorry." I didn't know what to expect as he watched me. Didn't know if he would snap on me or renege on his promise not to ever put his hands on me again.

But what I didn't expect was for him to kiss my lips and pull me closer to him. "So you really got a nigga back then, huh?" he asked.

I nodded. "For as long as you let me."

He nodded once. "I ain't saying I'm happy you did that shit, though. Don't ever go back to see that nigga like that without me. Ever. Will never trust that nigga. And, just so you know, he already assured me he would look out for me once I took Micah down. I just had to take over the DOA empire."

I kept quiet. Flesh started to crawl at the fact that Caltrone had played me. I listened to Enzo and had already made up my mind that Caltrone would never get that close to me without Enzo being there again. My chances of survival were slim to none, but since Caltrone wanted me to do something for him, he'd let me leave. I told Shawn everything Caltrone had told me, from wanting him to know the real reasons the Orlandos and the Tribe were beefing to the fact that the old man didn't care about being the evil he had come to be.

"Shy was going to let Drew talk to Caltrone at first but then she changed her mind. Said Drew had a lot of growing up to do before he would be able to sit in the presence of evil and come out sane," I said. "But, Caltrone wants Andrew. In order to help you like I asked him to do, he said he needs to see Andrew. I didn't know you'd already spoken to him. I'm sorry."

"Nah, don't be sorry. It's cool. When all this shit settles down, when the dust clears, we'll give Caltrone what he wants," Enzo said calmly. He was almost too calm. "And no, you won't take Andrew to Caltrone. If my mama said no, then no. She has her reasons."

"But, he won't help if I don't."

"So? We'll find another way. You did good, but nah. This nigga likes to be in control. I wanna see what he's like when he's not in control, feel me?"

I nodded. "So what now?"

"For now, we wait. We act like ain't shit changed. We control what the media says about us. You get to tell the world that you're a survivor. You get to show your strength."

"And you?"

"Me?" he asked with a slick smile. "I get to keep playing the game as if I never stopped."

I tried to get a handle on his emotions, on what he was really thinking. Tried to see if he felt anything after killing Micah and I saw nothing. Micah had taken him there. Had turned him into the monster he never wanted to be.

I asked him, "You okay?"

"Never been better. Just wanted to be left alone. He wouldn't leave me alone and this is the end result. All that nigga had to do was let me be and all would have been well, but you know how niggas are in this shit, B. They don't believe shit stank until they in the shit."

"What happened to Lilith?"

Enzo smirked. "My pops probably fucking her in hell," was all he said as he walked down the hall laughing like he knew something I didn't.

Chapter 21

Shy

It appeared that my role was never over, nor did I wish it to be. This was for my children and their future. It stopped being about me once I gained Shawn and Drew back in my life. Therefore, I stood listening to Bianca speaking to my son, who was now her husband, at his condo. A knowing smile slid across my face.

Before standing at this doorway accidently eavesdropping, I had to beg Mirror to take me and Drew to my son's condo to wait for him. Both Mirror and Drew wanted me to rest but I was hoping that Shawn would show up at his home first, which he did. I was busying myself folding his laundry and cleaning with both Mirror and Drew fussing at me when he came in. He walked right past me in a daze I was very familiar with, so I let him unwind on his own. That had me later going to check on him and Bianca when I overheard their conversation.

Bianca loved him deeply. In her eyes I saw a young me, with that familiar fear of the Orlandos I once had; but with her I saw something else, something grander. Bianca could see the good in him, and love him past the evil. It was even possible that she loved even that darkness. That meant I did all I could in raising Shawn to grow into a balance where he became his own man, his own version of an Orlando and a Banks. If she could continue giving him balance then I was at peace.

All my agenda's purpose had been was to give him and Drew normalcy and never this crime life, but I always knew they needed to be prepared in case my past, or the past of his ancestors, reigned over him, which it ultimately did. So now it was my agenda to fight for his normalcy, but also to fight for him to be his own man in this world he had been forced into.

It was several weeks later, after my son ceremoniously offed that bastard Micah. I sat reflecting and stressed out for my children's safety. It didn't help that I'd also received a phone call from Caltrone within that stressful week as well.

"So my grandson is more like me than I previously believed," I heard Caltrone drawl into my ear as I sat healing up in the sunroom.

A simmering hatred settled in my stomach but I kept it in control before responding, "It would appear so. This should make you very proud. Any thoughts that he wasn't can be shelved for now?"

Caltrone gave a deep chuckle then gave a satisfied rumble. "For now. It pleases me how he bestowed my Lilith upon me. Very skillful. I see your touch in his finesse with the blade and I see my mind in how he disposed of her without my blessing."

"I don't know what you're speaking about," I lied, and then reached for a blunt.

"I'm sure you don't," Caltrone coldly responded. "This leaves an opening for a new Lilith and you and I are due for a meeting."

Smoke trailed from my lips and I gave cold laugh. "But of course. After my son's arraignment, we will discuss where we are going in this new world of yours."

"We better. I'll see you in the courtroom, my queen. Until we see each other again. Also tell my grandson to keep up the good work. *Sí?* It might make a good tactic in prison, unless we have a deal? No? Bye, Iya," Caltrone rumbled then hung up with a laugh.

Sitting in the courtroom on the hard bench as the time ticked away was the most nerve-racking shit I have ever had to endure. Over time, more and more people filled the courtroom. Some of them had family members there to be arraigned. Most were there to see Shawn, including Caltrone, who sat in the back watching with fire in his eyes. I could tell by the manner in which he sat that he was making plans to off everyone against my son.

The judge sat in his big chair overlooking us all with glasses sitting on his nose as he thumbed through a folder in front of him. He was balding and his head appeared to be too big for his neck. His skin was pale, ashy, and blotchy. It seemed as if hours had passed before they brought my son out, when it was really only thirty minutes at the most. When he finally came out, I had to put my hand over my mouth to keep from verbally reacting the way I wanted to. He was shackled around his waist, hands cuffed in front of him, with shackles around his ankles. Even in death Micah still had power, the investigation he had going on before his death still a thorn in Shawn's side.

Enzo looked tired. His beard was growing in, and his normally cropped, razor-shaped haircut looked unkempt. Blood seemed to be seeping through the gauze on his face, which told me he had been in a fight that opened the wound back up. There were new cuts on his face and he moved slowly as if his upper body was sore. Drew blew out air as if blowing out steam, as Bianca's legs started to shake. My grip tightened on both of their hands and we all held it together as best we could. Enzo knew we were there, but he wouldn't look at us. I desperately wanted him to so he could know his family was in his corner.

Bianca, Drew, and I sat in that courtroom and watched as it seemed like the DA had tried and convicted Enzo before the trial. After Enzo pleaded not guilty, the DA instantly asked that bail be denied. The name Orlando had been a blessing and a curse in the end. The DA used the fact that my son was tied to the crime syndicate DOA to argue that he could jump ship and they would never see him again. The judge bought it and Enzo was set to be locked away until his trial.

When he did finally glance at us, they were taking him away again. Anger flickered through me.

I sat with Bianca and Drew for days waiting for my people to make a move, to do something, but reality finally set in. There was just no way in hell the good guy always came out on top. I didn't know what was taking my people so long, but seeing the way my son had been handled while he was in custody fucked with me.

After going back to my private home to finish my treatments with the healing I was going through I realized that as a mother, as a warrior in these streets, and as a survivor I just couldn't sit around, wait, and do nothing.

"Where are you attempting to go, love?" I heard Mirror ask me, which caused me to turn around.

Grabbing my purse, I exhaled. "My sons need me. Shawn needs me. I have many aces, but there's one that I need to force to help us in our favor."

Mirror walked up to me, rested his hand on my shoulder, then moved his hand to grip my chin. "Yuh know you got to keep a cool stress level, or the surgery you had will be for nothing. You need to be patient and not throw the Orlando name and power around, love."

Frustration had me moving out of his touch to grab more items. "I understand that, Mirror; however, time is of the essence. But Micah's hold is still on my son. We need to get him out so we can get him back on the field and also finish what we started with Caltrone."

"Yes, we do, love, but you need to put all the rubbish shit to the side, think clearly, and let me work my magic too. I'll take you to where you need to go but, trust, whatever happens he'll work it out, too. He's got your survival tactics in him; both of your sons do," he explained with a light kiss to my lips that had my anger melting away.

My hand reached up to touch his face then I dropped it. "Take me to the car. I'll direct you, but you have to stay in the car and wait for us when we leave."

"A'ight, I'm used to that role. Let us go then," Mirror said, leading me out of my room.

After blowing off steam with Mirror, Drew, Bianca, and I all sat in silence while we listened to every radio station in Atlanta go ham about Shawn's arraignment. Tears stung my eyes from what they spoke about, from his past in the Trap dealing with Dame, to the steps he took to being a rising young rookie in the game. My baby had put his heart and soul in his aspirations and goals of getting to the NFL. I was proud of him, proud of how hard he worked to get there. His dedication was everything. It had him having the Midas touch in some ways, from his success in school to the streets and football.

But now that was going to be washed away. I glanced at my baby boy, my other heartbeat. My arm reached around him and I kissed his temple watching him blush red. My gaze focused on Bianca, and I reached for her, doing the same. We all sat in our car outside of a simple blue bungalow-style home with a wraparound porch and a red oak door. A blacked-out armored Escalade sat in the drive, and I sighed. We were in Roswell and, how I had Bianca take us, we were hidden in a quiet, closed-off neighborhood we could not be trailed to.

Undoing my seat belt, I looked at them both. "I have one more ace up my sleeve, something I've kept from you all with good reason, that I had no control over."

A flash of concern and annoyance flickered in Bianca's warm brown eyes. I took her and Drew's hands in my own and squeezed. "Listen to me: this was out of my control, and for good reason."

"What are you keeping from us now, Mama? I mean damn! What we got to go through now?" Drew asked. His tone made my heart flutter in uncertainty.

"Just listen. I am a gatekeeper. Many of the secrets I keep are not my own to share, and many of them are. When I say I have resources I mean it and you all need to remember this one because it may be your saving grace one day," I explained.

Bowing my head, I went back to the past long ago when I was pregnant with Drew. His creation was the last straw for me, I explained. That day I had called every single living cousin, aunt, and uncle I had and said my good-byes. I was determined to leave this earth after Drew was born. I couldn't and wouldn't allow that man to damage me anymore. I was done. It was one day when I was about four months pregnant and hiding out in Prince George County, Maryland, in my mother and father's old vacation home, when my world changed.

Anika and the African Queens had been combing the streets for any intel they could get about the Orlandos, anything to take them out with, but it was no good. We had to change our scope on how to get that nigga Lu, and here I was, the only woman besides that nigga's real wife who knew every little thing about that man's operation. Hell, there were times when in order to keep him off me I had to help him build his kingdom up. So, here I sat with all that knowledge, not able to do a thing about it, until I felt a hand on my shoulder and a familiar nickname from my past.

"My Iy-Iy," I heard whispered low.

Turning their way, old tears spilled down my face and I wiped them away. "Only my father called me Iy-Iy. It had me abruptly standing to see the man who had been buried next to my mother, so I had thought. When I gasped that man moved to stand beside me. He was dressed to the nines, but what killed me to my core was the FBI badge he had on his belt."

Both Drew and Bianca stared at me in shock. "All that time, I had thought he was dead. All that time I thought I was alone. That I had to be the devil's sex doll and wifey. Yet there he stood. My heart broke and I hated him instantly, almost successfully put a bullet in his skull. But it was the fire that brought me back to life and gave me what I needed to fight for my sons."

"Damn," I heard Bianca mutter.

Drew shook his head and glanced at the house. "Is this that nigga's home? Our Grandpop Banks?"

"Yes. He has been my in. He became my in back then. He was the reason why Lu ended up locked up. I was his eyes, and I gave the testimony that brought that nigga down. My daddy picked up a drugged-up cokehead who was close to Lu's world and had her be my mouthpiece. We used her to help in the testimony then my father sent her off into hiding once his trial was over. The case was locked so tight that Caltrone couldn't use his own resources to save Lu, but at that point Caltrone didn't even care. Word has it that Caltrone even helped put his son away, but there has been no proof. So yes, I learned my father married my mother . . ." I gave a weak laugh and shook my head.

"He married into the game on purpose. To get close to your Great-grandfather Kulu. He wanted to take down the Tribe. But, like Micah, my father lost himself due to loving my mother and me and due to respecting what King Kulu's real agenda was. Anyway, after, Caltrone began cleaning out everyone in my family. It resulted in the death of my mother and father in a car accident, so I had thought. The FBI was able to come in after and pull them out. He explained that they hid him while he was in a coma, but they weren't able to save my mother. Then the rest became history," I explained.

"He never knew of my rapes until I was strong enough to tell him. He did not know of my sons until I was again strong enough to tell him and that was when my sister Sade died. When I gained Shawn and Andrew back and when it was a done deal that Lu was going to die in prison, I told him of my sons. The pictures you saw were what I gave him." I sighed, taking a moment to clear my mind before going on.

"Because of my father's work throughout the years, he's been promoted to a level of the FBI where he's considered dual CIA. He has power on a level none of us can fathom, and he's my protection when he's able to be. I know he's following this; he helped me with Micah. I know he'll help Shawn, we just . . . You all just need to know that using him is very limited because of his power. He is a card we never ever reveal. Only Anika and Phenom know. Each of us have used his help in some way. So, know you all know." My hands bunched in front of me upon my lap.

I felt an old ache in my stomach and sent up prayers. "I'll do whatever for my children. Even sacrificing myself for you, Drew, and for Shawn's protection. I did a lot of wrongs in my youth but I am proud to say that you and Shawn are mine."

The abrupt sound of Drew getting out of the car had me watching him. His hands were in his pockets. His head was bowed in thought. My son made me think of Shawn at that age. Drew had a lot of strength; with that and his bright mind I knew he'd be an incredible force, just like his big brother.

Drew walked around to my side of the car, dropped a hand, and opened the door. I stepped out and he hugged me tight. "I got a lot to learn but ya life has been crazy, Mom. I mean, I was just four when I came to you. Yeah, I remember my other mom, but really you raised me. I was with you the longest so yeah, you're my mama. Like, I can't say I ain't mad at some things, but Shawn got me listening so, like, thank you, Mama. Thank you for loving us like you do, and helping us."

Relief washed over me, and my grip on Drew tightened. I never wanted to let my baby boy go, ever, but already in his words I heard the man he was becoming and it made me proud. I felt Bianca's hand on the small of my back. She said nothing but gave me a soft smile and it was time for us to go in and meet their grandfather Banks. Time was of the essence and Shawn needed us just as much as we needed him. So, I used my key, walked in, and the scent of imported Cuban cigars filled the air. My dad had picked that up from Kulu and it made me smile that he even still drank the same African imported wine that Kulu had.

Pictures of us all, even me pregnant with Shawn, later holding Shawn, and the same with Andrew, sat on his mantle. I could smell BBQ and greens cooking. I could tell that both Bianca and Drew were impressed, especially with the large painting of several handsome young men in their prime hanging over his fireplace. It was the same one I had at my home and it touched my heart. Soft music played; it was Miriam Makeba. Dad was in a calm mode and I knew he was probably in the back, munching on snack cakes while cooking. As we made it to his backyard, he was.

His broad back was too tense. He was a tall, muscular man. His hair was cut low in waves and from the side of his jaw, he still had his bushy beard. I swore I saw a glimpse of a tear run down his face and it broke my heart. He knew.

"Daddy," I softly said.

The moment he turned, his large oak-colored hands dropped the tongs he used to turn the meat and they reached out for me to fall into him. The small talks we had were never enough, only lasting maybe hours; and it was always painful to leave him. He was still in a state of hiding, like Phenom, but as a grown woman I now could handle it better.

"So it is true, you are better? And is my grandson in jail?" his lightly-accented, bourbon-rich voice asked in concern.

"Yes, that is why I am here. That is why we are here. We need your help," I whispered in devotion and love. "Your grandchildren need you, and Shawn's wife needs you."

My father's hard body flinched. It had me gazing up to see the flash of the protective bear and lion I knew him to be, turn his face into a mask, before softening into its cocoa handsomeness. He kissed the crown of my head and walked up to Drew. His hand clapped on my son's shoulder and then he pulled him into a hug.

"You look like your mother with the scowl. Come here," he said and held him tight. He then let go and pulled Bianca to him. "I see why he chose you; you are a beauty. The both of you, come sit. I have cake; eat what you like and I'll finish this meat."

As usual, that was the way with my father. It was his nature to break bread and show his protectiveness in such a manner and I missed him. There was sadness in his eyes but also genuine love and happiness to meet his extended family.

"I heard the news. Been watching, and my people have been telling me everything. Eat. Drink. I have everything you sent my way, Iy-Iy," my father said.

He held a chair out for me and I took a seat, praying he could help. "Can you help us?"

"I move in shadows and in caution in my role. You can't get the fat from a pig before it's primed, and now that pig is ready to be gutted. I'll see what I can do, my Iy-Iy, on my word." My father moved to turn his grilling meat. He pulled out his cell phone and we sat back as he made some calls.

A familiar scent then brushed across my nose. I turned and an old pang hit my heart. See, people, especially some men, can underestimate the power of woman. It is for that very reason why the African Queens were founded to protect young women like Diamond, Gina, Bianca, and women like me and the ghost in front of me. I pushed up from my chair, and there was a gasp, then the drop of a bowl on a counter; and feet headed my way. It had me closing my eyes to center my spirit and accept the hug from a woman who had gone through as much pain as me and more.

Men always underestimated us, and that was one of the major weaknesses in the Orlando men. Caltrone felt we were bitches who needed to learn their place, and were never to be trusted; he was right about that in a sense. But, he also needed to understand that if you don't take down a bitch who becomes insane, then you leave yourself open for her to rip your throat from your body. Me and the voluptuous woman in a simple maxi dress I held were those types of bitches, made insane by the touch of an Orlando, so I smiled in remembrance of another secret I kept.

I turned her toward my son and toward Bianca and I knew this was going to change the game even more. "Andrew. Bianca. I would like you to meet my father's . . . life partner, Yolanda, also known as YoYo Orlando or Eve. Lu's only legal wife, and the woman who helped us end the devil," I explained.

Bianca's mouth opened then closed. She stared at the woman who was once a beauty queen, but who now had a scar on her face and a burn from her shoulder to her right arm from being the wife of a devil. She still was undeniably beautiful, but I guessed it was a blessing she gained those scars because they also kept her hidden and unrecognizable by the enemy.

"No way! Come on!" Drew barked.

I understood his angst, but I had to explain. "She kept me somewhat sane. She helped me a lot."

YoYo shook her head, held my hand, then gave a soft laugh. "No, stop playing. Shy was the one who told me how to get out by any means necessary and who led me to love her father. I'm indebted to the grave, so it's a blessing to meet you all. Whatever is needed I'll help."

Taking a seat, I let her tell them her story and I sat back in quiet thought observing everyone. I had many aces in my hands. I just knew it was time to use some to my advantage and I wasn't sorry about it in the least bit. There was power in this room, from all five of us. It made me proud because it was good power.

Yes, blood covered me from head to toe, but we all lived hardships, even my baby boy. However, it was our choices and determination that helped us get through it all. We were a mighty force, one to be reckoned with, that could bring as much evil as our enemy bought. But what counted was how we came out of that madness that made us so much better. As Nikki Giovanni said, "If now isn't a good time for the truth I don't see when we'll get to it." This is why we lived ENGA and even DOA.

Chapter 22

Angel

I sat slack jawed. Lu Orlando had an official wife? One who was now the life partner of Shy's father? And he was an FBI agent? What in all the unholy fuck was going on? I had to ask Shy to explain it all to me again because it was all set to drive me mad. Drew and I were on the same wavelength as we occasionally glanced at one another while listening to Yolanda's story. She, too, had been a young girl snared by the good looks and the faux charm of an Orlando. By the time she realized Lu was every bit of the monster the whispers of the hood said him to be, it was too late. She was married to him and once an Orlando claimed you as theirs your fate was signed, sealed, and delivered.

I looked at the woman and tried to see Dame in her. She must have realized what I was thinking because she quickly told me she wasn't their mother. Said that because she couldn't give him sons was another reason for his wrath. She told me the ways that Lu had wooed her, wined and dined her, and how it all had been a farce. Shit, still, I thought she had the good end of the stick compared to what he had done to Shy. I tried not to say too much. Couldn't help but stare at the long scar down her face, the slight limp in her leg, and the flesh mark of the burn on her shoulder. I couldn't imagine what that man had done to her.

It scared me. There I was married to an Orlando. There was nothing that Enzo could do to shock me. I'd seen him do the cruelest of things and yet, I knew, I believed him when he said he would never put his hands on me again. I missed him. Missed the hell out of that man like I was never going to see him again. He didn't want me to see him locked up. Refused to allow me to come and see him that way. Said he didn't want me to be that kind of wife. Didn't want me to fall into that stereotype of being another black woman holding her man down while he was locked away. He was talking like he was prepared to be locked away for the long haul.

Even with the news of Micah's disappearance all over the news, people still talked about Enzo being locked away in the same breath: one Nightwings manager missing and another Nightwings player locked away. So many times I'd cried myself to sleep thinking about Shawn. I trusted when he said we were a team. That was why I was kicking my own ass for going back to see his grandfather, alone, when he'd told me not to. It wasn't like I'd had a choice. Frederick and Mark had been waiting for me after I'd left practice for the Bounce Girls. Had been called back in to the police interrogation room as FBI agents questioned me about Micah again. I'd been trying to get back to the way my life should have been after Dame. Was trying to find that normal balance, but it seemed as if I was being thrown back into the abyss of the seventh level of hell.

I swallowed slowly as I slid into the back of the Escalade. Caltrone was sitting with his usual flair as he smoked a Cuban cigar.

"Wanted to see if you were still going to do what I asked of you, Angel," he smoothly said as smoke engulfed my lungs.

"I've been trying, but with all that's been going on, it's kind of hard to get Drew away from everybody," I explained. It was at least half true. No one would let Drew out of their sights for more than a few minutes.

"So you say," Caltrone commented.

I looked the old man right in his eyes. "It's the truth. They don't trust you and they never will."

He chuckled at this and leaned forward to look at me. Made me look him in the eyes as his spicy scent threatened to hypnotize me. No matter how vindictive and wicked the man was, he still had something that attracted women to him. I could easily see why.

"Marco, drive and let me show Enzo's Angel why this whole thing about them not trusting me is comical, *sí?*" he said.

I wanted to jump headfirst from the vehicle but knew he would just have one of them toss me back inside and keep it moving. All I could think about was the fact that Enzo was going to kill me. I was surprised when we pulled up to one of Micah's old apartments. It was one that I'd frequented many times when he would get me on weekends from Dame. The place was still cordoned off by police tape.

I had to ask, "Why are we here?"

"Need to show you something. Something you can take back to my grandson and let him know of, *sí?*" Caltrone smiled like he had the answer to all the world's problems.

I was nervous. Throat was dry. I still had on the Bounce Girls' training uniform. The shorts cupped my pussy, showcased my legs. Shirt had my tits on display for all to see. The only reason that stood out to me was because Caltrone couldn't take his eyes off any of it. If he had been Enzo, I would have spread my legs wider so he could have gotten a better look at it. But there would be no way I would play with that old man that way. He creeped me out. So I closed my legs tighter and placed my arms across my chest, which made him chuckle. I almost started to cry because I felt like I was that little girl in the back of Dame's truck again.

As I turned my attention to whatever was going on outside the truck, I spotted someone: the man who Shy had introduced me to days before as her father. He had walked out of the apartment with a box in his hand. I watched as he got into the back of a car parked near where we were. Caltrone rolled his back window down and gazed long at the man. I expected Shy's father to at least flinch, but he didn't. He nodded Caltrone's way. I started to feel numb. Shy's father couldn't see me, but I could see him.

Everything in me was numb. We'd made a deal with two devils. It was going to kill me to have to tell Shy that her father, too, was a devil. He and Caltrone worked in tandem to take down Micah. I realized they were two men cut from the same cloth as they spoke about Micah's demise.

"Iya wants me to keep Enzo out of jail. I think you should tell her you'd rather have him in there," Caltron said then laughed.

"My daughter is blinded by the fact that he's her son. I'll have to open her eyes to the fact that he's more than her son, Caltrone. He's your grandson and that itself is a problem."

Caltrone tilted his head, cast a glance at me, and then scowled at the man. "So because the boy has my blood, he's tainted, *sí?*"

"Take that however you want it."

Caltrone's face seemed to be transforming in front of me. All he did was stare straight ahead at me. Wanted me to see for myself that no matter how Enzo tried to show the world he wasn't a menace that would be all they would ever see him as. He was an Orlando. That last name was a blessing and a curse.

I found it ironic that both those niggas had found their way to Micah's apartment at the same time. I'd expected Shy's father and Caltrone to have an epic showdown, but was shocked when they seemed to be content in the fact that they had the same agenda. They talked from the back of their respective cars as we sat under the cover of nightfall. I saw Fuego walking across the street. Watched in silence as he placed little black squares on the sides of the building.

"You work fast, Caltrone," Shy's father said as he watched on.

"I always do," Caltrone answered.

I could tell neither man trusted the other. On Caltrone's lap his hand nestled a Desert Eagle that looked as if it could blow a hole clean through a bulletproof window. Although I couldn't see inside Shy's father's car, I wouldn't have been surprised if he, too, held a gun close to him. It was easy to cut the tension with a knife between the two men.

"Still trying to take down the Kulu Kings?" Caltrone taunted the man with a sick smile.

"The same as they're trying to rid the streets of you," he answered. "But that's neither here nor there. I'm here for another agenda altogether."

"Same as I."

For a moment there was heavy silence. The pressure in the air was thick. Just like I found out while at Caltrone's domain that his killers moved in silence, I was sure the same could be said for Shy's father. Smoked swirled around the back of the Escalade as Caltrone stared at me.

"My work here is done," Shy's father finally spoke up.

"Mine is just beginning," Caltrone said smoothly.

"I'm still coming for your head, Caltrone."

"I wouldn't expect anything less."

"You killed my wife like she was nothing. Tried to kill me."

"I enjoyed every minute of it."

"As will I when the time comes. Rest easy, Caltrone. You'll never see me coming," Shy's father threatened.

For some reason, I knew those were more than just words. I could feel the guarantee and finality in them.

"I wouldn't expect anything less. Just keep in mind you married into the Tribe. Papa Kulu is not in your blood. It's going to take a hell of a lot more to get to me from the likes of you," Caltrone told him.

"You'll never see me coming," was all Shy's father said before he drove off.

Minutes later, Caltrone's truck pulled off too and I watched in silence as the apartment building exploded and went up in flames.

"'The trust of the innocent is the liar's most useful tool,'" Caltrone casually said. "Stephen King said that. It has never been truer than it is now."

I couldn't say anything because I didn't know what to say.

A few minutes later I was dropped off at a safe house. Would never show the man where I really laid my head. I didn't look back as I unlocked the door and walked in. I wasn't surprised when I found Shy and Mirror waiting for me. Anika and Phenom were there as well.

I looked at Shy, the woman who had become my mother not just by law, but in my heart; she was the mother I never knew. She knew what I had done, the act of betraying her trust. There was no judgment in her eyes. She held her arms out to me and I rushed forward. For a long time I didn't say a word, I couldn't. I had to tell her about her father and that was killing me on the inside. Felt as if my stomach was being twisted into knots by the hand of Satan.

"Shhhh," she comforted me. "You did well. You did well. You came back alive because you followed your first instinct. No matter what it was, you did well," she said as she held me.

"He asked for Andrew again," I finally murmured.

Shy sighed low. "I expected him to."

"I have to bring him Andrew."

"I know."

I felt Anika as she walked over to where Shy and I stood. "She's a true queen now," she said as she joined Shy in hugging me.

"I never doubted she was."

Neither of them cared that I had just left the devil's lair. I had to tell them what I'd done. I told them how it all went down. Told Shy about her father and what had transpired between him and Caltrone. Spilled my guts like I was confessing my sins. I wanted to cleanse, purge myself of all the sins I'd witnessed. By the time I was done, Mirror had left to get Shawn. Shy, Mirror, and Phenom had agreed to let Caltrone speak with Andrew, and I realized that Shy knew exactly the devil her father was.

"Caltrone will never see him coming," was all she said as she looked off into the distance.

I could tell she was hurting behind it all. Could see those wheels in her head turning knowing her father, too, didn't see Enzo as a young man with a promising future. To him, he was just another Orlando.

Two hours later, after I'd showered and washed away my transgressions, Shawn walked in the room. I turned and looked into the eyes of another Orlando. He'd gone and gotten his hair and face together. No longer did he look like he was trying to grow a beard. The Enzo I knew was back. He was in black designer dress pants, wingtip dress shoes, and a red designer dress shirt. I rushed to hug him, but he backed away. I stopped.

It finally hit me that I would have to tell Enzo of my sins as well. I'd become a gatekeeper, but I wouldn't hide anything from him, would I? Did being a gatekeeper mean keeping secrets from the man I'd married? I finally figured out why Shy hadn't been in a relationship. She'd told me not many gatekeepers were. Some secrets you couldn't even tell to those you loved. Did he need to know that his other grandfather wanted his head on a platter too? Did he need to know I signed a deal with the devil to get him out of jail?

Without him even having to ask, I once again confessed my sins. Spilled everything that had happened from beginning to end. Told him of the conversation between both his grandfathers. I apologized to him for going behind his back and doing what he'd asked me not to. I didn't know what to expect. I could tell by the way he backed away from me that someone had already told him what I'd done. While he stood there staring at me, all I could do was wait.

"I don't know what happens from here, Angel. It's only going to get worse before it gets better," he said.

"I know that, Enzo," I said quietly, still not sure of what his reaction was going to be.

"Asked you not to go back to see that old man."

"I didn't have a choice. He sent two men to the stadium for me."

All he did was nod. "You down with me?"

I nodded.

"You sure? Because you can get out now."

"You divorcing me already?"

"No. Just giving you a way out. Shit could be get grimier than it is now. You'll still be my wife, but I can send you away. You can go to London."

My heart was slamming against my rib cage. "You trying to scare me?"

"Yep."

"It's not working," I lied.

He knew I was lying. Didn't have to divert my eyes for him to know I was lying. Fear lived in me like it belonged there. It was something I had to work on. I still didn't know if he was mad at me. He made me wait before he addressed that issue.

Chapter 23

Enzo

I once said a nigga's environment is what shapes him and I was a living byproduct of that reality. In the life of an average man who was facing going to prison, he would say it was a miracle that the charges were dropped; but for me that wasn't the case. Blessings had come through and my arraignment had been thrown out due to tampering and falsification of documents being found. How it all fell out, it was assumed that Micah ran from the law and had disappeared. After evidence showed the corruption was all a plant by Micah, they let me go.

The only thing I had to deal with was a fine for going at Micah. After that, Mirror and my PR rep sat me down with the NFL commissioner, the Nightwings owner, as well as my coaches, and bartered for me to get back on the Nightwings team and play the big game. It took only several hours for them to let me back, acknowledging that the suspicion had really been all Micah's doing. So after that, and after having to pay my fine, I was officially being allowed back in the game I was getting ready for. Shit was working out kinda.

I turned to Angel and then smoothed a calm hand down my dress shirt. "Nobody controls my destiny but me and whoever sits in the skies, feel me?"

"So, what does that mean? Are you mad at me?" Angel asked with nervousness in her voice.

My hands reached out for her and I pulled her by her hips to me. "No, you did what I asked, B. I want to not trust shit you do at this point but, for real, you did what I asked and you handled business as best as you could on your own. I can't be mad at it. I gotta respect that shit. Don't matter anyway. All we are are fucking pawns, but now with Micah KOS'd, it's time shit turned in our favor. Niggas gonna assume shit about me; it's time to show them something else altogether."

I let my lips press against Angel's parting mouth then moved around her in thought. Every move I made at this point needed to be specific to the overall end game. Caltrone was a smart nigga and every bit as crazy as the two niggas who were my brothers, and my father. Nigga liked to intimidate. So did I. I learned through this whole game that I enjoyed a lot of the things that he thought marked an Orlando and I intended to do whatever I had to to protect my own kingdom. So he wanted Drew now.

Scratching my jaw, I shrugged and smiled. My trust was in my baby brother, so if Caltrone wanted him, then he could have him. My grandfather, Aaron Banks, now wanted to come for me, and I welcomed it. However, people really needed to be specific about how they expressed such words. Everyone needed to get this game right. I wasn't a Kulu and I wasn't a Orlando; what I was was the son of a devil and his Lilith.

Rolling in my blackout, I slipped my hands in my pockets then gazed at Angel. She wrapped her arms around herself then stepped closer to me. "Your eyes are black. What are you going to do? What happened to Lilith?"

Touching Bianca's chin, I admired how she looked. She had a power to her that she was coming to understand. People were shaping us into monsters, and sooner or later she was going to have to accept it for being forced into a role she also didn't want.

"Shit, going to do exactly what I want: step to this Super Bowl pre-party, and be the Prince of Atlanta and like I said she's probably fucking my pops in hell. I handled her too and gifted her to my grandfather as a proper introduction to who I am and a tribute to him," I cooed as my hand slipped down her back.

"You did? But . . . but what about Caltrone?" she asked, her voice dropping in concern.

"Caltrone is going to give me everything he's been promising and, in the end, he's going to get everything he wants. Same with my grandpops Aaron. This war isn't about us, it's about them, so give them what they want and watch the shit burn," I explained.

"Besides, with what you spit at him when you met up with him, shit. You and my mom played that nigga Caltrone right where we needed him with y'all's plan," I said with a complimenting smirk.

Angel gave me a blushing smile then exhaled as if relieved about something. "Good. I wasn't sure. Like, I didn't know if you'd—"

Holding her hips, I allowed my hands to run over the curve of her ass then I squeezed to make her rise on her toes as I interrupted her. "If I'd put my hands on you? Nah. I meant what I said. I only put hands on bitches. I'm not going to beat you, B."

Angel gave me a light little shrug then looked down at her hands as I let her go. "I wasn't prepared to sit and break bread with him like that. I thought he was going to do me like Dame and it scared me."

Moving around the room, I plopped down on the bed in thought. "You may have to meet with him more often. He might make you do shit you don't wanna, like kill. First kills for someone like you is hard. I'll tell you this, when he asks you to do a real kill, not some squeezing your Glock and hoping a nigga dies like you do, only kill if you have to, a'ight, and be very, very, very smart about who you don't kill, a'ight?"

I could tell by how Angel turned my way that she was shocked by what I said.

"I wasn't always a killa, mama. I recognize when killing ain't for everyone. You need to just be about protecting this family, since you're a part of that. If that becomes your main objective and you not turncoating me, then I'm chill. Since I'm back in the game I usually take the anger on the field anyway," I explained to her to reassure her and make her smile.

It was confusing to watch Angel grab my bag and ready me to go to the stadium. I only had my mom do that for me back in the day; then it was just me handling business. It had me watching her, studying her body language. Shorty had proved that she was really down for me and I couldn't help but appreciate her more for that.

"You need to get your shit for the game and mine. I'll be in the car. We need to bounce," was all I said as I left Angel in my room.

Angel rushed out of the house a few minutes later. I knew we should have been on our way to the stadium, but something she had told me earlier stuck with me. It was eating away at me like cancer. I told Angel to direct me to the home of my maternal grandfather, Aaron Shawn Banks, the man who Shy had felt was worthy enough to give me one of his names. I was trying to remain calm, but truth be told, a nigga was furious. It pissed me off to no end that Aaron was no better than Micah. All he saw me as was an Orlando and the nigga had never even met me.

Angel and I sat in an unmarked vehicle. My skullcap sat low just like how I was sitting in the car. A voice in my mind had me swimming in black as I listened: *"Go make your introductions, son."*

I rubbed my temples as I spoke to the ghost I hated to the core. *You know how I make my introductions, nigga. That bum trick is the Feds. Nothing good will come from it.*

"*So? Fuck that trick. Nothing good is coming from it now anyway, my son, because you are of me. Now go make your introductions, nigga,*" the man who donated his seed to create me ordered.

My gaze narrowed and my fist clenched while I frowned. *Fuck no!*

"*Do that shit like I said! But do it with finesse, then come back and go to your little game. Be an Orlando!*" he barked out at me.

Frustration had me gripping the door until I was in a daze. I stepped out of the ride. I told Angel to stay in the car, but she didn't listen. I felt her try to stop me, but I was too far gone.

"Please don't do this, you don't have to," Angel pleaded.

Again, I heard nothing she had to say. Ignoring her, I walked up to the door, knocked on it, and waited.

A soft, feminine voice in my mind spoke to me this time, whispering, "*Be your own man. It's not Kulu, it's not Orlando, it's just you. Do what you need to survive.*" Shy's voice tried to calm me.

I thanked the voice that was my mother as that darkness kept me leveled but still felt amped.

A woman with a scar on her face peeked out at me from the panel of glass in the wooden door. She opened the door, and then stared at me as if I was a ghost.

"Is my grandfather home? I'm Enzo, his grandson," I introduced myself.

"He . . . he's not home," she told me.

Fear lined her eyes and I felt myself smile. "I wanted to introduce myself to my grandfather but I think you'll do just right. You live with him, so you conspired against me and my mother, so I have to say hello. Oh, and your husband Lu says, 'Fuck you, bitch.'"

Blood sprayed on the door as if I had thrown a can of paint on it. The woman's fear then pain seared on my brain as she fell before me and looked up at me in a vacant stare. I smelled savory food in the air, and saw the many pictures of a family Angel had told me my grandfather had worked to take down. It was time for a game changer and it felt like this woman's death would help the cause.

Dropping the knife that said DOA on it, I smirked. "Thank you for your help. Sorry that you had to escape only to die by an Orlando anyway. Blame the nigga you lie with who's gunning for me."

My father's laughter echoed in my mind. It had me exhaling and looking up at the light over my head in a daze. After coming back to earth, I turned then coolly walked away. Angel stared at me in shock before she got back in the car.

"We need to go," I quietly said, staring back at her.

Angel said nothing and still did not move.

Frustration had my lips curling in a scowl and I yelled, "Bianca! We need to go!"

It took several yells from me to get her drive off but eventually we did. She took me to a safe house where I cleaned up then we both headed to the stadium saying nothing about the murder I just committed. Yeah, it was crazy that I had just killed a woman in cold blood, but that was the price that was paid when I was messed with. When people didn't leave me alone and forced me to be a monster when I didn't have the desire to be about that life was when problems were created for them. One day, some muthafucka was going to understand that the first go-round and not test me.

But for now, the vibrancy of the stadium had me geeked; it brought me back to the middle of the game. Each memory of mine, all that prior energy, worked in tandem to fuel me as I ran. Air rushed in and out of my lungs and I glanced down the field. Madness fueled me. I kicked up my movements checking for the ball. I zipped past the sidelines hearing our Bounce Girls pump up the crowd.

"Welcome, Nightwings fans, as we celebrate another game of the season! The game is heating up and our city is putting it down! Rookie and rising star Shawn 'Enzo' Banks is back and bringing the pain as he takes us toward a win!" The words blasted throughout the stadium like a hurricane wrecking a town.

Sweat dripped into my eyes. My thighs, ass, and calf muscles clenched tight with a burning purpose as I jetted forward. Fans stomped their feet, clapping and shouting out in amazement as I leaped in the air over a diving offensive linebacker. I pivoted left and right, hitting them with a zigzag then pausing to make niggas crash into them.

My boy Dragon was flanking me through the whole game. I let my mind travel back to before the game, to reflect about everything that had gone down while I worked the field. Music blasted thumping with those niggas F.L.Y. spitting about swag surfing. I could see the chicks leading the crowd in a matching dance. Yellow, black, and silver lit up the stands and people cheered my name. It had me licking my lips and flashing the thumbs-up to the crowd. I sharply turned, dodging a nigga trying to tackle me so I could run for the money.

The sound of me being hit, the hard snap of a helmet against my helmet, and the hot liquid feel of my blood running over my mouthpiece had a simmering anger ebbing in me. The sensation was almost blissful and calming. I could hear the melodic thumping of my heart-beat in my ears as I tucked the ball to my stomach. Had I not been quick enough to check it, I would have lost the ball in my hand and let that helmet to helmet hit take me down. So like a map unfolding in front of me, I could see which ways I could do this. I could fall on my ass, or I could keep running.

These muthafuckas had hit me so hard that my skull rattled in my helmet but I wasn't about to let that shit keep me down. With everything in me I stayed on my feet and jetted forward. The crowed loved how I stayed in the game, how I brought the heat, and I loved the way they pumped me up.

The crowd erupted in an orgasmic-like euphoria as everyone collectively shouted, "Ooh!"

All around me, I heard my name being chanted, "Enzo, Enzo, Enzo!"

A snicker flashed across my face. While I worked the field, Dragon ran past me to protect my back with a thumbs-up. Stomping sounded in the stands, signaling for me to make my moves. Lights flashed, the Bounce Girls made it gutta, and I could see my coaches pointing for where I should go. I saw Dragon moving with me in sync.

My eyes narrowed and I shouted hard, "Let's take this shit, nigga!"

Dragon bowed his head then threw niggas left and right over his shoulders. I faked one way to throw the defense off only to do a quick break in the other direction. It really didn't serve a purpose but to make this shit look good as players came after me.

To my surprise, Dragon came from the right of me. Then, like the parting of the Red Sea, he sent his elbow into the throat of the bitch who came stupid at me. I gave Dragon a salute then sprinted forward, front flipped over a diving offense player, and landed with swag. The sound of the crowed exploding in hype had me gripping the ball, and saluting as I dropped to a knee, dipped low in a slow grind, then popped back up hopping up and down on the end zone.

Screams rent the stadium. "Ahhhhhh! Enzo, Enzo, Enzo. Dragon, Dragon!"

"Ladies and gentlemen! Nighthawks fans! Enzo and his Dragon have done it again for another win! We're going into the Super Bowl!" an announcer shouted while confetti spilled and lights flashed and flared.

Grinning hard while pulling off my helmet and dropping it in front of me, there was no damn way I was letting go of that shit. I glared at the opposing team. My teammates rushed forward then flanked me, lifting both Dragon and me up. I danced in the air, and saw the Bounce Girls come our way. Once we sat back down on the ground both Dragon and I fell into doing the Bernie Lean. We had made it and we were going to make Atlanta ours. It was now time to kick it and reintroduce myself back into the fold of the NFL world.

After the game, I sat in the locker room thinking about that woman's blood on my hands and Angel again while in the shower. Angel's previous words about my grandfather killed whatever trust was trying to form for the people around me. This life wasn't shit but games and other people's manipulations. I realized from the fucking womb that all of us kids were nothing but pawns in a bigger game. Micah had fallen to the game of his own building with me being his own trap. Now two niggas who wanted the extension of the Kulu Kings to go down wanted Drew and me. In my view, it wasn't really around anymore. Yeah, Phenom was being called Kulu King, but I never once heard the man call himself that title, which was interesting.

He had also taken down the men who had threatened his family, so who were his real enemies now? Yeah, my mom was of that lineage too but she was nothing but an African Queen who wanted her sons to have a life not part of the crime world. So that left what? A nigga who stepped into the Kulu lineage as a spy who was intent on now taking me out because of some shit he allowed? Then another nigga, a man who called himself my grandfather, who wanted Drew and me to turn into his pawns and continue the game?

Shit, Caltrone knew my hand in a sense. Knew I didn't trust him for shit, but what showed for me was that he really didn't know shit about who I was or my upbringing; same for Drew. What the adults were not factoring in was that they had dropped us kids into this game and just assumed we'd take on their fight and mantel. They all spit that shit that they had no agenda but, thanks to two men, both my grandfathers, we all were nothing but pieces in the overall game of control. Fuck that shit! The bullshit those two men were building was the reason why Lu's first wife was now dead and left as a pretty bloody gift at my other grandfather, Aaron's, door.

Watching the streams of soapy water travel down the planes of my naked body, the chants of my teammates brought me back to reality. We had a party to get to, one where I knew my family was at waiting on me. I was moving into my kingdom and had to play the role. I now had all of Atlanta loving me again, and I could also continue hamming it up as if I did not have blood on my hands.

It took only an hour to get fresh. I stood decked out in suave attire with my mother, Andrew, and Bianca at my side. From the shadows of the curtains behind me, my mother took the hand of the man I realized she had fallen in love with, and it made me proud in some way. She walked around as if she owned the place. To me she really did. So did Drew and Bianca.

Behind me was the rest of my true family: the Misfits. With Bianca's hand in mine, she kept me focused and also commanded the room with the backless dress she sported, while my mind calculated its game. Even though my real blood came from a long line of Orlandos, and although I once thought I was created out of evil, out of a sick man's obsession, I realized, no: Drew and I were created for another reason. To avenge the life taken from us kids.

So what was the best way to go into the gates of hell without a direct key? Be born into it. So I stood watching over everyone realizing that there was a whole bunch of so-called kings in this shit, but no fucking rulers, except those behind me and on the side of me, and I was going to enjoy ruling them all.

I headed to the bottom of the stairs, where my bodyguard Dragon and his wife stood waiting. The plans that led us here exceeded Micah's expectations. He had set us on this path of destruction and now Pandora's box was wide open. We saw Tino mixing and dipping amid various actors, actresses, and musicians flooding the massive manor. He would be our ears under Bianca's control. I noticed that Drew was shielding a little girl with matching eyes and a devious smirk on her pretty face, our niece. She then skipped away with a box Drew had given her. My baby brother then made his way to Caltrone with Dragon following. In the glimpse of my peripheral, I saw the blur of a kid with locs holding the hand of a pretty brown beauty with killer eyes as he took her to the dance floor.

Following them was my best friend, a gentle giant who could kill without even dropping a smile. With him was another pretty beauty with a madness that matched the multiethnic male who stalked behind them. This life was ours and the game had moved to the next level. We all moved from being players, and now it was time to make this world ours.

Micah really should have left me alone. I guessed he understood that now as he burned in hell, but now it was time for both of my grandfathers to learn the same. You don't fuck with true family, good or bad, and I was both ENGA and DOA. It was time for us young cats to take over and then Caltrone and Agent Aaron Banks would bow down to us or lose their lives.

The End